DEATH DANCE

DEATH DANCE

Suspenseful Stories of the Dance Macabre

TREVANIAN
Editor

Cumberland House
Nashville, Tennessee

FIC
DEATH
DANCE

Published by
    Cumberland House Publishing, Inc.
    431 Harding Industrial Drive
    Nashville, TN 37211
    www.cumberlandhouse.com

Cover design: Gore Studio, Inc.
Text design: Mary Sanford

Library of Congress Cataloging-in-Publication Data
    Death Dance : suspenseful stories of the dance macabre / Trevanian, editor.
       p. cm.
     ISBN 1-58182-250-2 (pbk. : alk. paper)
     1. Detective and mystery stories, American. 2. Dancers—Fiction. 3. Dance—
Fiction. I. Trevanian.
    PS648.D4 D418 2002
    813'.0872083527928—dc21
                                   2001052983

Printed in the United States of America

1 2 3 4 5 6 7—07 06 05 04 03 02

CONTENTS

INTRODUCTION
Trevanian

Good writing is not limited to academic or artsy literature, with its bias against "genre" writing, but is to be found in the best of the more popular narrative modes. Indeed, most "serious" literature could benefit from the clean, lucid style and the strong narrative drive that are characteristic of the best of popular fiction.

There is a tacit contract between the writer and the reader of genre fiction that obliges the writer to produce solid, clean, clear writing while keeping in mind the fact that most readers use popular fiction for restoration, relaxation, experience broadening, and vicarious adventure, as over against the uplifting and "improving" uses one makes of academic or "serious" literature. The successful genre writer also fulfills the readers' expectations by respecting his chosen genre's givens.

In the romance genre, for instance, the principle character must win the loved one after coming very close to losing him at least once. A modern alternative allows the strong heroine to decide finally that she doesn't need or want him, that she can do better. This can be a satisfying, even reassuring outcome of a romance story. Given this essential characteristic of the romance, only the nittiest of academic pickers would exclude the splendid and insightful novels of Jane Austen from that genre, but what Raymond Chandler called "genre snobbism" would make them wince to apply what they view as a diminishing label to Austen's work.

Similarly, the thriller genre must involve action and suspense, although the best thrillers also let their characters develop in the testing crucible of their quest, and the very best cast critical and mischievous lights on the self-satisfied cultures within which their anti-heroes operate.

Writers of the mystery/crime/detection genre are obliged to propose a problem or a puzzle, then reveal the solution. This can, of course, involve more than simple whodunit. The tale can turn on how it was done. Or why it was done. Or even on exactly what was done. Because no other genre has so strong a narrative engine driving the events from the first page to the final revelation, mystery/crime/detection fiction yearns to be clean, clear, and highly honed. The genre's natural celerity and leanness obliges the writer to work hard at those enriching and deepening "extras" of setting, ambiance, and character. But when this literary balancing act is pulled off gracefully, no other genre is more gratifying or has higher impact.

Most of the stories in this collection are crime or detective stories, and all were chosen because they satisfy the requirements of their genre—suspense, plot, logic, satisfying conclusion, etc.—in ways that are creative and entertaining. The quality of the writing weighed as much in the editor's decision as adherence to the genre givens.

These stories deal with death, danger, and harm occurring within a dance milieu: an evocative combination, since we do not normally associate dance with the sinister, the dangerous, the mysterious. Most of us think of dance as joyous and life-embracing; a celebration of movement, the corporal expression of our emotions, a glorification of the human form, its beauty, its sexuality. We view dance as a vehicle for romance, or think of its comic uses, its healing virtues, its expressive qualities, or even its ritualistic role in quest of nourishing rain, abundant harvests, and fertile unions.

But in these stories we find dance put to other, darker uses: as a means of luring prey; as a cold business proposition; as a bitter, hard-fought competition; as a form of aggression; as sociopolitical protest; as an expression of misogyny; as the physical manifestation of an unhealthy mind; or even as a pathway to madness.

．　．　．　．　．

Ruth Cavin's "The Mechanique Affair" is an amusing look at the world of modern dance, its tensions and rivalries, and a reminder that dance is not only an art form but also a business and, as such, subject to sharp practice. In "Jookin' 'n' Jivin'," Linda Kerslake takes us, by way of an old man's memories, back to the era of the Second World War and to some unfinished business there. The authentic "swing" stuff is one of the tale's satisfying elements. Barbara Burnett Smith combines an unusual setting: a children's dance class; an unlikely heroine: a doting grandmother; and a clever device for revealing whodunit in her "Death of a Damn Moose." Henry Slesar's "Change Partners" is a charming, light-hearted look at the vicious world of competitive ballroom dancing, in which marriage vows are puny things compared to the desire to win a cup. Carmen Iarrera's "Tango" takes us beyond the steps of the dance to the feelings it evokes in those who dance it, suggesting that the tango expresses and even influences how men and women feel about each other. The real villain of the piece by John Lutz, "Tango Was Her Life," is the crushing poverty of the region into which a lonely woman has wandered, nominally seeking dance tuition, in fact in search of love—local poverty which has turned its victims into predators. In Ina Bouman's "Mrs. Website's Dance," a woman seeks to use dance as a means of freeing a repressed man of his inhibitions. The tale is effective in its slow building up of an eerie internal ambiance. In "Dancing the Night Away," by Brendan DuBois, a nightclub tough guy meets a young woman on the dance floor and decides to pick her up. In fact, it is she who has chosen him, and with a different end in mind. "The Dance of the Apsara," by Joan Richter, explores the pain of lost love in the aftermath of war as reflected in the life of a damaged woman who clings desperately to a ritual dance as a spiritual life-line. "You Can Jump," by Mat Coward, is a tightly written and illuminating journey back through the punk era of the '70s, explaining what the Pogo was all about and leaving us with an uplifting message of political and personal expression. "In Our Part of the World," Andrew Kennedy's story of an unfaithful Basque folk dancer, introduces us to a fascinating rural society. Darkly folkloric in feeling, it is an effective atmospheric piece, and the action scenes are masterfully handled. Alexandra Whitaker's "The Trespasser" is a wicked and witty story of a love triangle, set in a dance school where the lost and lonely flock around a charismatic teacher. "At the Hop," by Judy and Bill Crider, is richly redolent of its era (late '50s, early '60s) with precious stuff of the hero wincing to hear his gal exposed to "dirty" words and such places as a men's toilet. The Criders have captured the era's (and the genre's) quibbling tone of the wise guy and his dame, and turned it upside down, to the wise dame and her guy. In "Dirty Dancing," Carole Nelson Douglas presents evocatively realistic insights into being a woman in her mid-fifties, alone in a mid-American world. The development toward women binding together to rid themselves of a male menace is very contemporary, as is the unresolved (but nonetheless richly satisfyingly) ending.

. . . . .

All these stories possess their genre's qualities of clean writing, strong plot lines, and dénouements that are both plausible and satisfying. But the moods they evoke, their settings, their writing styles, and the characters they reveal, are refreshingly varied. A good short story collection should be a meal consisting of many tempting little dishes: a sort of literary dim sum or smorgasbord. Readers use short story collections in different ways; some plough through steadfastly cover to cover, but most hop and skip, alighting here, then there, according to complex and quirky personal criteria. But for all readers, the juxtaposition of one story with another lends the subtleties of aftertaste and the piquancy of contrast, for each is read in the timbre/mood of the preceding one, and this lends a special flavor to the reading experience, making the collection greater than the sum of its parts, and leaving the reader both entertained and nourished by his light and varied meal.

Okay. That's it. *Tout le monde, à table!*

Trevanian
Ste. Engrâce
Autumn, 2001

IN OUR PART OF THE WORLD
Andrew Kennedy

You'll find our part of the world at the western end of the Pyrenean mountain chain, where the rolling grassy foothills steepen sharply and break here
and there into cliffs, where farms lie above or below one another, and where
lives criss-cross like the ancient paths, taking people up into the mountains
or down into the valley.

Joseph lived on a high mountain farm. He had a very old, heavy Bernard
hay cutter. Every time a piece on it broke, he took the broken piece down
to the lame mechanic in the valley and made love to the man's wife in secret
until it was fixed. Even when nothing had broken, but Joseph felt it was time
it had, he would find an old part in his barn and go down to the mechanic
just the same.

Joseph did the manly work about the farm (and manhandling the heavy
old Bernard was certainly a manly thing), but was happiest when drawn
down into the valleys. His wife looked after the sheep and seemed happiest
drawn upwards to the high pastures where mysteries and legends come alive.
Yet it was Joseph who would go up to the high ridges when it came to be
their turn to watch the village's combined flocks. He had many an assigna-
tion up there in the shepherd's hut during the stormy days of summer.

Joseph was a celebrated dancer of the region, and had directed a much
talked about pastorale. As was once the tradition in our part of the world,
great dancers became mayors, and naturally Joseph's name was once put forward for this important post, but his campaign failed. Malicious male
tongues said, as a joke, but half believing it all the same, during the after-

noons that stretched into mornings playing cards in the café, that Joseph had failed to find the number of sponsors he needed for his mayoral candidacy because he couldn't find eleven men in the mountains he hadn't cuckolded.

Joseph was the type of philanderer that women love and dogs mistrust. Women would love him until suddenly, between one day and the next, they wouldn't want to see him anymore. In the way we gorge on the plump June raspberries until we no longer have the taste for them, women fell in love with Joseph and then quickly turned away. But men were always happy to have his company and revel in the rumors of his exploits, since men enjoy the reflected glory of a womanizer as long as he leaves their wives alone. Joseph was perfectly discreet and, since no man in the café would ever consider the thought that his own woman would fall for him, and since those women who had fallen for him were always cool toward him afterwards, the men could believe he found his conquests elsewhere. Joseph was never directly suspected of cheating the men around him, but neither was he entirely clear of all suspicion, which is as it is, since a vague disquiet is, in our part of the world, felt about almost everyone's reputation. Joseph was a sharp observer of events, and could tell an amusing tale, even against himself—a very rare trait for the men in the café—while managing to keep the dignity natural to his early fame. And men would rather have a star among them, even a fading one, than a nobody.

Joseph was a lithe young fifty, taller by a brow than anyone around him. His name was Aramburu, which means "at the head of the valley," and he possessed what the professors of ethnology from Paris would consider a classic Basque face (among the Basque, of course, there's no such thing): very dark brown orb in a very bright white of eye, thin, slightly aquiline nose, and a straight mouth. He had a full head of dark hair, graying at the temples, which he wore longer than any farmer—or farmer's wife, come to that—in our part of the world.

Joseph had been clever at school, but a love of the girls kept him from any bookish success. As the youngest of four brothers, he had little hope of becoming anything but a laborer for the eldest, who would be the customary sole inheritor. So Joseph became a dancer.

Here, dancing is an athletic activity, and Joseph was born into the last epoch before the present, in which everyone believed only men could dance, only men *should* dance. Our dancing is a form of ballet, but not like the Paris ballet, full of moving hands and arms, where women are the stars and the men have to carry and lift as if they were in a gymnasium. Here, men keep their arms down, their heads up, and criss-cross their legs and feet in the air in fast precise movements. Basque dancers have given the world the *pas de basque*—the Basque step—which has been absorbed into the Celtic dances and spread everywhere. Basque dancing is athletic, precise, and very taxing. Joseph was very athletic, very precise, and handsome.

He became a star at only sixteen by dancing the role of Satan in the pastorale. In our part of the world, the pastorale is a play the origins of which are lost in time. The play is about many things, but it is also about how things go wrong, about how men and women get muddled in their dealings with one another. In the pastorale, tradition has it that Satan has a grudge against the Basque people because he is unable to master them or their language. So he meddles in their affairs and subverts the good intentions of heroes and heroines. It speaks to everyone in the audience for whom irrational trouble has caused great pain and for whom a good intention is sometimes flawed with a little bit of devilry. And for this reason the role of Satan was thought much too important for a young boy to play. But Joseph confounded every doubt and finished the last of the two performances to bracing cheers—a curious thing to happen to a devil.

As a star in his own small corner of the land, he was drawn to the coast and the wider world of Biarritz, where he spent two years at the new dance academy set up by "well-meaning cultural big-wigs to milk the ageless natural talent of the Basque hill people"—these are Joseph's own words on the subject—learning to dance a joke and to pick up English girls on holiday, mastering their language on the way.

When Maïté's hand came up for marriage, Joseph's suit beat all comers—and there were many—even though Joseph was ten years her senior. Maïté was the single lonely daughter of a lonely couple who had given up facing the hardships of the land and retired to the coast on an inheritance, leaving Maïté the small, but tidy, hill farm, the highest up the hillside. She had a house, eighteen hectares of land—some of which was gentle slope—a flock of ewes and a good complexion. There was a child before half a year was out, creating one of those subjects for gossip that no one could actually talk about. But the child was weak and died within days. At the time of the birth, Joseph was away in San Sebastian dancing in their fiesta. When he got back, the child was dead and he never saw it. Maïté said little and seemed to accept her fate with a tranquility that malicious tongues later called relief, but Joseph could not hide his sorrow and wept easily for some time.

No other children came their way. Joseph worked the land with minimal equipment and Maïté looked after the animals, building up a large healthy flock. She made consistently good cheese in the old-fashioned way that she sold to connoisseurs in spite of the new pasteurization laws designed to favor the large co-operatives, and she was admired for it. They kept in good order all the tools they had started with, and Maïté managed to save enough to impress the bank—an impressive feat in our part of the world, for those with no flat land. Although their farm was successful, Joseph's mind was always running down the valley slopes, through the cluster of houses about the old weir and mill, and on to the coast, and Maïté's escaped higher to the crests of the ridges and the places of old secrets. Dédé, the Aramburus' neighbor, was always being passed by one or the other of them going up or coming down. But then, Dédé saw more of the Aramburus than he needed to since, unlike the previous occupant of his farm, he did not interfere with their use of an old path that ran under the cliffs to the high pasture and which went past his house and barns. The men in the café thought that this was, although decent and neighborly, a curious inconvenience to accept.

The men in the café all agreed that Dédé was a strong and level man, but it was hard to read his intentions. As a young man, he had bought the hill farm next to the Aramburus, some years after Maïté's marriage, for a rumored sum that everyone knew, if it were true, was more than it was worth, and set-tled in to raising a flock of ewes and keeping to himself. He was certainly determined, and when he wanted something he patiently found a way to get it. "Look at the way he worked to get old Behegaray's land," someone would say, and the men in the café would nod, their minds divided in admiration of his purpose and anxiety over his suspected cunning. Old Behegaray, in spite of his hip, had claimed he would never sell, although there were many who wanted to buy, and, as they say in our part of the world, especially on market day, "you can sell to a man who doesn't want to buy, but you can't buy from a man who isn't selling."

Dédé seemed grave without there being any particular reason to be, and socialized little. When he did have a drink, he was more amiable—which is how it should be—but always polite, which earned him some regard. His mysterious air made him attractive to the older unmarried women, but for the young girls and the married women, Joseph was a more daring and alto-gether more worthwhile subject for romantic hopes.

Very soon after her marriage with Joseph, Maïté tired of dancing. She did not dance, nor did she want to hear about dancing, or even watch it at fêtes. Joseph, among the men, let it be known that it was his fault his wife was tired of dance. He had "demanded too much from her," he said. "She pleaded with me to stop, but I carried on. And now look, she doesn't want anyone to do it, and it embarrasses her to talk about it." In a clever way, Joseph made it seem as if he was talking about sex. Men smiled and winked at each other. It amused them to think that Maïté was getting too much of it. They would rather think that than think another man's wife could be get-ting too much of it from Joseph.

Maïté grew more handsome with the years. She had shapely, sturdy legs, and her body's upper and lower curves matched each other. Her pale, round face became brown and lean, fitting to her intelligence, and her patient gaze gave nothing away. About many a quiet and somber person hangs a suspicion of hidden passion. And that was true of Maïté, who was suspected of having lovers by inexperienced men who desired her. Although Maïté was correct and hospitable, the men were awkward with her because of her husband's rumored infidelities, and few women could confide in her because of their own betrayals, so she lived for much of the time among her own thoughts.

Lately, the men in the café were talking about a foreign dog, the English border collie, that was replacing their traditional working dogs and winning all the sheepdog championships up and down the country. In our valley, there was as yet only one example of such a dog. It was owned by the Aramburus' neighbor, Dédé, who was obsessed with it.

Dédé's border collie had been the puppy of a prize winner at a competition in the north years before, and he had paid a lot for it. He spoke to it in French, which it didn't seem to mind, and worked it so diligently that it had won a prize or two itself in the region. For a while, Dédé's dog was the envy of the valley. Now it's still the talk of the valley, but no one envies it. It got kicked by a horse—a common enough occurrence. It went into a seizure, like all dogs who get kicked in the head by a horse, and then came out of it, as most dogs do, and seemed perfectly normal, as most dogs are after such a thing. But the dog wasn't quite right, and for a working dog, its wrongness was a tragedy. It confused a single command. On the shout *"couché!"*—instead of lying down in front of the sheep, it would run at them on a tight curve, stampeding them.

Once he had found the answer to why his prized dog had made such a mess of driving his flock down from the hills after the accident, Dédé publicly set himself the task of re-training the dog. The prized collie went everywhere with him—even in his car—sitting in the front seat and gazing out of the window like an old woman with sad eyes, looking as if he understood Dédé's anguish but could not help him.

"They are smart dogs, those collies," Joseph said to the men in the café, "but do they understand the ewes the way our dogs do? Learning circus tricks for dog trials is one thing, but learning the traditions of the high pasture is another. Our dogs learn what they need to do from their mothers, as they learnt it from theirs. You can't teach that with shouts. Our dogs go distances beyond earshot. They move big flocks over dangerous steep terrain, not just a handful of penned sheep, who've never seen the mountains, around artificial barriers." Everyone agreed. This is the way men talk when confronted with a new idea. It is normal for men in the café to support the old ways. Each one there knew, however, as he savored his small coffee and large brandy, that each of the others was secretly looking out for one of those foreign dogs for himself.

The Aramburus had a sheepdog that Maïté was proud of, but who was no longer young. She was the great granddaughter of Maïté's first dog, and a fine example of the Pyrenean type. Quick intelligent face, robust, good stamina. She was perfect for broad hillsides and large flocks and she knew her job, having learnt it from her mother, which is as it should be. But Joseph and the dog were uncomfortable together. The dog's real master was Maïté, who was a gifted dog handler and had no trouble moving her flock around.

Maïté was interested in Dédé's dog, and though she wouldn't go to watch the trials herself, she made Joseph report in detail on Dédé's yearly attempt to re-instate his prize collie. Often Joseph hadn't witnessed the attempt and borrowed his report from someone else. This year, however, Joseph was attentive to the trials, explaining everything to two American girls whose enormous backpacks he had helped move to a secure spot under the stand.

It was a brilliant day, and the frail new stand was packed with spectators. A few mares' tails hung in the high blue, suggesting a weather change in a few days. But the high dark ridges all around the valley were hazy and Joseph knew the fine weather would continue. Joseph turned his head to the northern ridge and followed the line to where the forbidding gray cliff faces rose out of the dark bracken. He could just make out the shepherd's hut below the ridge crest and off to one side the mottled pale specks that were the village's combined flock of sheep. Joseph was happy at the thought of taking his turn up in the hut as guardian of the flock for the next week. It was September, his favorite season, after the tourists and before the hunters, when the weather was often calm and still for days, and the biting flies had gone, and the bracken was still green. The summer's hard work was done, the children were back at school, and women had a little more time for assignations. And of course, he reminded himself, as he drew his eyes down from the ridge, there were the American blondes!

Joseph charmed the two girls easily, drew out their story and their plans, brought them to the other café in the town. The girls felt relief, at first, at falling into a conversation they could understand, and then they felt the flattery of someone choosing to speak to them in their own language. They were hikers heading for the mountains, having come as far as they could by train.

The café was crowded and noisy. The girls' backpacks caused some cursing in the doorway, but Joseph returned every curse with a joke, defending the girls with laughter that also welcomed them into the heart of the room.

The talk was about Dédé's performance that afternoon. It had been a let-down. The dog had behaved miserably and Dédé had given up halfway through when the dog tried to run the sheep into the stand. In the bar, debate was squashed by a raucous table of drinkers who declared their faithful support for the border collie.

"Well," said Joseph to the packed café, "aren't these dogs flawed in some way?" He stood up and smiled conspiratorially at the girls. He stretched, and the drinkers somehow made him a little space, pressing back against one another to the walls. Then he curled himself forward a little, widening his eyes, opening his mouth and showing the hint of a tongue between his teeth. He went up on his toes and took a couple of cautious steps. Everyone recognized Dédé's dog, straining and eager in front of a flock. As Joseph danced lightly around the tables, darting his head at faces, people shifted, smiling, but nervous, keeping their distance. His neat steps and lithe legs mocked every dog gait, from a slow inching forward to a canter and a gallop. He moved precisely, following the shepherd's commands that he called out to himself, as he danced the mime of Dédé's dog rounding up sheep. He stopped in front of the raucous table, shoulders rocked forward. All eyes were on him, expecting one thing but not sure if they were going to see it. Without moving his lips, Joseph uttered the command in mimicry of the high flat voice that Dédé used in the trials, *"Couché!"*

Before the silence could settle, Joseph barked and darted to one side of the table, snapping his teeth. In spite of their expectations, it startled those at the table, who gave a fair imitation of frightened sheep. One surprised old man threw himself back too far and turned his chair over, an outflung arm with a fist enclosing a brandy glass hitting the man to his left in the face and knocking him over as well. The pair collapsed on each other while the bar erupted in applause and a great deal of laughter that lingered on.

"You see," said Joseph, "these collies are flawed." He returned to the girls, whose faces gleamed with admiration.

"Those packs," he said, when the café had settled down, "they make beautiful girls so ugly. Look." He mimed a hunchback. "How can you show your elegance and sweetness?" He straightened up. "How can you lift your chin, toss your hair with disdain at the lover who leaves you? These"—he hefted the little pagodas—"are an abomination."

"We have to carry our tents and sleeping bags."

"You are not gypsies. You have a right to live like people. Here." He showed them on their map. "You want to climb this peak and you want to see this valley and you want to go into Spain." He moved his finger slowly along the contours until it came to rest on a small black mark. "You want somewhere you can lie down, go to sleep, in comfort.

"You can do all these things you want to do with the comfort of a home. This is my cabin. There is water, a hearth, a place to sleep, a place to wash also, and . . ."

"Toilet?"

"Yes, of course, toilet." The girls looked at each other. They had been in the half-world of traveling for so long they were ready for anything that seemed like a home. "I can show you, and you can decide," Joseph continued. "We can go from here. You have the place to yourselves for a week, then I shall come to stay for the sheep."

Joseph knew that hospitality was an easy thing in America. To these girls, he thought that such an offer would not sound out of place. He did not say that his tour of duty up there began that night. He did not want to give them any reason to refuse.

Joseph drove the girls up to the hut in his nondescript Lada jeep, of which there are many in our part of the world. The girls hung out of the windows commentating excitedly on every view. The girl behind him had to grip hard to the back of Joseph's seat at many of the rough passages, and her blonde hair, flying free, often brushed the back of his neck. Maïté's dog—Joseph always thought of her as that—clung to the packs in the back, silent as only the worried can be.

They arrived at dusk. The girls squealed with delight and ran around the hut not knowing what to examine first. Joseph could hear from the clang of bells that the flock was nearby and safe, and he didn't feel any need to seek them out quite yet. The dog, who knew the hut well, made a quick examination and then sat by the doorway with her tongue out, her experienced eyes half closed, and her back to Joseph.

The hut sat on a small shelf just below the brow of the ridge and looked south over the valley that stretched east and west far below it. In front of the hut was a pole-fenced paddock and corridor where the sheep could be penned for milking. By the door was a trough to which water from a spring was piped and where the shepherds used to wash out their large copper cheese pans in the days when they milked hundreds of sheep a day and made themselves rich from the large roundels of pure sheep's cheese they cured in racks beneath the platform where they slept. Cut into the slope beside the hut was a small gully where the spring emerged. Two short oaks grew in it, and beneath them was a flattened rock on which those who were not afraid of laminak could sleep in the shade, out of the midsummer sun.

In our part of the world, laminak are tough female fairies who are the construction gangs of the nether world. They will help humans occasionally but they drive hard bargains and don't like being crossed. Joseph, who approved of tradition but ridiculed myth, had made love many times on that flat rock, taking a risk from being out in the open since there are few places in our part of the world not observed by someone. Maïté, too, had given herself to persistent Dédé on that rock two months before she married Joseph, in the summer when the suitors came calling. She hadn't wanted it to happen, but it happened anyway. It was from then that she believed the place to be special to the laminak. And often, since the death of the son she had made with Dédé, she had approached that rock and talked to the mysterious creatures, hoping they might give her an answer as to why she could not face Dédé again or have children with Joseph. Sometimes she would walk to lür galdüa, another place ruled by laminak, hoping to find them there, but she never did.

She loved lür galdüa because it was a pure place, and she loved its name, which Joseph had given it. Joseph had read the book *The Lost World*, and many times as a boy, walking along the ridges in boredom, he had imagined himself an explorer discovering a lost world. He was impressed by the inaccessible tableland described in the story and, years later, named a similar feature on the ridge near the shepherd's hut *lür galdüa*—"the lost world." This name stuck with the shepherds, replacing the old name, which few had known, given to the tableland when laminak were thought to have made it.

Lür galdüa was a circular column of sheer rock with a flat turfed top, joined to the hillside by a grassy causeway that sloped down to it from the ridge. Part of its circumference was bordered by rocks, but elsewhere the grass grew right to the edge of the sheer drop over the cliff. To anyone down below in the valley, lür galdüa was indistinguishable from the line of sheer cliffs that rose out of the broad ridge at the entrance to the valley. Even those who knew it could not make it out against the backdrop of ridge and rock face. The sheep liked the spot because the grass was rich, so the shepherds let them use it, especially in autumn when good grass was scarce. But the downhill slope of the causeway would often draw more sheep onto the tableland than it could comfortably handle.

Getting a large flock out of lür galdüa was difficult because there was only one access, and a shepherd would have to approach the tableland along the only exit for the sheep. A wise shepherd would leave his dog in the hut, since in a large flock of sheep there are many ideas of which way to run. Until a flock is running like a stream, each sheep will tend to start off in the direction it faces, so many of them, when faced with an intruder—like a dog trying to do its job—will as likely jump over the cliff as head for the way out. The men in the café were all agreed that letting the flock eat its fill, and then leave, in its own quiet way, was probably best, but the experienced shepherds knew that even then there was a risk of losing some animals over the edge, especially lambs.

In the hut, Joseph made a fire, set out a simple meal and wine. Joseph's experience was wide. When he stopped at the general store to buy up the last of the bread, he picked out a packet of marshmallows from the sweet rack. In the cabin, he made little toasting forks from oak twigs, and they huddled round the fire to toast the small soft sweets. The girls softened in the same way. Joseph could almost taste their sweetness.

Behind them was the sleeping floor—a raised platform under the roof where sleepers might profit from the heat of the fire the longest. The girls had laid out their sleeping bags and emptied their sacks up there. Joseph had not made any indication of where he was to spend the night, and the girls had not asked.

After the wine, Joseph felt softened but powerful. He led the girls outside with an old paraffin lantern, which he set in the empty trough by the door. Then he led them away from the hut and told them to look up. The girls gasped. Here in the Pyrenees, the air is very clear, and the dome of the heavens is startling at the end of the summer when the night air is dry and warm. Right above them, dividing the sky in half, was the great ribbon of the Milky Way, visible in all its contours and breaks.

The girls craned their necks, turning this way and that, trying to take it all in.

"Up there," Joseph said, lifting his arm and pointing to an arbitrary point in the ribbon of light, "is the center of this galaxy. If you took all the stars right away, yes, turned them right off, the sky would still look exactly like this, only the little lights would not be stars, they would be other galaxies."

"Wow!" the girls exclaimed.

"I, too, am a star," he said and took up a comic pose. "It's time for you to learn to dance. You know the fandango?" He held his arms up and crossed his feet rapidly, moving from side to side. His style was both elegant and satirical.

The girls laughed. "That's a fandango?"

"A fandango of the south, over the mountains. Come, let us do it together." Joseph pulled the girls into a line, put an arm around each waist, and patiently went through the steps with them. "Now," he said, "together." And he hummed the melody to which all three moved. The girls laughed and shook their hair, arms raised, fingers snapping. They were relaxed and easy with Joseph's light touch, and when they were sure of the steps, they let go and danced apart, turning this way and that to the rhythm that he clapped for them.

From the darkness beneath the oak trees by the spring, Maïté sat and watched Joseph cavort with the two girls. She heard their laughter and smelled the earth that their busy feet kicked up in front of the hut. She had been at the flat rock all afternoon, waiting for the laminak, who had not come. They had not come the last two times she had made the climb from her house. Did they have nothing more to say to her? In the way of people who have set out to find something and feel confused when they find it, Maïté felt confused. At the last new moon, the laminak had given her an answer, but had she understood it? Could she trust it?

Maïté kept her eyes on the girls in front of her, but she was not looking at them. She was contemplating the youth that the girls had brought to this old place. She did not feel old either. She felt light and shining, like them. Now, the meaning of the laminak's answer was clear and unmistakable: she would, at last, try for another child. The laminak had shown her how. She was fertile still, and younger than many new mothers.

Joseph made the girls sit down, refilled their glasses. "Now," he said, "I'll show you real dancing." And in his frayed espadrilles, on the bare earth by the hut, he began to describe his first role—Satan in the village pastorale. His words carried easily to Maïté who watched, not simply with her eyes, but with all the energy of her mind.

"Satan and his lieutenant approach," Joseph said, "from below the stage, from the underworld. He hopped from one foot to the other making a scissor with his free foot, like this." Then back and forth he went in a lilting stride. He began to recite the words from his pastorale. "So, master, you have been a long time in this valley. What do you intend for the people of Esquiague?" Joseph changed his voice. "The good lady has a weakness for superstition and I shall turn her mind from her duke. I will set maiden against man and leave no faithful in the church. Look how our dance will set heart against heart."

And Joseph sprang in the air like an arrow, the simple movement made vivid by the dark shadows thrown by the lamp. His face was radiant with the joy of his strength and control. Maïté stared as if her whole mind was reaching forward through the darkness toward the dancing man. She saw his all-consuming self-regard that, in the end, brought nothing to life! A barren vanity!

Joseph's body extended out to her and occupied her vantage point. His movements were inescapable. They touched her, penetrated her skin, and spread into her bones. She was held down as if by a weight, while her soul was being slowly drawn out of her toward the stars. Paralyzed, she did not recognize anyone or herself anymore. It was as if all people had vanished from the hills and only the twisting coils of the devil held her in his illicit and extinguishing grip.

After Joseph had danced, he kissed both girls and, arm around each waist, led them slowly into the hut. He undressed them both delicately and made love to the first while the other lay in quiet contemplation beside. When the first girl sighed and let her arms drop, Joseph turned to the other and began to pleasure her slowly. Later they slept in a confusion of limbs.

Under the oaks, Maïté regained her awareness, and her eyes focused once more on the dark shadow of the hut and the dark emptiness around it. She knew where to go. She knew that it was the perfect time, and he would receive her willingly. Had he not spent his whole life waiting for this one moment? Later the laminak would have to be paid, but she knew how.

At first light, Joseph was awakened by the sound of wild barking way off in the distance in the direction of the escarpment. He looked down from the sleeping platform and saw Maïté's old dog still lying by the fire, head on her paws, old eyes looking up at Joseph. Joseph slid down the little wooden ladder with his clothes and dressed quickly. He opened the door. The air was fresh but the day would have heat in it. The two girls shifted in sleep as he called to the dog, but the dog only stared at him. Joseph cursed her under his breath and closed the door. Where were the sheep? He heard the bark again. Was it familiar? It came from the direction of the "lost world."

When Joseph breasted the ridge and looked down upon lür galdüa, he cursed. The villagers' combined flock was crowded tight onto the grassy tableland. A thousand sheep were in an area that would have looked small with a hundred. A wild dog must have done this. He could not see the dog in the half-light, but he knew it must be somewhere, among the big boulders on the main ridge, and that meant he had no option but to try to move the flock out before the crazy dog came again and ran the sheep over the cliffs.

Joseph set off down the slope slowly and then veered to the cliff-top on the right. He grabbed several of the first line of sheep and flung them up the causeway, but they bleated in fear and pushed back into the flock. There was nothing for it but to get behind them. He had never done this before, but the technique had been discussed in the café. A careful man should be able to work his way along the circumference of the tableland to the point furthest from the causeway, and then, with gentle persuasion, urge the flock away from him and up the causeway slope to the main ridge. The rocks bordering the cliff edge were damp with dew. Joseph slipped once or twice, and was thankful that the gloom hid the sheer drop beneath his heels. As he crept along, he had to push aside sheep that were being edged closer and closer to the precipice by the agitations of the pack. When he touched their backs, they jerked up their heads, lips curled and eyes rolling. They smelled of sweat and fear and their droppings trodden into the slick grass. They were so tightly packed their bells were muffled. One tried to leap away from him, its feet landing on the back of the animal in front. Joseph wondered if he could grab its fleece to steady himself, but likely as not that would start the panic he feared, or pull the animal down with him.

His foot shot out from under him and a rock bolted into the darkness. He caught at a grassy tuft while he waited for the crash below. Nothing! He straightened up and found a new foothold. Then he heard the faint liquid sound of the rock smashing itself to pieces below. His skin rippled with fear. He was higher than he thought.

There were stinging nettles in every crevice, and his hands tingled as if they had been electrocuted, which made him rage at the sheep. Slowly, Joseph inched his way around, but before he had got to the spot opposite the causeway, he ran out of boulders to cling to. There was only a clean drop where the grass met the air. "So much for the men in the café," Joseph muttered to himself, "this is impossible." He let go of his last handhold and stood up among the sheep with his back to the cliff.

He pushed the animal in front of him. "Ha!" he said quietly to encourage it. The sheep leant back into his hands, telling him there was nowhere to go. The flock was stilled. Something was holding them. Joseph was puzzled. He rose on the balls of his feet and peered up the causeway in the dawning light. He saw something—a flash of white! The dog! He could just make out the shape. It was sitting at the entrance. No wonder the sheep wouldn't move. A white throat! There was only one dog with a white throat. "Dédé!" Joseph called out. "It's me, Joseph. I'm trapped at the back." There was no answer. "For the love of God, Dédé, call off your dog. Dédé!"

Then he saw her—or at least, he saw her silhouette. Her face was in darkness. "Maïté? What are you doing up here?" he shouted too loudly, and the flock shifted and pressed against him. He could feel their strength and knew they would batter anything with their heads when desperate. He struggled to keep his balance.

There was no answer to fill the long pause, and Joseph was at a loss. Eventually he said, "How did you get the dog? Dédé never lets it out of his sight." No answer. "Maïté! Is it because of the girls? For heaven's sake, they are just girls, a bit of fun!" Her silence drove him to silence. He tried to push against the sheep, but they were becoming increasingly uneasy. Then he said in a cajoling voice, "What have I done that you haven't known about? What's different? You've always known about me. We went our separate ways—it was what you wanted." Silence. It was lighter now. Joseph could see Maïté's face, staring into another distance, Dédé's English collie in front of her, immobile but straining forward at the flock with eagerness. "So, the children didn't come. It was not my fault." Maïté's head seemed to jerk stiffly from side to side at those words. "I had a son but he died. That was that. Many live with that sorrow. Maïté, what is it? We can confess to each other. We've been together so long. We know each other." Again, Joseph thought he saw Maïté's head shake in small mechanical movements. "Maïté!" he shouted, suddenly impatient and fearful. His mind was dry of possibilities. His hands and legs trembled as they used to before an important performance. "Maïté! Say something, for the love of God!"

Maïté turned her head to the dog. In a firm and resolute voice she commanded, *"Couché!"*

DIRTY DANCING
Carole Nelson Douglas

The orange flyer featured drawings of balloons, cocktail glasses, and confetti, its centerpiece a crude picture of a fifties-vintage convertible. Words angled here and there: "Drinks," "Dancing," "Disco."

"'Portnoy's.' Sounds like a place my kids would go against my best advice," I complained when the girls at work flourished the flyer for the monthly employees' club outing. "What is it?"

"Oh, a singles' bar, really," said Mary Lou, "but our group booked it earlier in the evening, before the rush." She is an outgoing bottle redhead who is becoming pleasantly plump now that menopause has come and gone. "It'll be fun. They have a huge buffet, and drinks, of course, and pool tables and stuff."

"Sounds like a blast," Connie said, her choice of words revealing her own fifties generation and taking me back to my single years, which had suddenly come again.

Connie was younger than Mary Lou and me, a thin, forbidding-looking fashion plate who was actually a cream puff at heart.

"Why not the usual daytime outing?" I wondered. "I don't even know what to wear to that kind of place."

"Oh, we'll dress up, I imagine," said Mary Lou. "You know, something middle-aged-respectable but a little kicky. Listen, we old broads would never dare go to a place like that if it weren't under company auspices. Some guy in accounting is program chair and he set it up. We can see how the aerobic set lives."

"You make it sound like a strip bar," I fussed. My upbringing always inclined me to step wide around the nonrespectable.

"It's not," Mary Lou assured me. "My kids have been there. Do you think I'd let them go anyplace tacky?"

I wasn't keen on going to a place that appealed to my friends' kids: Unlike many parents, I knew that kids like to do things that their parents would never approve of.

But I'd never missed a company outing, so I went.

I didn't expect to be nervous, any more than I had expected to be suddenly single. And I know I'm out of touch with the modern-day cult of the deliberately crass, but the smooth, unexceptional course of my life has isolated me from the ruder realities. I grew up in the midwest and attended college long enough to acquire a degree and a fiancé.

His name was Jim, and he was, of course, a gentleman.

We had two children, who never gave us more than the expected minor trouble. When they were both in high school, I entered the working world. College loomed, and while Jim was doing well working for the city, additional income was nothing to sniff at. Besides, we wanted other things than the necessities; we weren't getting any younger.

I was as giddy as a girl graduate to win my first paid position at a large bank in town, and while the ins and outs of finance are more arcane than most, I thrived on the challenge and a new circle of work friends, many women like myself, either single parents or working wives.

Despite one or two women vice presidents—who avoided fraternizing with the other women employees, not wanting to be mistaken for less than what they were—women mostly filled the firm's support jobs and had the sort of easy camaraderie that made going to work stimulating.

The kids moved on to college in that smooth slipstream all middle-class families dream of. Everything was wonderful. Jim and I were even planning a modest cruise for Christmas.

Then he died. Suddenly, at work. I was notified at my desk, but my rush to the hospital was a mere formality. The heart attack had been unheralded and immediate.

At fifty-two, I was a widow, a bewildered widow who'd had no warning. Everything I'd done, everything I'd assumed, had been Jim and I. Now "I" was at sea. The cruise seemed pointless, although the kids urged me to go anyway. The kids were always urging me to do something atypical after Jim died, as if they worried that I would wither if not exposed to stimuli.

Work proved to be a blessing, of course, especially my women coworkers. Women form a certain sisterhood because of the unspoken fact that they expect to last the longest, and live alone the longest.

So Mary Lou and Connie, my middle-aged girlfriends, made sure I went now and then to movies I didn't really like, and out shopping for clothes, and to the monthly office outings.

We met at Connie's house at seven-thirty, then she drove us in her Taurus to the highway that looped the city. We moved through a river of black asphalt shimmering with the head- and taillights of heavy traffic.

"I had no idea the Loop was so clogged this far past rush hour," I said from the front passenger seat.

"You've been in a rut, Linda." Mary Lou, in the backseat, sat forward to talk to me, bracing her hand on Connie's headrest. "This section of the Loop is teeming with superstores and trendy restaurants. That's a pretty dress; where did you get it?"

"Mallow's." I touched the full chiffon skirt figured in a floral swirl of dusky rose, purple, and green. "I bought it for the cruise."

They were silent for a bit. I noticed the streetlights glinting off of Mary Lou's wedding ring as we passed under them. I still wore mine, of course; it had never occurred to me to take it off.

Portnoy's announced itself with racy outlines of red and lavender neon. Except for that garish decoration, it resembled the nearby upscale franchise restaurants that squatted on black islands of asphalt parking lots all along the freeway—a one-story sprawling building tricked out with ersatz Art Deco architectural details. The facade's wavy glass block windows reflected the red neon, making it look as if bloody, agitated water washed against them.

Inside the place was dim and barnlike, the bar a neon-outlined altar winking with glassware and bottles. A wooden dance floor adjoined the bar, and the only other seating was the far banquettes that rimmed the perimeter and a few tiny round tables on stilts.

I recognized a sprinkle of faces there as we headed for the banquettes. Unused to wearing high heels except to weddings, I stepped gingerly over the polished parquet dance floor.

Everyday faces had altered in that lurid nightclub atmosphere. The other women had chosen dressy clothes as well, thank God; the men, of course, looked the same. Suits are suits.

After the women complimented each other on their outfits, our group hunted for a table. I realized that the banquettes had to be mounted by a step, and that the only occasional chairs were actually high stools.

"This is silly." Mary Lou giggled, hopping up on a stool despite her high heels. "I'm too old to do this without jiggling like a bowl full of jelly in all the wrong places."

"Maybe this is the wrong place," I suggested.

A willowy woman definitely young enough to hop on and off a hundred barstools without jiggling anywhere but where it draws applause passed our table. "Drinks, ladies?"

We eyed each other. "A margarita," Connie ordered with aplomb. Mary Lou rolled her lively eyes. "I can never make up my mind—how about a . . . lite beer?"

The girl nodded, then eyed me with the bright, expectant look of a begging squirrel that I assumed was her workaday mask. I can never decide either.

"A Bloody Mary," I finally said.

She sashayed off with the round brown empty tray and I noticed then that her skirt barely covered her bottom.

"The men will love this place," Mary Lou predicted, in a low, laughing voice.

"I like the family outings better," I said. "With our failing eyes, we can hardly see in this barn. Wasn't the sleigh ride in December fun? Or that June trip to the water park? What are we going to do here, except drink and talk to only the people we know?"

"It's good to see how the other half lives," Mary Lou said. "And I hated wearing a bathing suit in front of all my coworkers. Some things are meant to be kept between an older woman and her Maker, like cellulite. Gosh, look at this place. I forgot what it was like being meat on the hook and single."

A few young customers were edging into the cavernous space, all dressed with casual care and all wearing a wary, hopeful look in their eyes. The place was otherwise deserted except for our group, but suddenly the music system shuddered into loud life.

"Goll-y." Mary Lou clapped her palms over the red curls covering her ears. "I thought our hearing was supposed to be going too."

Already the cigarette smoke from a banquette behind us was drifting into my nostrils, tickling my allergies. The pounding bass beat made the stool legs and the tabletop vibrate, a slight, shrilly annoying sensation that made me move my hands to the boxy black satin evening bag sitting on my perilously slanted lap.

Then an odd thing happened. I found my feet tapping the stool's wooden rail to the thunderous beat. Jim and I used to dance when we were dating, standing apart but near, gyrating to music not quite as loud but just as insistent. Married life and responsibilities had made that phase less than a memory. Now, here, unexpectedly, it came back. The Jim of those days came back—tall, thin, a bit raw, but so likable . . . and ultimately, so lovable.

I would not dissolve into more widow's tears; not in public. Jim's death had shown me how repressive the fifties had been: A public place was nowhere to display affection, fears, tears, or even opinions that might ruffle someone.

I wished that I had been less inhibited and had gone to work sooner, had not neglected myself while I fulfilled the roles of wife and mother. Now husband and kids were gone, and I was like some gawky, awkward spinster despite my devotion to husband, home, and family. I was alone and aging, linked by telephones to my nearest and dearest. If I hadn't had work . . .

A new song—if you can call contemporary music that—came on. No, not a new one—an old one. The forgotten but familiar guitar twangs snapped my senses like a barrage of rubber bands. "Johnny B. Goode."

"Oh," I said impulsively to Mary Lou. "Jim and I used to dance to that all the time when we were young. That rhythm makes me want to beat my feet on some floor all night."

Mary Lou glanced around the dim room. "Too bad there aren't any suitable partners in the employees' club—unless you want to ask the night security guard to dance," she added with a snicker. "He's here alone."

Harvey was a retiree past seventy—genial and paunchy, with a slight limp.

I jerked an elbow into her side. "Shhh!" With the music so blaring, I had to talk loud even to urge discretion. "I wouldn't ask anyone to dance, but I sure love that music. Oh! Listen to it! Doesn't it get your blood pumping? I loved to dance to that song." The deserted dance floor begged for some young people gyrating on it, even if they were only ghosts.

"Say," came a voice from the nearest banquette. "Jerry likes to dance and I don't. Why don't you two hit the floor?"

She was a beautiful young woman—dark-haired with classic features, and more, a kind face. Startled, I eyed her escort, a man I'd never seen at the company. He was perfectly presentable, a classic thirtysomething with curly blond hair and the eager, energetic smile of a born salesman. Maybe his slight buck teeth enhanced that notion.

"I couldn't! I haven't danced in years."

"Go ahead," the young woman urged. "I hate to deprive Jerry."

He was getting up and coming toward me, his friendly grin as unwelcome to me as a sinister leer. I was appalled. I wasn't used to making a spectacle of myself. For thirty years, not doing that had been my vocation. How was I going to untangle myself gracefully from the damn high chair?

And still, at my back, the music's beat beckoned, making me giddy, making me reckless.

Who cared what a woman past fifty did? Jim and I had planned to dance again, a little, on the cruise. This unknown young man couldn't possibly be construed as anything but a "safe" sexless partner for a woman my age.

Besides, he was pulling back my stool. Before I knew it, I was tipped onto my tottery feet—the shoes were new—and we were threading past the empty tables to that empty, garishly lit dance floor where a ghost of a me I'd forgotten was urging, *Hurry up, the song will end. This is your last chance.*

"Do you whoosh dance?" he asked from behind me.

"What? I can't hear over the music."

"Push dance?"

"Push? No, I never heard of it."

We were on the floor and I turned to my providential partner, hoping I wouldn't look too silly doing the gyrations of thirty years ago, the Swim and the Jerk. Maybe I would pick up some updated moves from him.

He grabbed my hand.

No! We danced alone, in the old days, without touching, without accommodating ourselves to a partner. Didn't they still do that? Isn't that what was on MTV all the time nowadays?

He swung me behind him, his strength unexpected in such a wiry short man, jerking me around like a Raggedy Ann doll. I turned, dazed, and he jerked me in the opposite direction. I was dizzy already, and disoriented, and the soles of my untried high heels skidded over the slick floor.

He never let me go. He never let me stand in one place. It didn't matter what I did, I was an object he manipulated. He twirled me under his arm and I felt the underarm seam of my new dress rip. I wasn't dressed for this kind of workout, this kind of wrenching.

Around me, the seductively throbbing music had become a relentless cage of lyrics and never-ending beat.

Way down in Louisiana close to New Orleans . . .

Spun, turned, twisted, jerked in unanticipated directions, then snapped in the opposite direction . . . dizzy . . . as if trapped for endless minutes on a carnival ride you regret going on the moment it starts hurtling you in some unnatural motion. . . .

This wasn't dancing as I knew it, as I had expected, where I stood alone on my own two feet and was in control of myself. This was like a French Apache dance. The only hand-holding dance I had ever done was the sedate lindy hop as a preteen; this was a frenetic jitterbug. I could only hope he wouldn't lift me off the floor and throw me around like they used to.

Then, midway through a powerful jerk, his fingers released mine. I saw his grinning face. In the lurid light it looked demonic.

He had released me in midmotion. Like any thrown object, I kept moving, out of control. My shoe slipped on the floor. I was spinning, downward. To the floor. Hard.

The music—I had thought it was a short song, but perhaps it had been a shorter dance than the forever it felt like—twanged on. I was sitting on the floor looking like a fool, an incompetent old fool, breathless with the shock of the fall.

He came to help me up, but I pulled away, feeling my face redden as it hadn't in years, and struggled gracelessly to my feet, my high heels snagging in the full chiffon skirt.

When I turned, trying not to look beyond the dance floor to my watching coworkers, I saw him waiting for me.

"I wanted to dance alone," I shouted over the scream of the sound system. "Separately." My arms gestured apart.

He grabbed one.

I couldn't believe that he wouldn't stop, wouldn't let me go.

Jerk. I was pulled beyond him into the dark, noisy outer space beyond the shining neon planet of the dance floor, where people I knew and didn't know were grinning at the spectacle I made.

Just when I thought I would hurl into merciful darkness, his arm jerked me back into the vortex of noise and neon and his grinning face. Twirl. Pull. Spin. Jerk.

Dizziness had escalated to utter disorientation. I didn't know where dance floor or watchers were, where dark and light began and ended. I just tried to keep on my feet until the damn, driving music ended and freed me.

It did just that far too late. He released my hand.

"What were you doing?" I demanded in the quiet moment before another selection began.

"Dancing," he said, still grinning.

"I didn't know that dance."

He shrugged. Was it a matter of pride with him, that he was a short man strong enough to jerk even an inexperienced partner around the floor? You would think a good dancer, a gentleman, would not want to try anything so athletic with an unknown partner that it would send her to the floor. You would think.

I was steady enough to walk back to my table, imagining what my friends thought, or would say, but I was too numb to say anything more. Our drinks had arrived. Connie and Mary Lou were studiously sipping away before their sympathetic eyes met mine.

"We'll have to try it again sometime," he said blandly in parting. I couldn't believe his nonchalance about it all, like he tossed women to the floor every day.

"I don't think so."

He smiled again, grinned. "Sometime when we haven't been drinking."

"I was perfectly sober," I said indignantly, knowing that such assertions

33

always sounded like their opposite, but my Bloody Mary hadn't even arrived until now.

With a smug and disbelieving smile, he vanished back to his young woman, who was also smiling. I understood now why the lovely young lady with the kind face wouldn't dance with him.

. . . . .

"Forget it," Mary Lou said in the ladies' room at work the next day, fluffing her moussed curls with a metal pick. "He's just a jerk."

"But he made me look like a fool! Why? And then he acted as if it was my fault, like I was a lush or something."

She shrugged. "Nobody will remember that you fell in a few days."

"Everybody will think I'd been drinking."

"Maybe. But hey, you've got reason to let loose a little. They've all done something like that."

"I don't even know who that young couple was, where they work."

"Accounting, I think, both of them. Those people come and go."

"Not soon enough."

. . . . .

Martha in Personnel was an elevator friend of mine; we only chatted going up or down together, but we did a lot of that.

"Jerry in Accounting?" She frowned, her darkly penciled brows drawing together. She had the lacquered hair and nails of a woman groomed to greet the public, a longtime receptionist. "We've got more than one. Why are you interested?"

I lowered my voice and told her. Martha was about my age. She raised an irked eyebrow.

"What a dirty trick! And you didn't even know that push dancing is a cousin to slam dancing. You don't do that kind of a dance with a partner you haven't practiced with, or who doesn't know the dance pretty well."

"Slam dancing," I said in horror, for even I had heard of that violent exercise. "How do you know about this 'push dancing'?"

"My kids, of course," she said. "It's like jitterbug, and it's getting popular again, but it's not for amateurs. Tell you what, I'll look him up in the computer."

Her nails clicked on her clacking keyboard. "Got a Jerry Snyder . . . or a Kimball."

Inspired, I asked, "Which one is on the employee club board?"

"That info wouldn't be in here."

"I don't suppose his description is in his file."

"This ain't police headquarters, honey. But . . ."

She glanced around. "You could always go down to Accounting and check it out."

"I don't want to see him again," I said between tight teeth. "I just want to tell him off from a safe distance, so I don't kill him. If I had his phone number, I'd tell him what he did so he doesn't do it again to anyone else."

"Don't you think he knows what he did?"

"No! I think he's a thoughtless creep without any manners who imagines himself God's gift to dancing women."

"Tell you what." Martha's lethally long crimson fingernail tapped the edge of her keyboard. "You make sure it's the right Jerry, and I'll get you his home phone number."

. . . . .

Accounting was foreign territory to me; my work never called me down there. The place was a maze of the latest office cubicles, sleek, neutral-colored, and impersonal. I wandered through, feeling like an awkward intruder, ready to jump if my particular bogeyman popped up from a cubicle like a jack-in-the-box. Every cubicle I peeked into was a potential bomb of unwanted recognition for me.

"Oh."

I had not found him, but I had found her. The nameplate on her inner cubicle wall read "Misty Weatherall."

"Hi." She looked as surprised as I did.

"I'm . . . looking for your young man."

"Jerry?"

"Yeah."

"He's not my young man. I just went out with him a couple of times. I won't anymore."

"Why not?"

"He's kind of . . . got a chip on his shoulder."

"Why did you suggest I dance with him?"

"I overheard you saying you wanted to dance, and I don't dance."

"You don't push dance? Have you ever danced with Jerry?"

"Once. The second time we went out."

"And?"

Her eyes evaded mine. "I didn't fall, but I didn't like it."

"Is that why you sicced him on me?"

"Listen, you said you wanted to dance. I thought you knew how, that you could handle that kind of thing. And I sure didn't want to dance with him."

"Is that the only reason you aren't going out with him again?"

"Well, there's you. Once you two hit the floor, it was obvious that you weren't up to his speed. He should have stopped."

"Thanks."

"And he's awfully bitter about his ex-wife. It gets tiresome hearing him going on about it. Actually, I dated him because I felt sorry for him; then I felt sorry for me." She frowned. "He doesn't take no for an answer. He's going to be hard to cut loose. I guess we both made a mistake."

"Do you have his phone number?"

"Never needed it."

"What's his last name, anyway?"

"Snyder."

"Is he on the employee club committee?"

"Sure, he's program chairman now. Why do you think we all ended up in his favorite venue?"

"Wait a minute, if you overheard me wishing I could dance, did you both overhear me complaining that a singles' nightclub wasn't a great place for a meeting?"

Her dark eyes shifted to her computer screen, where a complex table of numbers stood frozen in their amber rankings. She tapped a key and the screen went black. "I heard it."

"Could he have?"

"I guess, but it was my idea to suggest the two of you dance."

"You didn't suggest the kind of dance, though."

She shrugged again and looked at me. "Jerry doesn't do any other kind of dancing."

I went back to Martha and got the phone number.

. . . . .

It did me no good.

I called it in the evenings, several evenings. All I ever got was an answering machine and a smarmy recorded message that Jerry was "out having fun."

I never left a message. I wanted to hear him respond when I told him what he had done; how irresponsible he had been. How my dress was too fragile and my shoes too new for such gymnastics, how boorish it was to hurl a strange woman old enough to be his mother around a dance floor in such a violent manner. I wanted to tell him what a cad he was to blame my fall on alcohol. All right, "cad" was a melodrama word. I wanted to tell him what a jerk he was.

"He never answers his phone himself," I complained to Connie one day. "Probably people are standing in line to tell him off."

"Why not confront him at work?"

"I've made enough scenes in front of my coworkers."

Mary Lou had overheard us and bustled over, waving papers. "I told her to forget the jerk," she explained to Connie. "He doesn't care anyway."

"Yeah." Connie's smooth blond head nodded without disturbing a hair. "Some guys are like that; they get a kick out of rattling women's cages."

"That's just it. I felt like I was caged with a wild animal out there on the dance floor. I could have seriously injured myself when I fell, broken a leg. It was . . . social assault."

"God, you women." Gene, the assistant manager, was suddenly behind me. "Everything's rape nowadays."

Speechless, I watched him walk away before I could answer, feeling rage boil over.

"He's a jerk, too," Connie said softly. "Mary Lou's right. Forget it. There isn't anything you can do about it."

. . . . .

Some acts in life are too uncivil to be borne, and sometimes they seem very small things on the surface.

I can't help feeling that way. I was reared in a generation in which children were to be seen and not heard, when politeness was an expected feature of daily life, and when most people were assumed to mean well. If knighthood was no longer in flower (I'm not that old), men—except for the most illiterate types who still spat in the street—were expected to behave like gentlemen.

I began calling Jerry Snyder impolitely early in the morning when he would be getting ready for the office, and even on weekends. Always the answering machine. Jerry was out "having fun." I even tried calling at three in the morning one night when I couldn't sleep. I was having trouble sleeping; I kept going over and over the incident in my mind, wondering if he did it deliberately because I had criticized his idea of entertainment, deciding what I would say to him when I finally cornered the rat. He deserved a good dressing down.

Martha got me his address as well, with only a lift of her eyebrow for comment.

I looked it up on the city map: deep in a nest of new apartment complexes for young singles on the city fringes.

I drove by one Saturday, looking for his unit. The buildings suggested Swiss chalets. A flashy fountain spit high into the air in an artificial pond near the complex's center. Complex was the name for the place, although it was pretentiously called Woodwinds. Laid out at angles, each building's numbers hid discreetly. I finally found number 66—a second-story unit reached by both exterior stairs and an internal elevator.

If all else failed, I could waylay him; confront him in person at his door. That meant I had to park our '85 gray Honda Civic and wait. He would have to come back to that apartment sometime.

But he didn't, not all day Saturday, and not as late as ten o'clock, when I finally gave up and left.

I needed more information than Martha's user friendly personnel files would provide. I thought about it. With his car license and description, I could find his car in the employee section of the parking ramp and follow him home after work, just like a lost dog.

The telephone again. Stomach fluttering, I called the Motor Vehicles department.

"I have a problem," I told the woman who answered, wanting to sound flustered and innocent and having no trouble doing that. I wasn't used to extracting possibly confidential information. "A gentleman and I got into a fender bender the other day. He gave me his card, but I'm in sales and call on a lot of people who give me cards, and the accident shook me up. Now my insurance company needs the information. I think I know which card it is, and have a likely name. Could you tell me what the car looks like from your records, and then I'll be sure it's the right person?"

The pause made my heart beat triple time. "I'll transfer you to someone who can help."

I repeated my spiel to a man this time, my nervousness all the more genuine. I'm sure he was thinking, "just like a woman," when he looked up the name. The computer, he told me, would take a few moments to sift through all those names for the right one in the right town.

"Two cars, ma'am. A yellow eighty-six Corvette and a black seventy-two Chevrolet Impala."

"Oh, it was the black Chevrolet. I remember it was an older car," I exclaimed with honest relief. "I certainly would have remembered the Corvair."

"Corvette," he corrected in a weary, condescending tone.

Good. I had been made to look like a fool on the dance floor, and now I was discovering that it could serve my purpose to look like one elsewhere. The clerk would never be suspicious of such a ditsy middle-aged woman.

I didn't have the license numbers—I didn't want to stir doubts by asking for too much. Better safe than sorry; I knew that from recent experience.

On my lunch hour I prowled the employee parking levels. Parking ramps are eerie, echoing places. Women are always urged to be wary in them, but now I relished the deserted air, the scrape of my shoes on cement and the squeal of cars turning down the exit ramp the only sounds. Our employees invariably ate at their desks or downtown.

Not being an expert in cars, I had purchased a Blue Book and went down the rows, proud when I stood before the broad black rear of the correct car. I jotted down the license number on my notepad.

I always got off half an hour earlier than Accounting employees. All I would have to do is drive out and park on the street near the exit—not easy during rush hour with limited spots, but if I went round and round until something turned up, it should work. And I should wear a hat or scarf, so he wouldn't recognize me. Tonight. I would put the plan into operation right after work tonight.

Everything went perfectly. I bought a nondescript scarf on my lunch hour. I looked like a grandmother, but all the better. *Oh, what big eyes you have, Grandmother!* I thanked God now that Jim and I hadn't been able to afford a flashy new car someone might notice. My hands gripped the Civic's wheel, even though I was parked; the motor was running and I was ready.

As cars poured in a relentless stream from the parking ramp's mouth, I had only a moment to identify the right vehicle. This was the hardest part. Cars all looked alike to me, except for the most obviously different ones. And so many people had black, gray, and white cars these days. With dirt and dust, they all faded into one monotonous neutral stream.

Then—a large, dusty-black silhouette, a flash of blond curly hair. I wrenched the steering wheel and checked the traffic stream in my left mirror—a truck coming fast in my entry lane.

I pressed the accelerator and spun out of the parking place. Behind me an angry trucker honked. I didn't care; I was only a car behind the black '72 Chevrolet.

I stayed behind, but it never went onto the Loop, toward Woodwinds. That unnerved me. I knew how to get there. I didn't know where the car would take me now.

Then, after we left the crowded downtown and I did get an idea, I didn't like where it was leading me—out to the dingy circle of deteriorating neighborhoods that ringed the downtown, we drove. Out where makeshift Vietnamese restaurants stand next door to pawnshops and laundromats and missions, and even big, belching, city buses drive by fast. Out where gangs wage war and men lie like the dead in alleyways, drunk or drugged or even really dead.

It was still broad daylight, but driving through that area dimmed my vision; I was as nervous as if nightfall veiled my senses.

Jerry stopped his car before a seedy-looking three-story brick apartment building from the twenties. He vanished inside. Too scared to venture after him, I decided to wait for him to come out again.

And, again, he didn't, at least not by eight o'clock, which was as long as I dared stay, even with all the car doors locked.

I decided I had to follow him again, and I needed more protection than locks. I was able to purchase a can of pepper spray from the gun section of the local mall's sports outlet. Standing at the glass counter with all the mechanical black and silver weapons laid out on shelves beneath me was . . . nerve-racking. The young man behind the counter even assumed I wanted to buy a gun.

"Can just anybody do that?" I asked with an uneasy laugh.

"Yes, ma'am. Just fill out a form and wait a few days. Want to see anything?"

I eyed the foreign instruments. That's what they looked like, instruments for some strange manufacturing process. "No, thanks. The human bug spray should do it."

. . . . .

"How about a movie tonight? *Jurassic Park* should be running out of hordes of kids by now at the cheapie theaters."

Connie and Mary Lou stood beside my desk like the Bobbsey Twins, radiating innocent eagerness.

"No . . . uh, thanks. I have to volunteer at the old folks' home tonight."

They finally left, after more idle chitchat, which I had no time for. I had things to do.

Driving behind Jerry after work that day was a picnic. In fact, I had brought along a thermos of coffee and had packed a sandwich and raw veggies with a cookie in an Igloo cooler—I hadn't made lunches like that since the kids were in grade school. I was prepared for the long haul. He was not going to elude me this time. Besides, it was so fascinating to watch the smartly suited young accountant vanish into that disreputable building. Why?

This time I didn't park the moment he went in. I drove around the block, undeterred by overflowing Dumpsters and a ragged man shuffling down the alley behind Jerry's place. Alley! On the next cruise through, I turned down that narrow way lined with dented silver garbage cans and littered with trash.

I counted the buildings as I drove and—yes! A shambling wooden garage for four cars hunkered behind Jerry's building. The alley was narrower, dimmer, meaner than the street, but I found a deserted garage to park by. Then I slumped behind the wheel and waited.

None too soon. A dirty door in Jerry's garage began crawling upward on its tracks, screeching with age. Shortly after, a sleek, low yellow rear bumper edged out. Jerry backed the Corvette in the absolutely wrong direction to the way I was facing. Frantic, I balled up my fists, then started the car and seesawed it out of the cramped spot. The Corvette was gone when I was once more pointed down the alley, but I hit the accelerator and sped at forty miles an hour down the lane. One wasn't supposed to drive more than twenty in an alley, I remembered from my long-ago driver's test, but this was an emergency.

My car paused for the side street as I peered right and left. A yellow glint at my right made me jerk the wheel that way. The old car squealed at such treatment; Jim would know why a steering wheel always did that when cranked too hard. I didn't care. I followed the car back onto the street in front of the apartment buildings.

The Corvette was attracting greedy street glances now, but Jerry was impervious, fleeing this sad neighborhood. My car attracted no notice, from the street men or from Jerry.

We headed for the Loop at last, and I was mentally rehearsing my diatribe against him, which by now had become quite a production. He would finally face what he had done and realize his behavior had been thoughtless at best and caddish at worst.

But the yellow Corvette did not take the exit for Woodwinds.

Instead of entering an affluent apartment complex, I finally found my car sitting in the parking lot in front of a big, boxy building identified only by a big, boxy, cheap-looking sign high on a pole beside it. "Foxy Chix," it read, none too legibly. "Topless dancing. Beautiful babes."

I sighed and set about eating dinner and drinking coffee and waiting for dark, which no longer scared me, because then I would be invisible.

With the pepper spray in my right hand, I waited past eleven. The yellow—atrocious color for a car, and yet how fitting to his poisonous personality!—Corvette was impossible to miss, even at night in the dimly lit parking lot. Sinister customized vans hiding who-knows-what in their roomy, secret interiors; pickup trucks; junkers; sports cars whose names I didn't know; and massive motorcycles sprinkled the lot around me. It was only a weeknight, after all.

About eleven-thirty I noticed movement by the Corvette and sat up straight.

I dared to roll down the window a bit. Voices, abrading voices, drifted in through it. A man's and a woman's.

"I told you to leave me alone, Jerry! Damn it, why do you come here?" Her voice was ragged, raw, and on the verge of sobs. "I'm working."

"I pay for my drinks like anybody else. I can watch you like anybody else, Tiffany." He sneered the name, obvious pseudonym that it was.

"I don't want to see you anymore."

"But I can see you any time I want, all of you. Come on, get in the car."

"No! I just want you out of here. Get a life, get another girl, get one who wants you. I don't."

Something rang in the air, the clap of a hand on a face. I started the motor, thinking of my own two daughters, who would never be caught dead in a place like this, yet. . . .

I shifted into gear. I didn't want to . . . to blow my cover, but I could see the two figures interlocked, and this time the push dancing was serious.

I pulled on my headlights and pointed my car at them. They were framed and frozen by lights like deer on the highway.

Jerry's face wore the same leer/sneer I knew so well from my one nightmarish dance with him. The girl who was shaken in his grasp, being pulled this way and that, now suddenly jerked to face the lights. Her expression was unforgettable, fear and struggle masking her pretty, made-up features. I was aware of long, bare legs and arms, of white boots and some skimpy sort of cover-up, of flying long red hair etched into flaming tendrils against the car's garish yellow background.

"Let me go, Jerry," she begged as she saw her opportunity. "Just let go and don't come back."

He glared into the corona of my headlights, looking for someone to blame behind the wheel. Then he released her so quickly that she fell, fell hard against the car. My foot pressed the accelerator as he jumped into the Corvette's low front seat.

In a moment he had roared away with taillights as red as the devil's eyes glaring back at us. I slowed to cruise past the dazed and shaken girl. She stared mindlessly into my driver's window as I passed. I knew that in the dark it was only a blank, black grease-blob of glass, and that I was nameless and faceless, just another passerby in the night.

. . . . .

The phone was ringing when I got home.

"Linda! Mary Lou and I were worried sick! If you're going to be out so late, let us know."

"What did you call for?"

"Well, we wanted to take you out to dinner. You've been keeping to yourself so much lately. You dash out of work every night like a rabbit scurrying home to its burrow. We're worried that silly incident at Portnoy's is turning you into a hermit."

I tried not to laugh.

.   .   .   .   .

The next day, I decided my investigation needed to take a new tack. Martha could help me again.

"Ex-wife?" She frowned at her computer screen. "I doubt we'd have that."

"She wasn't always 'ex.' Maybe she was listed as next of kin when he applied for work here."

"Why do you want it?"

"Oh, it's silly, but I thought . . . maybe if I understood him, if I knew why he was so hostile to women that he took it out on me, a complete stranger—old enough to be his mother, for heaven's sake—I'd be a little more understanding of what happened."

Martha grinned up at me. "*Cherchez le* shrink, huh?"

"Who knows a man better than an ex-wife?"

Maybe an ex-dance partner was beginning to.

.   .   .   .   .

I looked so respectable that she let me into her apartment almost immediately. Her name was Karen. She was a tiny woman almost overwhelmed by her cloud of bouffant brown hair, the painfully thin kind who always look cold, hunched somehow, but pretty if habitual anxiety hadn't sharpened her face. When I told her I was there about Jerry, her haunted features grew even starker, all cheekbones and big eyes and soft, scared mouth.

"Oh, God, I can't even stand to hear his name. I just want to forget him, I just want him to—please, God—forget me."

I told her why I couldn't forget him, and she just nodded. "Listen . . ."

"Linda."

"Listen, Linda, he is such bad news. You're lucky that all he threw you around was a dance floor. And his hate just escalates."

I glanced at the impressive battery of locks and chains on the front door.

She nodded. "My name's not on the mailbox and I have an unpublished number. Every time it rings I'm afraid it might be him anyway. I'm just grateful he found that stripper. I had a lawyer who was trying to represent my rights in the divorce, but Jerry got so . . . ugly that I finally just took the divorce papers and ran, left him everything. God, I am so glad to be out of there."

"So now she's got him," I mused. "Looks like the only way to escape him is if he finds another victim."

"Look, it's not like that. I wouldn't wish him on anybody. But he doesn't let go easily." She shook her head and bit her already raw lip. "And I don't understand the creepy apartment near downtown, the two cars . . . although I bet he got the 'Vette with what would have been my part of the divorce settlement. All I know is that he was meaner than a junkyard dog, abusive, obsessive, and he was just getting worse. I'm lucky to be alive."

I stood to leave. "Thanks for the insight. I'm shocked but not surprised. This puts my dance from hell into a different light."

.   .   .   .   .

When I left I kept seeing Karen's old-young face and hearing her soft, tremulous voice. I thought about my two distant, happily married, wholesome daughters and their dull textbook husbands and suburban houses. I thanked God, and I knew I couldn't stop now.

The sleazy street in front of Jerry Snyder's apartment building was never deserted. I wore an old raincoat I'd kept for yard work in cold weather and the dowdy scarf and tennis shoes. I parked a half a block away and shuffled toward his building, ignoring the men on the street, my pepper spray clutched in a fist tucked into a pocket.

The building's deserted lobby was like a movie set: peeling gray paint, cigarette butts and advertising flyers stuck to the vinyl tile floor, a battered rank of painted gray metal mailboxes. Tattered pieces of paper identified some of the units as occupied; last names were the only clue to who lived there. Once this tawdry puzzle-board with half the words missing would have stymied me, brought me to the brink of tears with frustration. Now I wasn't so easily put off. Of course, "Jerry Snyder" was nowhere listed. One word caught my eye. Rider. It rhymed with Snyder and sounded like a C.B. radio handle, a second, secret self-identity a macho-man would take. Rider. Maybe. A man with two cars and two lives.

The landlady was what I'd expected—buxom, blowsy, indifferent, her television baby-sitting four fussing kids in the background. Her aquiline nose and challenging eyes didn't promise easy cooperation, but I softly told her that I'd come to town to tell my son that his daddy had died and I didn't know anywhere else to reach him and who knows where he was during the day. . . .

My sad tale didn't soften her heard-it-all facade, but she didn't care about apartment house rules anyway. When I told her my name was Rider, she nodded.

"He doesn't hang around here much anyway, but he always pays his rent on time."

"Oh, I'm glad to hear that, about the rent, I mean."

She looked at me as if I were the most naïve mother in the world. Obviously she found Rider's long absences suspiciously criminal, as did I. But she gave me the extra key. I trudged up three flights of filthy stairs and finally stood before door number nine.

The place was as grim inside as the untended hall outside. An ugly plaid sofa on its last legs was the only furniture in the living room. The tiny kitchen beyond was relatively clean, and equipped with a small microwave. The cupboards were sparsely stocked with instant coffee and discount-store eating utensils, glasses, cups, and dishes. The microwave dishes looked new. A bottom cupboard had an extensive if purely functional bar. In the ancient white refrigerator frozen meals crammed the frost-caked freezer—all trendy, low-fat entrees with angel hair pasta and the like. I thought of Jerry's curly blond cherub hair and shook my head.

Besides a front-room closet, mostly empty, only one other room opened off the living area. I opened the bedroom door and felt my knees go weak.

The room was wallpapered with women, women frozen in photographic pornography—some the softcore, soft-focus images seen in shrink-wrapped magazines; most of it vile, sadistic stuff I'd never imagined. Ordinary, innocent snapshots of Jerry's ex-wife, Karen, were tacked up among the raw stuff, and lots of black-and-white photos of the girl I'd seen him arguing with outside Foxy Chix, obviously taken while she was performing. I inched along the photo-papered walls.

Stark black-and-white photos of other real women punctuated the lushly colored and brutal images of anonymous, writhing women: women spread-eagled, women bound, whipped, chained, raped. One small photo of a smiling, pretty young girl had obviously been cut from a high school yearbook. Another subject of a "real" photo, I saw with a shudder, was just a child. I forced myself to study the pornography, the women's faces contorted in pain passing for passion. Then, between the spread thighs of a leather-masked woman, I spotted a small black-and-white photo of myself. Self-recognition was a body blow; my heart pounded even harder when I realized the photo's source. The employees' club monthly newsletter. I had been cited as a top employee of my department two years before. I was a trophy, too, carefully recorded, though a small one.

In the bedroom closet I waded past sadomasochistic props to find boxes of copper-tipped bullets, huge heavy-handled knives, hunting knives, I think. No gun here, but I found lots of the same used, nondescript clothing I wore now, suspended from cheap wire hangers like empty carcasses.

I returned the key and left, wondering if the landlady would bother to tell Rider his mother had called.

· · · · ·

I called the police, like a good citizen. Finally referred to a harried-sounding woman detective, I was told that until Jerry did something provable and punishable, nothing in his behavior or his lifestyle was a crime. They could watch him to see if he was involved in a pornography ring if I would give them his name. . . . She addressed me as "ma'am" every other sentence. I hung up.

. . . . .

Karen was easy to disguise; just slap some makeup on her whitewashed face and draw her hair back into a sleek ponytail. We bought her a black leather jacket so she would look a little tougher. I wore a blond wig my second daughter had to have when she was eighteen and left behind when she married, and junked up my clothes as best I could.

The taped hard rock music inside Foxy Chix was earsplitting. It made Portnoy's seem like a wake. I identified Jerry's latest girl the moment the stage spotlights hit her long red hair. The show didn't shock me. What these women did was pretty tame, and even playful, compared to the wall of photographs, even though they both fed the same sick needs in a working woman's simple quest to survive. . . .

It was easy to talk to Tiffany—after finishing their acts, the women strolled topless among the tables of men. I hooked her attention with a fifty-dollar bill. Maybe lesbians came in here occasionally, but I doubted that. It didn't bother me if anyone thought that's what I was, anyway.

Karen and I took her to an all-night diner nearby, where we huddled in a back booth and everybody had hot fudge sundaes on me.

We told her what Jerry had done to us. She told us what Jerry had done to her, which was worse, much worse. She didn't have to tell us how scared she was. She would leave the planet to escape him, if she could, but she had to work, she had to live somewhere. She could be found. I told her what I'd already told Karen—about Jerry's secret life and how his sanctuary was equipped for bloody murder.

"He's got to be stopped," I said.

Tiffany slurped the last sweet liquid from the bottom of her glass, "Do you mean what I think you do? I don't have the nerve—"

"I'll buy the gun," I said quickly. "I know just where to go. The young man behind the counter said he'd 'walk me through it,' whatever that means. A woman my age, a widow suddenly living alone, logically feels the need for home protection. We should clean out his hole. Mama Rider can do it. The landlady won't care if he never comes back as long as the apartment is empty and clean. The police may ask you two some questions. Have good answers."

"But . . ." Karen's thin face showed hope for the first time. "What about that incident with Jerry on the dance floor? You could be a suspect if something happened to him."

I shook my head to dismiss that objection. I had finally put that sad little episode into the proper proportion.

"Don't worry about that. Like my friends kept telling me, I was making a mountain out of a molehill. Dancing with intent to humiliate is not a killing offense, for heaven's sake. Everybody's forgotten about it. Everybody."

CHANGE PARTNERS
Henry Slesar

Bernardo completed the Simple Twinkle and then made a quick turn right into the Counter Promenade Position. Nadine reacted perfectly as always; she was always flawless with American waltzes, this one peculiarly named the Beanbag. She wasn't winded in the least, no trace of the emphysema so gravely hinted at by Dr. Forbush.

They glided by the judges stand, and Bernardo felt the vibrations of their approval, and his heart leaped into his throat. They were going to win! It had been two years since they had walked away with the Big Silver Cup (to say nothing of the cash prize) but he felt their time had come. Blessings on the head of the Program Director who had declared the Waltz to be the final dance of the Vancouver contest. It was an Over-Forty competition, which might explain the choice. Bernardo was over forty. He wrote down forty-six on the entry form, even though he was fifty-four. But still nimble! Smooth and controlled! Not even his wife, ten years his junior, could match his lyrical movements.

He was perspiring heavily as they awaited the results, the sweat of anxiety, he told himself, rather than exertion. Nadine clutched his hand in her cold marble fingers. Her grip weakened when they announced their second place finish.

In the bus, on their way back to the City Center Motor Hotel, Nadine sat shrouded in the guilt she always felt when First Prize eluded them. She was as diffident about her dancing skill as Bernardo was confident of his own. He was already thinking about their next event, the Hawaii Star Ball in September.

"It's at the Sheraton," he said, "right on Waikiki Beach. Kathy and Gene are going to take a crack at it. So are the Lowrys. You remember them, they won the Latin championship at the Constitution State Challenge."

She was conscious of the weariness in her voice when she answered. "I think I'd better talk it over with Dr. Forbush first. He said something about treatments."

"Forbush is an idiot," Bernardo snorted. "First he says its chronic fatigue syndrome, now he says emphysema. Next week he'll be telling you it's mad cow disease." He smiled and patted her hand. Two rows in front of him, a woman turned and looked at him. There was something vaguely familiar about the tilt of her head, the cascade of her blonde hair.

Nadine fell asleep ten minutes after their return to the hotel. Bernardo was too keyed up to feel tired. He decided to go to the hotel bar for a drink. He checked himself out in the full-length mirror first. Okay, he thought, okay, denying the slight paunch he was developing, the puffiness under his eyes. He liked the thin moustache he had nurtured. It gave him a vaguely Latin aspect, like the name to which he had appended an O.

There were only three people in the small cocktail lounge, but one of them was the blonde from the bus. He was almost sure she had been in one of the competitions. Not the Over-Forty; she was too young. He seated himself three stools away and ordered a martini. She smiled in his direction and said: "Congratulations. I thought you'd make the First."

Bernardo was tingling with pleasure. He took the seat next to her, and found out she was in the Pro-Am, that her name was Angelica, that she lost because her partner Theobald was a big show-off who smothered her best moves.

"That's so wrong," Bernardo said sympathetically, "I had a dance teacher who told me, the man is the frame, but the woman is the painting."

"Not Theobald Kessler! He wanted to be the whole picture. That's why we split up."

"Really?" Bernardo said, more intrigued than ever.

"Theobald needs a wimpy partner, someone who'll take orders. He's a drill sergeant, not a dancer." She looked deeply into his eyes. "I could see the way you danced that you really respected your partner. Is she your wife?"

"Yes," Bernardo said glumly.

"That's too bad," she answered lightly. "Since I'm in the market for a new partner." She laughed to show it was only a joke.

"Then you and Theobald . . ."

"We aren't married, thank God. No strings attached." Her lashes fluttered like butterfly wings. She wasn't beautiful. The bridge of her nose was too high, there were too many lines radiating from the corners of her topaz eyes. But her figure was perfect. Perfect! The way most dancers had to be. She emitted waves of energy. He thought of Nadine's increasing fatigue, and his yearning became almost wistful. He found himself talking about her.

"She's sick, or thinks she is. Tired all the time. Doctor says her pulse is too slow, her metabolism is out of whack. He wants her to see a cardiologist, have something called an echocardiogram."

"Where is she now?"

"She's already asleep. What time is it?"

"Ten-fifteen," the blonde said.

"See what I mean?" Bernardo saw her glass was empty. "Can I buy you another?"

He could, and he had another for himself. They talked about Vancouver, about the beauty of the countryside. She said she had a spectacular view of the mountains from her room. He said they never even opened the curtains.

Two drinks later Bernardo saw the view for himself. Angelica slipped a cassette into the player, a seductive Tango. When he turned from the window, she was holding out her arms to him, waggling her fingers in the sign language that said, come on, come on. He went into her arms and they danced.

. . . . .

Nadine came home with an inconclusive verdict. There weren't any magic pills for her condition, so Forbush didn't prescribe any medication. He just told her to rest up for a few weeks. She knew Bernardo would be disappointed. It meant they would miss the Hawaiian Star Ball, and Bernardo loved tropical milieus.

"He said you should call him," Nadine said. "Will you?"

"Of course." Bernardo took her frail body in his arms. "And never mind about Hawaii. We'll get you all better for the San Francisco Dancesport. We've always had good luck in Frisco, haven't we?"

"Yes," Nadine said. "That Meringue Competition in '89. Our first Cup!"

"The whole Latin thing is coming back," Bernardo said happily. "We can freshen up the Meringue, or maybe do a Mambo or Samba. . . ." He steered her into a Controlled Cuban Motion and Nadine laughed as he hummed the music, did a basic chasse that led to Away and Together. His moves were gentle, but Nadine started to breathe rapidly.

"I'm sorry," she said. "It was a tiring day."

"Of course," Bernardo said. "Early bedtime for you, Pavlova." She smiled; it had been a long time since he had used the pet name. "Maybe I'll go see Kathy and Gene, find out if they're going to Frisco, too. We might split expenses."

Bernardo didn't visit their friends. Having spoken to Gene that morning, he knew they had gone out of town to visit relatives. Instead, he went to the Philadelphia hotel where Angelica had moved the week before. Angelica had no permanent home, and Philly was as good a town as any. Bernardo's presence made it even more desirable.

She wanted him to stay the night, but Bernardo didn't think he could explain a long absence to Nadine.

"Why don't you just tell her you have a new partner?" Angelica said mischievously.

Bernardo was shocked. "I could never do that. I owe her too much. Maybe eight hundred thousand too much," he added ruefully.

Naturally, he had to explain the remark. There was no money in competitive dance, and since it was their sole occupation they needed another means of support. Nadine's money had supplied it for the past eighteen years. She was the beneficiary of her late parents' considerable bequest.

Angelica had to admit he had a point. She was supporting her own dance mania by waiting on tables or working in bars. Once in a while, she managed to get into a chorus line in road company musicals. She leaned her head on his shoulder and said, "I bet we would have made a great team." Her expression turned sunny. "Why don't we find out? Tomorrow? The Rosetta Ballroom?"

Bernardo had no trouble finding an excuse for his late afternoon dalliance. He was going to the Terps, a club frequented by retired dancers. In actual fact, he went to the Rosetta Ballroom downtown. Angelica was looking pretty and svelte in her black satin leotards. The first number was a Mambo. They did Cross Rocks and the Chase and a Breakaway to Cuddles, and Bernardo was ecstatic. He felt as if he was holding a silver cup in his arms.

The next morning, he kept his appointment with Dr. Forbush. He turned out to be white-haired, elderly.

"Basically, it's her heart," Forbush said. "It's simply not pumping enough blood. That's why she's tired all the time. That's why I recommend less dancing for Nadine, especially in those stressful competitions."

"I see," Bernardo said sadly.

"I didn't have the heart to tell her the truth." The physician smiled slightly at his inadvertent pun. "Anyway, I think it would be better coming from you, since it affects you both."

"Yes," Bernardo said.

On the way out, he asked Forbush about Nadine's next appointment.

"It won't be with me," Forbush said. "I'm sorry to say—no, happy to say, to be truthful—that I'm retiring this month. My nurse will be glad to give your wife a referral to another physician."

Nadine was waiting anxiously for his return. When she saw Bernardo's face, her own expression brightened.

"You're going to be fine," he told her. "It's only a temporary condition. All you've got to do is regain your strength."

"But how?"

Bernardo grinned, expanding his thin moustache. "Why, through exercise! The best exercise in the world. Dancing!"

Nadine looked dismayed, but only for a moment. The next thing she knew she was whirling in her husband's arms, in an unorthodox quick-time waltz that almost swept her off the ground. He laughed and released her. She was panting, but he didn't seem to notice.

"We'll start tomorrow," he said. "We'll go to the Rosetta. I've got some new ideas—a Samba, a variation of the Boto Fogos! Wait 'til you see it!" He laughed and embraced her.

The ballroom orchestra didn't play a Samba that night, but there were two other inspiring Latin numbers, a vigorous Rumba, a Tango version of "Jealousy." He felt Nadine faltering in his arms, glimpsed the sweat on her forehead, but he pretended not to notice. When she weakly suggested an intermission, he scoffed, dragged her to the center of the ballroom floor and did a Jazz Dance so intricate that all the other couples on the floor backed off to the perimeter, a tribute not often seen at the Rosetta Ballroom. There was even some applause, but Bernardo barely heard it. His ears were ringing.

Nadine went straight to bed when they got home. Bernardo thought about calling Angelica, but he knew she would want him to sneak out and, what else? go dancing. He made himself some hot chocolate and watched a ball game on television, falling asleep at the start of the third inning. And what did he dream about? What else?

In the morning, Nadine didn't want to get out of bed. She apologized meekly, but she had suffered muscle cramps all night. The problem was she had an appointment with her accountant. She asked Bernardo to call him.

Bernardo did better than that. He visited Mr. Hofnagel in person. Hofnagel had known Nadine for decades; he was an ideal confidante. When the accountant asked after her health, Bernardo said mournfully: "She isn't well, poor thing. Heart trouble. I'm doing everything I can for her." Which was true.

Hofnagel asked if money could help; there was still a good deal of it in her account, or rather, their account. Bernardo was relieved to hear it.

When his business was concluded, he went to see Angelica. She wanted to go to the Rosetta, but he said it wouldn't be wise. He wasn't pleased when she suddenly pulled away from his embrace and began pushing the hotel furniture against the walls. Then she tried to roll up the carpeting, but it was too well adhered to the floorboards. She didn't give up. Giggling, she took off her shoes and insisted that Bernardo do the same. They danced that way for two hours, to the cassette-recorded music she carried everywhere.

Nadine was grateful for the respite she had that night, but Bernardo knew he couldn't allow it to continue. "Exercise," he reminded her. "It's the only way you'll get well, Nadine. And remember, San Francisco is only three weeks from today!"

The Rosetta had a new orchestra, a group called the Vorhees. Swing was back, the leader announced, Swing was the thing! The Vorhees' drummer pounded out rhythms like a madman. The older dancers were aroused by their nostalgia, the kids were amused. Bernardo and Nadine were the instant stars of the Ballroom. Bernardo insisted on the wildest possible gyrations, spinning his wife around like a top, performing his own version of the Jitterbug dances of two generations ago. She began to look panic-stricken, and at one point breathed into his ear and said, "Bernardo! I have to stop!"

He pretended not to hear her. But when the dance was over, he took her home. She had a restless night, and so did he.

In the morning, he announced that he had reserved the rental dance hall at the Terps, where they could practice the routines they would be performing at the San Francisco Dancesport.

Nadine said, "Bernardo, I can't."

"Of course you can!" he told her. "Look, I'm tired, too. But we've only got ten days to go! If we stop now, we'll lose the momentum! And—lose the competition!"

"There isn't any Over-Forty this year," she said. "We'll be competing against twentysomethings, Bernardo!"

"Our experience will be the difference! But we have to stay in training!"

There were two bands at the Rosetta. The Vorhees were followed by the Klassic Dance Band playing Golden Oldies. Bernardo wouldn't let her sit out a single number. Nadine danced the final Rumba with tears in her eyes. . . .

. . . . .

The funeral was an impressive affair. Kathy and Gene Stevens made all the arrangements, with the acquiescence of Mr. Hofnagel, who agreed that the money should be spent.

At the funeral home, someone had the idea of placing their fifteen trophies on top of the closed casket. Gene thought the idea bordered on tacky, but it was done anyway. Conrad Williams, publisher of *Dance Topics* magazine, delivered the eulogy. It was a touching tribute to the love of Dance more than a farewell to the departed, but nobody minded. Kathy Stevens wept openly when he said: "Who can doubt that Bernardo gave his heart to the glory of the Dance?"

There were a dozen cars in the procession that followed the hearse to the cemetery. Theobald Kessler offered his limousine to the grieving widow. To the casual observer, his arm around Nadine's shoulder appeared to be only a comforting gesture. Nobody saw the small smile on her face, or the way their feet moved in unison on the carpeted floor.

DANCING THE NIGHT AWAY
Brendan DuBois

Even several blocks away, Maria could make out the beacons around the Jupiter Dance Club, long beams of light lancing up into the muggy night sky. She drove along Beach Road, scouting for a parking space, and made a left down one of the crowded side streets. There. Looked like a rental car, filled with gray hairs, moving slowly out into the road. She managed to insert her tiny Ford Escort into the small space, frowning as a rear tire ran up the side of the curb. She had a flash of memory, of her older brother Hector, and how he had—in vain, of course—tried to teach her how to drive.

She retrieved her purse from underneath the front seat, gave her face a quick glance in the rearview mirror—the lights from the bars and the hotels illuminating the car's interior—and got out, locking the door behind her. The sidewalks were crowded with tourists and assorted creepy-crawlies, and she kept on walking, swinging her purse from one hand. She rounded the corner and walked past the well-lit hotels and restaurants—neon-bright in this early part of the summer—wincing a bit at the pain caused by her new high-heeled pumps. A warm breeze rolled in from the ocean off to the right, past the wide sands of South Beach, and she felt herself begin to perspire. It was hard to believe that she had grown up near here, just a couple of miles away, and she remembered those hot nights, when the wheezing and rattling air conditioner wouldn't do more than just stir the air. Unlike anyone else in her family, when she had gotten old enough to realize there was more to the world than just the highway and neighborhoods and high-rises, that there were places with cool nights and frost on the lawns in the morning, she had gladly moved out.

Now she was closer to the Jupiter Club. It was a squat, two-story building, colored pink coral, with thin, tall windows. At each corner of the building, searchlights aimed straight up to the sky. Neon decorations in the shapes of planets, comets, and stars studded the outside walls. Cars were double-parked near the entrance, but at this early hour, there didn't seem to be much of a line. As she got closer to the building, she was amazed that even outdoors she could make out the sound of the music inside, a deep, bass *thump-thump* that seemed to make the sidewalk quiver.

She stood in line, behind a couple chattering in Portuguese. The wall to the right was made of some kind of reflective metal, and she checked herself in the mirror image. Short, simple black dress, with black high-heeled pumps and black stockings. Gold chain around her neck, gold stud earrings in her ears, and a gold ankle bracelet. Nothing too fancy, nothing too daring, no tight Spandex or plunging neckline. No hairstyle done up in swirls and curves. Nope, her long blonde hair just pulled back in a ponytail. Blonde. She still hadn't gotten used to the new color. It looked like she was wearing a wig. The line moved up and she paid a young lady twenty dollars, almost feeling sick at how much the entrance fee was. Twenty dollars!

Her hand was stamped with some sort of ink that showed up under blacklight, and the line moved forward again, through a checkpoint. She shook her head. Plans would have to change, no doubt about it. Two large men, wearing acid-washed jeans and black polo shirts with the club's logo on the chest, took a quiet look at everyone passing through, and they used hand-held metal detectors on most of the males. The women, she was amused to see, were let right on through. She also went through the checkpoint with no problem, and then the line widened as people started going up a wide carpeted stairway. Now the music was much louder, so loud she had to resist an urge to bring her hands up to her ears. At the top of the stairs, the lights and the noise and the moving shapes almost made her dizzy, and she had to step aside from the lines of people that threatened to bowl her over. She took a deep breath and tried to take everything in.

There was one large sunken dance floor, accessed by four sets of stairs, one at each corner. There were four other raised dance floors, much smaller and at different levels. There were areas for drinking as well, with a long bar set on each wall, and there were tables, scattered around the dance area. A few velvet roped-off areas, where private parties kept an eye on the display. The DJ was in a transparent cube, projected over the floor. He wore a blue jumpsuit with flags and patches and a pair of earphones, as he hunched over twin turntables. People of all sizes, colors, and shapes massed together on the dance floors, moving with the steady *thump-thump* of the music. Some wore neon-bright necklaces around their wrists or necks, others waved plastic wands filled with fluorescent chemicals. The music was so loud she couldn't even tell what language was being used in the lyrics. All that could be understood was the *thump-thump* of the sound, a frantic rhythmic beat that seemed to drive all the dancers. She had a flash of thought, of a dance gene, passed down from generation to generation, beginning thousands of years ago on the grassy steppes of Africa, as tribes celebrated life and death and the success of the hunt.

Such a thought.

She spent the next few minutes moving around, looking, searching, looking out at all the faces. Some looked happy, others looked energetic, and many looked impassive, as if they were here because there was no other place to go. She felt a flush of embarrassment, remembering how as a teenager in high school she had never really enjoyed the school dances every month. There was too much swaggering from the boys, too much gossiping from the girls in the rest rooms, too much of the give and take of the old mating ritual. She had always felt out of place, just like tonight, in this dance club, for if she had her druthers, she'd be home at her tiny apartment, watching a rented video, eating microwave popcorn, and dreaming of moving back up to Vermont.

But she had to be here. Had to. There was no other choice.

There. In the far corner, a roped-off area. Empty. A large round table, comfortable chairs. The Jupiter Club was packed, but that place looked off limits. Whoever had claim to it had not yet arrived.

She stood by a cement pillar that rose up to the curved ceiling. More neon displays of planets and comets and spaceships. The music continued, one tune blending into another, and the flashing lights and laser beams were starting to give her a headache. She wondered how—

A voice. By her ear.

She turned. A young man, with earrings in both ears, a goatee. Dark slacks and polo shirt with the club logo, carrying a drink tray.

He leaned in. "Can I get you something?" he yelled.

"Sure," she yelled back. "Club soda, with a twist."

He nodded, moved back into the mass of people. She wondered how long it would take for him to find her, if she decided to move. What the hell. She was getting thirsty, and it was going to be a long night. So she stayed.

There, moving like a little ship, through a mess of other ships; the young man came back, and she took the drink. "Seven dollars," he yelled.

Seven dollars. . . . She put the drink back on the tray, went into her small purse, and laid eight singles on the tray and took the drink back. He smiled, leaned in again. "New here, aren't you?"

"Yes."

He nodded. "A fun place. But watch yourself."

"Why?"

He shrugged, backed away, and she sipped at her drink, watching the people, listening to the music. Eventually she emptied the glass and gave it to a passing young lady holding a tray, and then slung her purse across her shoulders and went out on the dance floor. She danced alone and then danced a few times with men who thought they were dancing with her, and after a while she found that she was actually enjoying it some. The movement, the joy of just doing something mindless and fun, without all the worries, without all the troubles. She was beginning to see why such clubs were popular. With the noise and the lights and the drinks, it was an easy place to step out of life for a while, to leave everything behind.

Yet, as she danced the night away, she kept on glancing up at the roped-off area in the corner. Still empty.

Still empty.

. . . . .

The next morning, she had to fight yawns as she processed reports at the sixth-floor nurse's station at the university hospital, about ten miles north of the Jupiter Club. She was working on her third cup of coffee, and it still felt like she hadn't jump-started the day. She had stayed at the club until 2 A.M., had danced numerous times and had drunk two more club sodas. Even without drinking alcohol, her tongue and mouth felt fuzzy, her ears still rang from the rhythmic music of the night, and her feet ached from the new shoes.

"Maria?"

She looked up. A woman was there, dressed in a dark gray business suit. Red hair, cut short. Elizabeth something, from Human Resources. The woman who had hired her less than a month ago.

"Yes, Elizabeth?"

The woman glanced down at a file folder she was carrying. "Maria, just checking. That social security number you provided us, it's incorrect."

She didn't feel so tired anymore. "Really?"

A nod. "Really."

"Well, I guess I made a mistake. I'll get you the right number tomorrow."

"You don't know it offhand?"

Maria managed a smile. "I thought I did, but the fact that you're here tells me otherwise. Sorry, Elizabeth, my social security card is somewhere at home. I'll have to go look it up and get back to you."

Elizabeth made a check mark with a pen on the file folder. "Very good. I'll look forward to seeing it." She turned and started down the corridor, and then stopped. "Maria?"

She looked up, her ears still ringing. *Thump-thump.* "Yes, Elizabeth. I'm still right here."

"It's just that . . . well, your supervisor, she tells me that you're doing a superb job. You obviously have skills and drive for something more challenging. Why don't you reapply for something else here at the hospital? She'd give you a good recommendation."

Maria paused, hands over the keyboard. Careful, girl, she thought. Don't give this cow any more excuses. "Maybe I will, Elizabeth. Thank you. I'll look into it."

"Very good," she said, and she walked away.

Maria went back to the pile of patients' reports at her elbow, continued typing in the information. It had taken a lot of work, a lot of research and questions, to find this particular nurse's station, and she wasn't leaving here until things got done.

A couple of the nurses at the other end of the station—being nurses, they were polite and gracious and made no secret of the fact that they thought Maria didn't count because she wasn't a nurse—got up and loudly announced to all within earshot that they were going to lunch. Maria watched as they ducked into the nearby elevator. She watched the indicator lights flash on, until they reached the first floor, where the cafeteria was located. She waited for a few more minutes, and in a well-practiced move, got up from her workstation and walked over to where the nurses had been sitting. Underneath a counter were four or five purses, lined up in a row. She went to the second one in, made of multicolored cloth, and popped it open. There. Key chain, with lots of keys and one magnetic keycard. She picked up the keys and walked away from the station, moving purposefully and quickly down a hallway that had no patients' rooms.

There again. Door with keycard reader. Large orange and black sign. AUTHORIZED PERSONNEL ONLY.

She looked around. She was alone. She slipped the keycard through and opened the door.

"As authorized as it's going to get," she said.

· · · · ·

After work, she drove for a half hour to a place that brought back lots of memories. One-story homes, made of concrete and glass. Lawns padded down to brown dirt by generations of children running around. She parked in front of a house that caused her to catch her breath for a moment. Home, such as it was. She got out and locked the car doors, looked around at the young men, most of them shirtless and wearing shorts, gold jewelry around their wrists and necks. How things had changed. This had been a safe neighborhood, hell, a safe town, once upon a time, when she had been a young girl.

She got up to the house, carrying her purse—heavier now than it was last night—and unlocked the metal gate on the front door, and then the main door itself. "Mama?" she called out, not wanting to frighten the old woman. "Mama, it's me. Maria."

A weak voice. "Come in, come in, daughter."

She went into the living room, carefully locking the doors behind her. The visiting nurse who spent the night here would be along in a while, and she wanted some private time before that happened. She passed through the living room—past the old furniture, the framed family photos up on the wall, and the framed painting of the Sacred Jesus over the television set. She went into the bedroom and there was Mama, laying in bed, the air conditioner whispering along, the television set on the Univision channel, watching some Mexican soap opera.

"Mama," she said, bending over to kiss her cheek.

"Maria," she sighed in pleasure, grasping a hand with both of her own wrinkled hands. "You look so thin. . . ."

She pulled up a straight-back chair, sitting close to her. The bedroom was cluttered with more family and religious photos, and it was hard to look at the family photos without choking up. Mama was approaching her eighth decade and was parchment and bones and a smile and gray hair, but when she was younger, she had been such a beautiful woman. Father was a stern man, with a thick moustache, who had been gone now for almost twenty years. Maria had only a few memories of Father, and not many of them were nice. A lot of loud yells, slaps, and just a few kisses. That's all. And in the photos, of course, besides a younger Maria, was her older brother Hector. Handsome, forever handsome, up there in the framed photos.

"Maria, your hair . . . when are you going to stop looking like an Anglo, hmmm?"

"Soon, Mama, soon. Are you thirsty?"

She nodded. "Of course."

"Hold on."

She went out to the kitchen—noting that it was clean, at least the daytime home health aides were good at something—and came back with a glass of ice water. Mama drank it gratefully and settled back on her pillow. "That was good, Maria. Very good."

"I'm glad, Mama."

"Tell me, dear . . ."

"Yes?"

"Your brother, Hector. I miss him so."

Her eyes suddenly teared up. "I do, too, Mama."

"Why won't he visit anymore?" her mother asked plaintively. "He's not mad at me, is he?"

She bent over to kiss her cheek. "Of course not. Everyone loves you, Mama. Everyone."

She smiled back. "That's nice of you to say. I just . . . I just would like to see my boy."

Maria reached over, squeezed the tiny hand. "So would I."

. . . . .

The visit lasted another half hour, until the evening visiting nurse rang the doorbell and she let her in, an older Jamaican woman with a thick accent and a wide smile, who said as she was leaving, "You be careful out there, girl. Some bad men about, it looks like."

Maria walked out to her car, saw what the nurse had been saying. The men—four of them—were lounging on and about her car, drinking from bottles wrapped in brown paper bags. They whistled as she approached, making yelping and barking noises, and one of them, the tallest, sprang up from the fender and said, "Hey there, babe-of-mine, where are you going tonight?"

"Away from here," she snapped back, and the other young men laughed. The one who had spoken slapped a hand to his chest, where lightning bolts and daggers had been tattooed. "Come on, love-dove, the night's still young. You and me, we can have some fun. Right?"

She got closer, noticed the stench of beer and sweat on them. Two were leaning on the trunk, one was resting on the hood of her car, and the leader was blocking the driver's door. She sighed, letting the purse swing from her hand.

"No, wrong," Maria said. "Now, please, get off my car, okay? Go find some other girls to play with. Girls dumb enough to be seen in public with you."

More hoots and hollers from three of the young men, but the tall one stepped closer, his eyes tightened in anger, his hand holding the beer bottle even tighter. "You tryin' to make me look bad, eh? Is that so?"

She turned and looked around at the neighborhood, the one that once upon a time had such happy memories. Where had it all gone?

"No," she said. "I'm not looking to make you look bad. I'm just looking for you to leave so I can go home."

He turned to his friends for more laughter and support. Then he turned back and said, "You gonna make me, little one?"

Maria moved quickly, like she had done so many times before. Within seconds the purse was open and the 9 mm semiautomatic was in her hand, and even with the traffic noises and the jets overhead going to the airport, the *click* as the hammer was pulled back was loud enough to make everyone take notice.

"No," said Maria, holding the pistol in the approved two-handed combat stance. "I'm not going to make you. But I'm going to try to appeal to your better nature. Is that possible?"

One by one, the other three men moved off and away from the car. The leader slowly put up his hands. "Sure, babe. Anything's possible."

"Good. I'm so glad."

Within another few seconds, they were gone, across the street and down an alley, and she was in her car, driving away, not allowing her hands or legs to tremble, not once.

. . . . .

Another day to recover, and back to the Jupiter Club.

Tonight she was trying something different, so she had on red high heels, a cropped tank top that showed off her belly—and she didn't like how saggy it looked, compared to some of the drum-tight bellies she saw about her—and tight white Capri pants. Before she left she debated on what to wear underneath the pants, and finally went with a pair of white thong underwear. Her butt was big enough without having a panty line showing, but it still got some getting used to, having that tight piece of cloth seesaw through her behind.

This time, she was surprised at how the music didn't seem as loud. Maybe her ears were deadened, maybe she was getting used to the *thump-thump* and the pounding sound of feet upon the dance floor. She went through the line and again felt lucky that the two brutes at the doorway with the hand-held metal detectors let her in without comment. Oh, one of them looked her up and down and gave her a wide smile, and she got into the act and smiled right back, and then got back inside.

Again, on the dance floor, moving with the music, and again—surprise, surprise—she was amazed at how she was enjoying herself, no matter which dark thoughts were living back there in the deep caverns of her mind. She just let the music take her over, just let her body sway and twist and jostle to the music. Men and sometimes women came by before her, trying to pretend at least that they were sharing a moment with her, and she let them be with a smile. Three times she was offered a drink—twice by men and once by a woman—and each time she graciously refused, as gracious as one could do with such close quarters and loudness. As the night progressed, she would look up every now and then, at that familiar empty corner, and it was empty again tonight. She wondered if she was timing it wrong, and she pushed that thought out of her mind. Just go with the music, go with the rhythms.

After she had been in the club for an hour, she was getting thirsty, and she was pleased to find the drink server again, the young man with the earrings and goatee. She ordered the same drink as before—club soda with a twist—and after paying him she laughed as he shouted in her ear: "You're not bored yet?"

"No, not yet!" she yelled back.

"Good," he said. "But watch yourself."

He turned to walk away and she grasped his elbow, almost causing him to drop his drink tray. He looked concerned and she yelled at him, "That's the second time you've said that! Why?"

He shook his head, leaned in again. He smelled of cigarette smoke and old sweat. "You're young, you're fresh, you're new. A dangerous combo for some of the types here. Just watch it."

She smiled, to let him know she wasn't bothered. "Okay, I will."

Maria took her drink and leaned up against one of the pillars, on which was displayed a rocketship in neon lights, climbing up to the stars overhead. There wasn't an empty chair in sight and she found that by leaning against the concrete pillar, she could give her feet a rest. She sipped at her drink, looked out at the dance floor, seeing the writhing bodies, the glow-tubes being tossed about and thrown up in the air. She finished her drink, found a wide spot on a railing to put the empty glass down, and then turned and went back to the dance floor.

She glanced up.

The empty corner wasn't empty anymore.

. . . . .

She forced herself to continue, to go out onto the floor. Nothing out of the ordinary, nothing drastic. Just keep on going like everything was cool, which was true. Things were fine. But as she danced, she let herself drift over, until she got a good view of the corner table.

There were three men there, and three women. Two of the men looked like brothers, with thick moustaches and dark eyes that wandered about the room. Both wore jackets, and she instantly knew why: to cover up whatever weapons they were carrying, and she also instantly knew that these two had no problems passing through the metal detector checkpoint by the stairway. The three women were wearing a mishmash of skirts, Spandex, heavy earrings, and bracelets, and they seemed content to huddle together, gossiping, sharing cigarettes and lighters. But it was the third man who caught her eye. Even at this distance, she made out the dark slacks, black shoes, and simple pressed white shirt, unbuttoned to the chest, the sleeves rolled up. No over-abundance of gold jewelry for this man. There was a wristwatch, maybe a ring or two, and a simple gold chain about his throat. His eyes weren't as active as his mates, but they had a laughing quality about them, like the entire club and its occupants were placed here for his pleasure. He leaned back in his chair, his thick black hair swept back, and as he talked to one of the two men, a free hand was gently caressing the hair of one of the young women. And as Maria watched, catching glimpses every now and then, his gentle strokes would become fierce tugs, as if reminding the woman who she belonged to.

Maria was thirsty again, but she forced herself to look away for a few minutes. She knew what was going on behind those eyes, the eyes that ignored nothing and took everything in. She couldn't chance a problem, not now, not at all. She kept on dancing through another set, and looked up.

The corner was empty again.

She looked around.

No wonder. They were on the dance floor, about six feet away from her.

. . . . .

The two men with moustaches looked uncomfortable, as if this was the first time they had ever ventured someplace where they were required to dance. The three women were doing fairly well, moving about, and one of them had a bright orange glow-tube that snaked about her arm. But the man at the center of it all, the little leader of the club, he took center stage and he danced, and he was good, and he knew it. Not only did he move in motion with the rhythmic sounds of the music, the trumpets, the drums, the wailing guitars, but he always seemed to be a half step ahead of himself, like he could sense where the music was taking him. He moved in a wide range of motion, sometimes close to the ground, other times stretching out, like he was try-ing to reach the ceiling, and his muscles were visible under his shirt and slacks, moving with him. She was reminded of the grace and presence and stealth of a panther, on the prowl, moving quietly through the jungle, and before she knew it, he was there, before her.

She swallowed, her throat dried. He smiled. She smiled back, and then let everything fall free from her mind, focusing on him, focusing on the dancing. The music changed a beat and a tempo, became something where the dancers partnered off, and without asking permission or saying a word, like it was meant to be, he moved toward her and took her in his arms. She could feel the muscles now, moving and rippling under her touch, and she saw how he danced, staring right into her, a little smile on his face, just the faintest blue-black stubble along his jaw and cheeks. He smelled of some sort of cologne, but nothing heavy or overpowering. No, something confident, something quite confident, like this man before her.

Maria tried to give as good as she got, and as she swirled about, she sensed anger and a sharp look from one of the three young ladies, but she paid it no mind. She just stared right back at him, moving along, and as the music slowed, she allowed herself to be brought in closer, pressing her breasts into him, and she froze every reflex she had, as one of his hands drifted down her hot and sweaty back to rest on the swell of her butt.

He bent his head down, lips grazing her ear. "Please. Join me for a drink."

She moved her head back, looked up at him. "I'd love to."

. . . . .

Up in the corner introductions were made, and she knew his name, of course, Ramon, and everyone else's name she quickly forgot. So sorry and all that, but Maria knew none of them really mattered. Only Ramon mattered. When they were only a few feet away from the corner, one of the club's staff came in, carrying a spare chair, as if they were reading the man's mind. He said something to the man carrying the chair, who nodded and quickly left. Maria followed the man's lead, sitting right next to him, and in a matter of moments, the club employee came back, carrying a champagne stand, with a bottle in ice sitting nice and proud. Ramon made another request as the champagne was being poured, and the employee took out a little hand-held radio, and bang, just like that, the DJ lowered the tempo and volume of the music. Just like that. The employee left and the three women stared at her with barely disguised hate, while the two guards just stared, and Ramon leaned over, put a hand on her leg, and said, "Now we can talk, eh, just for a few minutes. Before the music starts up again. Here, please, drink."

She smiled, sipped the champagne, which she hated. Too many bubbles, too much sharpness. "Thank you," she said to him. "It's delicious."

"Of course," he said, his hand still on her leg. "I like the way you move."

"You, too," she said, putting the glass down. "You're quite good."

"Ah, it's just a gift, I suppose."

"No, really, I can tell," she said. "Out of all the men here, you are the very best. I have never seen anyone with so much grace, so much passion."

One of the woman whispered something to her companion, but Ramon didn't notice. He just preened some and said, "I find this place, it is a refuge. A place for me to relax, to unwind, to forget all my business troubles."

"You are a businessman, then?"

"I am," he said. "And you?"

"I work at the university hospital."

At that, one of the guards said something to the other, and both laughed. Maria went on, "It's quite a nice job. Up on one of the research floors."

"Are you a nurse, then? Will you take my temperature?"

She lowered her eyes, smiled. "No, not a nurse. A data technician. But if you'd like, I'll take your temperature. That is, if you are feeling ill."

He slapped a hand to his chest. "I am fine. I have the stamina and energy of a bull. You'll see, I am fine."

"I have no doubt," she said.

They talked for a little bit longer, about the weather—hot—and politics—ridiculous, as always—and when the music roared back to its usual volume, he put out a hand and she joined him without hesitation, out on the dance floor, moving about, feeling the eyes of everyone upon them, for while she was just a moderately fine dancer, he was a great one. And the women—especially the ones who had accompanied him—gave her such looks of contempt and envy, all evening long.

. . . . .

Back in the corner a couple of hours later, still sipping her first glass of champagne, resisting the offers of a refill. Ramon had drunk four or five glasses, but he was a happy drunk. There are ugly drunks, who sour and stew and look for fights, but Ramon seemed happier and happier as the night progressed. His hand had started just above the knee as the evening had begun, but now it was at her upper thigh.

Maria glanced at her watch. It was time. She gathered her purse and leaned over and said, "I am so sorry, but I must leave."

"So soon? The night is just beginning."

She frowned, pouting, hoping it would work. "I am so sorry, but I have to go to work tomorrow."

He waved a hand dismissively. "Call in sick. Don't show up. Please, I'd like to spend more time with you."

"I am sorry, but I'm still on probation. I don't want to be fired. Please. Will you be back here later? Tomorrow, perhaps?"

He smiled. "No, not tomorrow. The night after. Saturday. Then you won't have an excuse, will you? You can stay all night, until morning."

She took a breath, reached over and kissed him, feeling his tongue move against hers, the rough stubble scrape her skin. His hand squeezed her thigh quite strongly.

"Yes, Saturday night, that will be fine," she said.

Another squeeze of the thigh. "I look forward to it, Maria. I most certainly do."

And she got up and walked out of the dance hall, legs shaking, and when she got outside in the muggy air, she still tasted him on her lips. She found an alleyway and an overflowing Dumpster, and she leaned over and vomited into the darkness.

. . . . .

The next day at work, her head was throbbing from the lack of sleep, the loud music, and the memory of spending the evening with Ramon. She had taken two aspirin in the morning, another two at mid-day, and she was working hard on drinking water, trying to rehydrate herself.

Maria came back from the ladies' room just before lunch, to find Elizabeth from Human Resources waiting for her at her work station. Maria paused, made a show of slapping her forehead with her hand.

"Social security number, jeez, Elizabeth, I'm sorry, I forgot," Maria said.

Elizabeth shook her head. "Well, that's quite irregular; I hope you realize that. I simply need an accurate social security number from you, Maria, or we're going to . . . well, let's just say, we need that correct number."

"I know, I'm sorry, I'll make sure you get it. I promise."

Elizabeth looked down at her file folder, and Maria wondered if the woman knew how to talk and breathe without having a folder in her hands. "One more thing. It seems like your transcript . . . well, the registrar's office, from the college you attended, they said it's all wrong."

"How's that?"

"Well, the name is the same, but the birth date is wrong. It's for a woman much older." Elizabeth stared right at her. "Do you know anything about that?"

She shook her head. "That's an old paperwork problem, one that's haunted me for a long time. Seems like me and another woman, the same name, our records got mixed up. I have a friend at the school. I'll make sure it gets straightened out."

Elizabeth closed the file folder. "Good. Maria, like I said, your work has been exemplary. But these loose ends . . . well, they need to be tidied up."

"I understand."

"Good."

Elizabeth started to walk away when there came some raised voices, from a meeting room just off of the nurse's station. Elizabeth turned her head to the noise and shook her head.

"What's that all about?" Maria asked.

"Oh, an inventory was done this morning, and the records don't match," she said, walking past her. "Can you believe that?"

Maria looked at the closed door of the conference room. "No, I can't."

. . . . .

At night, she was back in her mama's room, and Mama was doing a little better, but not much. Sometimes she dozed in and out, watching Univision, and while sometimes she was right on the mark when it came to the right date and place, other times, well, other times it made Maria's heart ache at what she said.

Like now. "Dear one," she asked. "Where's your brother? Where's Hector?"

"He's not here, you know that," Maria said.

"My poor boy," Mama whispered. "Have you been out on his boat lately? Such a handsome boy, the captain of his own fishing boat. I'm so proud of him."

She stroked her hair. "No, Mama, I haven't been out on his boat. Not for a while."

"I miss him so," she said. "Won't you call him?"

"Later, Mama, later," Maria said.

Mama closed her eyes, breathed some more, and said, "I miss him so. I miss my Hector."

"Me, too, Mama, me too."

A few more minutes of sleeping passed, and then Mama woke up and smiled. "Look at you, the color of your hair. It's so bright. When are you going to change it back? When?"

She squeezed her thin hand. "Soon, Mama, soon."

And then, a thought: "Mama?"

"Yes, daughter?"

"Mama, would you like to live with me for a while? Would you?"

A faint smile. "That would be nice. But you'd let Hector know, wouldn't you?"

She brought the thin hand up to her lips, kissed the rough skin. "Of course."

. . . . .

Just before her third night at the Jupiter Club, Maria was in her apartment, ready to get dressed. As she stood in the tiny bedroom, the pictures on the walls rattled as a jet flew overhead, going to the international airport, just a few miles away. She didn't mind the noise that much, for it meant the rent was relatively cheap. And since she had signed a six-month lease and was planning to skip out on the lease about five months ahead of schedule, having a low rent made sense. There was nothing in the small place that belonged to her, save some clothing, a few personal items and her pictures, up on the walls. Once she had conducted a little practice drill, and found that she could empty the place of everything she valued in just under ten minutes. A good drill.

Maria was drying her hair with a long towel, looking at the clothing and other items spread out on the bed before her. She frowned, looking at the black bra and matching thong panties, black hose, a black dress even shorter than the one she had worn the first night. Things were clicking but she still hated what she had to do, to be ready for what was about to happen.

Next to her clothing was her purse, and beside that was the 9 mm pistol she had used the other night to scare away the homies, or whatever they were calling themselves this year, who had been sprawled out on her car. That had been something, a task she was more comfortable with than tarting herself up and going dancing.

She tossed the towel away. No time for brooding. Just time to get to work and to do what had to be done. She picked up the pantyhose, tossed them away. Bare legs tonight. She picked up the bra and tossed it aside as well. Mama would be horrified, but so be it. She got dressed quickly, gathering up the pistol and the purse, and as she slipped out of the bedroom, she kissed her fingertips and pressed them against a family portrait, a young man standing proudly next to his younger sister.

. . . . .

Back at the Jupiter Club, she had a brief scare as one of the bouncers with a hand-held metal detector waved her aside, and she grasped her purse even tighter. But just then a guy getting scanned by the other bouncer started tossing around an attitude, and the second bouncer went over to provide backup, just waving her on ahead. She felt her legs totter some, going up the stairs, and she felt the eyes of all the men about her, and she knew why. With bare legs and no bra and what little she was wearing, it was like she was sending out signals to any male in rut in the room.

But she blew by them and made her way to the dance floor and began dancing, looking up at the empty corner, feeling just the tiniest bit disappointed. He had promised! She shook her head. Grow up. He'll be back.

After a couple of sets on the dance floor, where some of the men hovered about her like spacecraft orbiting a planet, she ducked away to one of the bars and nodded at the drink server she had seen the previous two nights. He crisply nodded in reply and came over with a drink, and she paid and tipped him as well, and he went away and then came back, like he was bothered with something. He shouted in her ear, "I warned you!"

"What do you mean?" she yelled back.

"I warned you to be careful!" he shouted. "That man, Ramon, he is a beautiful dancer, the best I've ever seen! But he's . . ."

"He's what?" she demanded.

It was like he thought better of everything, and he walked back behind the bar and she sipped her drink, and when she turned around, there was Ramon, on the dance floor. No female companions. Just the same two guards as before, and he watched her as he danced, so muscular and lithe, and then he smiled widely and crooked his finger at her, and she laughed and put her drink down, and she went out and joined him on the dance floor, the *thump-thump* of the music making her feet and legs and hips move.

. . . . .

It was like he was hungering for a release, for something, for Ramon refused to leave the dance floor for long minutes. Once he just said, "I need to dance, I need to dance more than life itself! Come, don't stop, my love!"

He grasped her and moved her about, his strong hands moving up along her ribs, along her back, briefly cupping her buttocks one time, and another time, briefly caressing the side of her breasts, and she could tell from the look on his face that he enjoyed feeling no brassiere there. They danced and danced, moving almost as one, and during one quiet point, his lips up against her ear, he said, "Maria, you are so beautiful."

She forced a laugh. "I think you say that to many women, eh?"

He squeezed her at the small of her back. "Only to blondes. A curse, I know, but I am only attracted to blondes. Something my mother and sisters always argued with me about."

"And how about this blonde before you?" she asked teasingly.

Another squeeze. "This blonde, I want to take her to my home. As soon as possible."

She fought the nausea in her stomach, raised herself and kissed him deeply, tasting his sweat and feeling the rough patch of his unshaven skin against her own. "Then let's go. Right now."

He broke free and grasped her arm, and then said a solitary, quick phrase, and his two men quickly fell in behind him, and they left the Jupiter Club, the music *thump-thumping* in her ears, all the way out to the sidewalk.

. . . . .

She wanted to follow him in her own vehicle, but he would have nothing to do with it, and despite some good-mannered arguing on her part, she found herself in the back of a black stretch limousine, being chauffeured to Ramon's house. She sat in the large interior, Ramon before her, his bodyguard—Juan, perhaps?—sitting next to him. Juan stared and stared at her, and she felt herself begin to shrink away from that steady gaze.

Ramon opened a small bottle of champagne from the limo's mini-fridge, and as she sipped it he said, "My dear, your purse, please."

She slowly brought her glass down. "I'm sorry, what did you say?"

His expression had changed, and he was no longer the smiling man on the dance floor. The drink server was certainly correct. "Your purse. Now. Hand it over to Juan. Now."

"But—"

Juan moved snap-quick, grabbing the purse from her side, tugging it away. She froze, watched as he unsnapped the top and dumped the belongings on the floor. Ramon and Juan and she looked down, as Juan stirred the little mess with his foot: a mascara kit, eyedrops, packet of tissues, keys, a folded-over collection of currency, lipstick, and some change. Ramon looked up, and now the happy dancer's face had returned. "My apologies, my dear. It seems . . . well, I'm a very prominent businessman. I have many, many enemies. Some who would not hesitate to send someone as lovely as you to harm me. Juan."

The guard bent over to pick up the purse and the belongings, but Maria tossed her champagne in his face. As the man sputtered and sat back, she got down and put everything back in the purse, looking up and saying, "Stop the car. Now."

Ramon laughed. "Maria, please, I don't want to—"

"You've insulted me. You've insulted me and hurt me, and I don't want to go anywhere with you. Not for another second. Stop the car."

Then Ramon came over, knelt down, and picked up her hand and kissed her fingers. "Please, my dear. I was wrong. I was so very wrong. This has been a special night for me. Please. Can't the special night continue, just for a while?"

She looked down at his handsome face, the bright eyes, and he kissed her fingers again. She made a point of sitting back against the limo's cushions. "All right," she finally said. "This special night can continue."

· · · · ·

An hour later, Maria was in a bathroom off the master bedroom, a bathroom almost the size of the tiny apartment she had been renting. She had just taken a long shower, trying to wash away the man's scent and touch and fluids, and it hadn't worked. Not one bit. The only thing that would work would be a little mountain stream, near her home in Vermont, and if all went well, by tomorrow morning, she would be there, naked in the water, washing away everything from what had just happened.

Shivering, she wrapped a towel around her, felt another roller-coaster of nausea race through her. Steady, girl, she thought. Steady. Almost there. She opened up her purse and took out the mascara kit and the eyedrops, and she went to work. Just a minute or so, that's all, and then she went out in the bedroom, holding the towel wrapped around her with her right hand.

Ramon was on his side, on his bed, naked except for the satin sheets about his strong body. He smiled at her and said, "Feel better?"

"Oh, yes," she said. "Much, much, better. And you?"

"Couldn't be finer," he said. "Are we ready for another dance lesson? Hmmm?"

She managed a smile. "Of course."

The bed looked like it could sleep five, and the view of the harbor was magnificent, and a large-screen television in one corner was set to a Miami Heat basketball game. She walked around the foot of the bed and came up behind him, caressing the back of his neck with her free hand. "Ramon, dear, what's the score?"

"It's—"

He wasn't able to finish the sentence. She let the towel drop and moved quickly, to his exposed back. In her hand, cupped there from whatever prying eyes might be watching, was the eyedrop bottle, and screwed at the top of the bottle—previously hidden in a mascara brush handle —was a tiny needle. She pushed the needle into his spine, squeezed the bottle, and just as quickly, cupped it back into her hand. She giggled and rolled him over on his back, and kissed his lips. His eyes were wide and his breathing was becoming labored.

"Don't fret," she whispered. "You've not been poisoned. You're not going to die. Not at all. But I must tell you something. I know who you are, what you do, and what you've done. I know where you go and that you like blonde women. I know everything about you, Ramon, especially about someone you killed, just a few months ago."

His lips were moving, but no sound was coming out. "Shhh," she said. "Don't even bother trying. Sometimes, people get in your way, don't they? One of these people was a fisherman, who didn't want to import things for you, things from a cargo ship, out in the straits. And to make an example of him to the other fishermen, you killed him. Without even a second thought."

She kissed him again. "Ah, dear one, that was my older brother. You murdered my older brother, took him away from me and my family, all without worrying about what might happen to you later. So this is later, Ramon. So here I am, his sister. To avenge."

Maria took the towel and re-wrapped herself, and then bent down, to kiss him again. She could barely hear his breathing. "But to avenge . . . it would be so difficult to prove what you did, to give you jail time. Even for me, a cop from Vermont, it would be difficult to put the case together. And to kill someone as well guarded as you . . . well, many other men, with many more resources than I, have tried and failed. Correct?"

She stroked his forehead, leaned down, looked into his wide eyes. "So I thought I'd take away the thing you loved the most, the thing you said you loved more than life itself. You see, dear one, where I worked at the university hospital, I stole something. Not much. Just a little experimental derivative of curare, a paralyzing agent. And the wonderful thing—well, not wonderful for you, of course—is that there is no cure. No cure at all."

One more kiss. "There, my dear. You are young and healthy and will live a long, long time, and during each second and minute and hour and every year, you won't be able to move even a finger. Not even a toe. Not even a word will be able to escape those handsome lips. You will be fed and washed and changed, just like a baby, and every time you close your eyes, you will remember me."

She got up and got dressed, as he laid there, looking up at the ceiling. Maria gathered her purse and went over and looked down at him and said, "Yes, you will remember me, you'll remember this special night, and you'll never forget your last dance, will you?"

And she left the bedroom, gently closing the door behind her.

THE TRESPASSER
Alexandra Whitaker

Knowing Antonio, or seeming to know him, was at least as important to his students as learning to dance. They vied to buy him beers between sessions and to be seen joshing with him, because Antonio possessed qualities that his students admired, but lacked. Most people take ballroom dance lessons because they are awkward socially, yet they want to mix with people. Because they just might meet a nice man or a nice woman there, you never know. (But you do know you won't meet him sitting at home night after night, so give it a try. Go on, what do you have to lose?) So they came to Antonio's academy seeking companionship, but also self-assurance, poise, social as well as physical grace—all qualities Antonio had in abundance, which is why they clustered around him, hoping that as he taught them dance steps, so would he also impart some of his sparkling charm and glamour.

In addition to classes two evenings a week, there were dances every Friday and Saturday night where students could practice and perfect what they had learned during the week. In fact, what these rather gauche people were buying for their monthly dance tuition was a social life, somewhere to go every Friday and Saturday night, a place where they were guaranteed a warm welcome, because socially unsure people are especially warm with each other, since warmth reflects well on the one confident enough to reach out to others. And of course it sounded good, dashing even, to say that you went dancing every weekend. You could mention it casually at the office. "Tango, rumba, you name it. I do it all." People were impressed. It was all a very good deal for just eight thousand pesetas a month.

But don't imagine that anyone there considered himself to be wanting in social skills or personal attractiveness. No, just a little shy, that's all, and too busy—that was it, really—too busy to spend much time cultivating friendships. (Although each was quick enough to recognize the lack of polish in his fellow students.) There was no feeling of solidarity amongst the underdogs, only strenuous efforts not to wind up at the very bottom of the social heap. Obviously, the closer you seemed to be to Antonio, the cooler you were, so the students competed for his attention and tried to demonstrate that they knew him well and could be casual, even offhand with him. Sure, Antonio and I go way back together. Way back.

It was easy to laugh and joke with Antonio because he was that kind of a guy. It was too easy. The real test, the real way to prove you were "in" with Antonio, was to know, or seem to know, Conchi, and to voice the opinion—or to agree quickly in an I've-known-that-all-my-life kind of way—that Antonio would be nowhere without her. He owed it all to her. He was the front man, charming and talented, but she was the power behind him, the pillar of the school. He shone on the dance floor; she kept the books. He joked with the students and flattered them; she made sure they paid promptly every month, sending cute little reminders through the mail when necessary. Under their combined efforts, the dance academy flourished.

Conchi was always around the school somewhere, but in the background. While Antonio occupied center stage, she hovered in the wings, always present, always busy. Sometimes she was down in the crowded little office doing the accounts, or she was in the back room sorting through costumes, but most often she was installed at her own little table at the back of the dance studio, working on something, publicity posters for the school, or organizing the next big ball, and at the same time keeping an eye on things. She was always over-worked, her eyes rolling, her curly dark hair falling down from its clasp to be blown up tiredly out of her face. She gave off that behind-the-scenes-in-showbiz air that was all flap and martyrdom and inviting of sympathy. She always carried things with her: folders and files, clipboards, stacks of invitations, armloads of fabric. The correct greeting to Conchi, by those lucky enough to be able to greet her familiarly, was: "Conchi, you poor thing! Up to your eyes in work!" And she would smile wearily in a someone's-got-to-do-it way, or simply close her eyes in resignation with a small tightening of the lips, and everyone would *ooh* and frown in a tender, admiring way, and wonder just where Antonio would be without her, and she would shrug in a way that, while not meaning to run Antonio down, had to admit that the answer was "nowhere at all."

But Conchi was not just some dogsbody around the school. She was Antonio's girlfriend, and what's more, his dance partner. It was a very special treat to see the two of them dance, which they did only rarely and then only if the students requested it ardently enough and if one of them dragged Conchi onto the floor by the hand. Only then would she and Antonio agree to do one—just one!—number together, usually a flashy tango, after which all the students would break into thunderous applause and shake their heads in admiring wonder, their eyes shining with the brilliance of the performance. They would elbow each other and make self-abasing jokes about how they could never, ever, in a month of Sundays learn how to do it like that.

The new student trying to make his way into the sacred inner circle would have to be careful to mask his surprise upon learning that Conchi was Antonio's partner, on and off the dance floor. Certainly, on the surface, they seemed to be an oddly matched couple, and she did not correspond to many people's notion of a dancer. Conchi was a big woman. For a dancer, quite surprisingly big, and in the little-girl dance costumes she confected for herself, grotesquely so. Antonio was very strong and he could do a masterful job of leading, whirling, and dipping her, but he could not lift her off the ground. Her size was the reason it was so important not to betray any surprise upon learning she was his partner. And it was why established students, when pointing her out to a newcomer, always stressed defensively, "She dances like an angel."

One of the qualities often attributed to the heavy-set is that they are "light on their feet" and gifted with unusual grace. This was not the case with Conchi. She was a competent dancer, excellently taught by Antonio, terribly hard-working, and able to do what was required of her, but she would never be an inspired dancer, much less star material. Antonio felt that he, however, might well have the makings of a star. And if he did not, he would like, at the very least, to be able to find that out for himself. But as long as he danced with Conchita, entering into competition was out of the question. Equally out of the question was his ever taking another dance partner. This disparity between their talents was not a topic they could broach. As a couple, they ran the academy together, honed their dance skills in intensive courses on the coast for two months every summer, organized endless shows with the school, and by God, that kept them busy enough! They didn't have *time* to compete; that's how they put it to each other.

And the fact that Antonio was a better dancer was mitigated by the fact that he actually did owe it all to Conchi. They had grown up together in a dusty small town in the province of Seville, where dancing meant flamenco, and ballroom dancing was considered risible, inoffensive but silly, in much the same way as homosexuality was considered, and for that reason among others, the two things seemed to the townsfolk to go hand in hand. As chance would have it, Antonio, a passionate fan of ballroom dancing since childhood, was also pestered by doubts during his adolescence as to which sex he found most attractive. He sampled sex with both, and remained unsure. But Conchi settled that matter for him, as well as most others. She loved him first from afar, then befriended him, learned to dance from him, lent him money to open a little school in the town, painted and prepared that first studio, rounded up the first batch of students, fought for him and his school until it was up and running, working tirelessly and for no pay. It was the night of their triumphant inauguration of the school that he, dizzy with elation and wine, slept with her for the first time. It was inevitable. She was so devoted, so hard-working, so adoring that she had made his dream her own. And it was a relief to him to resolve his secret worry once and for all, nestled safely in the soft comfort of her ample and curvaceous form. She was all woman, and a lot of woman. Who could doubt the heterosexuality of a man who possessed this much woman? They worked hard until they were able to make the important move to the capital. Sensing that in the big city he might find distractions and temptations, dangers that had not existed in their small pueblo, Conchi sought to assure her place at Antonio's side by the exhausting but efficacious method of making herself indispensable. She partnered him on and off the dance floor, cooked and cleaned their apartment, washed and ironed his clothes, polished his shoes, ran his business, organized the school shows, and practiced new steps late into the night to assure that she would be up to scratch on the dance floor. All that was left for Antonio to do was to charm the students, teach the lessons, and choreograph the shows.

Nonetheless, the fact that Antonio was held back from competition by Conchi hovered, all unspoken, between them, making Conchi all the more hard-working, and lending to Antonio, laughing and joking though he was, a little air of melancholy that some of his students, many women and the occasional man, found really very attractive.

Which brings me to another reason Conchi was so popular: she meant that Antonio was taken. Thanks to her, there was no friction amongst Antonio's secret admirers in the school. Had he been free, things might have gotten ugly with all those lonely people fighting for him. But this way he was nobody's, he was Conchi's, and that was as it should be. Everyone's to dream of, no one's to have.

Not, that is, until Inma arrived.

．　．　．　．　．

Inma was unlike Conchi in every way. She had a tiny waist, an athletic boyish build, pale short-cropped hair, and she danced with verve and grace and assurance. Her body responded to the slightest touch of her partner, almost divining his intention before he signaled it. She didn't have much dancing experience, but she had great innate talent, and she caught on intuitively to what it took Conchi long weeks of practice to achieve.

Like Antonio, there was an alive, crackling quality to Inma. She was also lippy, and could sling his jokes back at him. There was a tingling in the air between them. His body was dense and muscled and perfectly rhythmic, hers was lithe and light and biddable. They laughed, dancing together the first day, and at one moment, when their eyes met, there was the sudden understanding between them that soon they would be having sex. When that first class was over, Antonio went down to the office and dug through his desk, hunting ineffectually for a blank enrollment form for her. Conchi usually handled all this, but she was away that afternoon on errands. He glanced up, and there was Inma, looking in the half-open door. He was surprised to see her so soon, and yet not so surprised. She stepped into the tiny office, and suddenly nothing existed in the world except the fact that they were close to each other and alone together. Their awareness of this became so overwhelming that it was like the booming of a bass speaker, drowning out their voices and confusing their thoughts. Antonio made an inane joke about there being so little space, and she answered something with a nervous laugh, but he didn't know what. He realized he was babbling foolishly, but he needn't have worried because she couldn't hear what he was saying either. He drew her into the room because he had to shut the door in order to open the filing cabinet, and as he rolled the drawer open, he backed into her gently, pressing her against the closed door, so that when he finally turned to her, their lips were already almost touching. With the first kiss, the booming sound stopped abruptly. In the quiet, their two bodies locked into each other in a perfect fit. Her body melted around his as it pushed against hers, and then came some of that fumbling with clothing that is only comic in retrospect. When they ran back up the steps to the dance studio, both smiling and apparently normal, but not daring to look at each other, they were lovers.

The next day during class Antonio avoided Inma's eyes and spoke to her only once, sharply, when she made a mistake. He was proud of what he had done, as a sign of his virility, but he was also faintly appalled. He hadn't often been unfaithful to Conchi, and never twice with the same person. What he liked was flirting. Being free to flirt, but "taken," so that he could be seductive, yet avoid being put to the test. The fact is, his sexuality was somewhat low wattage—not that it had been with Inma! Fiery spontaneous sex with a total stranger, well, well.

But maybe that was enough of that kind of thing.

Inma didn't give up so easily. After class, she brought her enrollment form, neatly filled out, down to him in his office. "Hi, again," she said softly, eyes shining.

"I have a girlfriend, do you know that?" he said accusingly. "And she's right upstairs." As she began to close the door, he hissed, "Don't do that! She could come down any minute!"

But she closed it anyway. "I'll never tell her," she said calmly. "I give you my word that she'll never learn about this from me. And she'll never guess. How could she possibly guess that we're already lovers? It takes a certain progression to arouse suspicion. But we . . . we've been lovers since we first looked at each other."

Antonio hesitated—those words had a good ring—and Inma saw that she had won. She took his hand and pressed it to her face. "Don't worry," she whispered, her lips brushing his fingers. "I won't give you away. I promise you." He sighed with combined irritation and desire, then hugged her hard to his chest. They stood that way for a moment, their hearts beating against each other's. Then she slipped out the door.

This time, she thought as she climbed the stairs, *this* time everything is going to be all right. I'm going to be good and safe and loved. Nothing will go wrong this time. Maybe you have wondered what an attractive woman like Inma was doing in this dance school full of losers. The short answer is that she was something of a misfit herself. She didn't know what was wrong, but she seemed to alienate people, burn through them, fall out with them, use them up. She was always having to move on to new places, new lovers, new friends. Something was always not quite right. But this time, this time would be different. This was a fresh start. Inma felt she had found her place, and in it she would be different and new and better.

A little later Antonio left his office and ran up the stairs to the top, where he faced his students. He clapped for their attention and tossed his hair in his usual boyish way. "Okay, people, let's go! Let's dance! Okay, Juana? Carmen, what's up? Let's go! El Mambo!" But as his glance swept over the room, he was startled to see that Inma had not left; she was cozily installed at Conchi's table at the back, and the two of them were laughing about something. When he dared to look again, she was leaving, and he could relax. Inma threw a last word to Conchi, waved, and broke through the swinging doors still laughing. Outside, in the cool dark air, her smile subsided into an intent look of satisfaction. He was hers now. She was sure of it.

They met once or twice a week in a bleak room in a cheap pensión across from the old Córdova Station. Inma led in bed as surely and masterfully as Antonio did on the dance floor, and their bodies followed and matched each other's as surely. He was bewitched by her vigor, her slightness, her suppleness. Exotic little boy, writhing and powerful, but so wonderfully small. As if by a miracle, once or twice a week, in this tatty pensión, this strange little naked creature belonged to him. During the first weeks satisfying their pent-up sexual longing for each other took all their time together, leaving only a few minutes for lying in each other's arms and gazing languidly at each other. They almost never spoke, except for pronouncing each other's names yearningly.

Laughter and banter they saved for the dance studio. Inma raced from the beginners' class, to intermediate, and then advanced, all in a couple of months. To explain away her unusual talent, she pretended to all but Antonio that she had done ballroom dancing since childhood, and she was just brushing up on old skills. Oh, that explains it! Well, no wonder! This satisfied people who would have been uncomfortable with the fact that she was simply more gifted than they were. Or rather, it nearly satisfied them. Inma was not popular among the students. She made no effort to join in, she occupied too much of Antonio's attention during class, and, most galling of all, she had wormed her way far too fast into Conchita's affections.

Inma was rigorously careful to denigrate her dancing ability around Conchi, so that their friendship might continue to flourish. She pretended to be bewildered by new steps, asked Conchi's advice frequently, and faked despair at ever mastering them. By systematically and ceaselessly downplaying any area where she might possibly outshine Conchi, negating any personal attractiveness, calling her looks "tomboyish," her body "bony," with a shrug of "But who cares anyway?" Inma managed to keep Conchi placated. It was a lot of work. Inma stepped and fetched for Conchi like a nimble little servant, and flattered the larger woman. She applied whatever emotional balm Conchi required, taking her cues faultlessly and speedily, dispensing on demand, like a faithful vending machine, praise, sympathy, admiration, indignation. She was Conchi's helper, Conchi's eunuch, Conchi's little dancing puppet.

Like most heavy people, Conchi maintained that her weight had nothing to do with the amount of food she consumed. It was a question of metabolism. Inma was only too eager to agree. She saw, however, that her new friend was always peckish, so she began to bring an assortment of snacks in her rucksack, which they shared as they worked and chatted side by side at Conchi's table, addressing envelopes or pinning up hems. Inma brought the kind of food she ate, fruit and nuts and flasks of herbal tea. Conchi called it "rabbit food," but she managed to put away a lot of it. Inma was skillful at putting a positive spin on Conchi's corpulence. For example when Conchi was trying on a frilly new costume which could not be zipped up over the bulges of flesh on her back, Inma said, "It's because you're so buxom, lucky you." Conchi smiled down at her plump breasts and cast a pitying look at

Inma's nearly flat chest. Inma did the same, and shrugged apologetically. But inwardly Inma snickered at the image she conjured up of her own poor Antonio laboring away over—or even worse under!—that jiggling mountain of flab. Probably damp with sweat. Yuk!

In contrast to the scrawny and servile Inma, Conchi felt herself to be deliciously feminine, wise, funny, a source of everything plentiful and good, and so Conchi grew to enjoy Inma's company. And yet . . . and *yet*. Conchi never came to feel perfectly at ease with her new friend. Inma was simply too thin. It is a recognized fact, but one rarely expressed, that friendship between women can almost never thrive where there is a weight difference of over ten kilos. And here the difference was easily thirty. Also Inma danced far too well to be any sort of true friend to Conchi, and although Inma's easy, laughing relationship with Antonio did not worry Conchi particularly, something about watching the two of them dance together did. Conchi felt no immediate danger, but she would keep an eye on things all the same. In the meantime, Inma was gratifying company, and quite useful around the school as well.

Eventually, as the aphrodisiac of newness wore off, Antonio and Inma began to talk during their trysts at the pensión, and the more they talked, the more difficult their relationship became. Or perhaps they talked because it had already become so. Antonio didn't like how Inma had befriended Conchi; he thought the double betrayal excessive. But Inma said it was necessary; that Conchi's rumbling jealousy, never far below the surface, would erupt if Inma were not diligent in tamping it down. Inma, for her part, was getting sick of waiting for Antonio to leave Conchi. It was so obvious that Inma was better suited to him in every way, on and off the dance floor, in and out of bed, that she couldn't see what was holding things up. Antonio explained to her, of course, what every student already knew: that he owed it all to Conchi; how without her, he would still be stuck in the pueblo, miserable and misunderstood. But times change, Inma pointed out, things evolve, people move on. Healthy people do, anyway!

One afternoon, casting about for reasons why he couldn't leave Conchi, Antonio tried a new tack, one he hoped would come across as melancholy and dutiful: if he left Conchi, what would she do? Who would she find to love her? After all, she wasn't exactly every man's physical ideal. She would end up all alone.

Inma digested this in silence for a moment, then said in a flat voice, "You're saying you can't dump her because she's fat."

"Don't be vulgar!"

Inma's temper snapped. "That's the best reason for overeating I've ever heard! I tell you what, how about if I put her on a diet and get her to lose twenty kilos? Will you leave her then?" Antonio decided to laugh this off, and reached out in a mollifying gesture, but she batted his hand away. "Twenty-five kilos then! Would *that* do it? How about if I make her skinny *and* beautiful *and* find her a new man? Can I have you then? Or is there always going to be *something*? Jesus, you're like a spoiled child with your whining: "I can't leave my girlfriend because she's too useful and too fat!"

Now Antonio had had enough. He leapt up and pulled on his trousers. "Let's just forget it, shall we?" She watched his fingers fumble angrily as they did up his belt, and got a feeling like a cold dark hole opening in her chest. *Oh no, he's going. Please don't go.*

"I'm sorry, Antonio," she said. "I'm sorry!"

He yanked on his shirt. "You obviously have no idea whatsoever of the complexity of human relations. You understand nothing at all!" He shoved his feet into his well-polished shoes and swept up his keys and change. Then he held his hands out, palms up, let out a snort of angry laughter and addressed the ceiling. "This is madness! What am I doing here?"

"I said I'm sorry, please, Antonio, don't leave, please!"

But he swept out of the room, his voice carrying back to her from down the hall, "I must really be losing my mind!" punctuated by a bark of that phony laughter.

How she hated that, that theatrical talking to the gods, or the heavens, or the camera, as if he were starring in a movie. He, the star, and she some shitty walk-on. She lay on the sagging bed in the damp spot of their cold, congealing passions while he pranced away dry and clean, light and free, his anger cleansing away his guilt and leaving him feeling refreshed and self-righteous. The room was shabby and grim without him. He's leaving, she thought. I'm using him up. The cold dark hole in her chest felt so wide and deep that she might fall in forever. She curled up in the bed, out of the wet spot, and lay listening to the whoosh and beeping of the traffic below, and to the sickly sound of the wavering horn section of a band practicing across the river for Holy Week.

. . . . .

But they continued to dance beautifully together. Inma knew instinctively that this was the one way she had, her only chance, of making Antonio love her. One day in class they were fox-trotting so magically that one by one the other couples stopped dancing until they were alone on the floor. "Like Fred Astaire and Ginger Rogers," was the murmur around the studio. Conchi looked on stonily from her table in the corner. When they were done, the students broke into spontaneous applause, and Conchi flushed deeply. Applause . . . when applause was supposed to be reserved for Antonio and Conchi! The dancers left the floor hand in hand and went laughing to the bar, where Antonio swept up his bottle of beer and took a swig from it. Then he passed the bottle absentmindedly to Inma, who drank from it as though nothing could be more natural. The kind of slip-up that happens. Sharing applause, sharing a bottle of beer. What wouldn't they be sharing next, Conchi wondered? The casualness of their gesture struck her to the heart. This was it, the little sign she had been on the alert for. It was time to take action before this thing got out of hand. Conchi munched one of Inma's carrot sticks, eyes narrowed, and decided to go ahead and do what she had been contemplating for some time.

. . . . .

Word of Conchi's pregnancy spread quickly through the dance academy, students competing to demonstrate that they had been the first to know.

"Yes, I know! Conchi told me last week. I was thrilled!"

"I didn't even need to be told. I'd seen it in her face."

"If it's a boy, they're going to call him Antoñito."

"Well, obviously!"

. . . . .

"That's it, then," Antonio said with a sigh to Inma in their pensión. "She's got me by the balls. There's no leaving her now."

"But do you want this baby?"

"Of course not! What do I want with a baby? More responsibility, more ties? I want to dance, that's all. Dance! Dance!" He pounded the wall with his fist, then let his head drop in a pose of defeat. In the privacy of his mind, however, he was far from displeased by the news. While Conchi was pregnant, and later when she was looking after the baby, he would be free to seek a new dance partner. Competitions this summer! But he was careful not to illuminate this side of the question for Inma. Instead he would use the baby as a heaven-sent way out of this now tiresome relationship.

"If you don't want it, don't have it! She can't make you do anything you don't want to do, pregnant or not! It's the oldest trick in the book! Stand up for yourself!"

"My love," Antonio said, for the first time, and Inma caught her breath. "My love, if I could spend my life with you, I would. But that's not possible now. And it will be my sorrow forever." What the hell, he was as good as out of there already, he might as well give the poor kid a thrill, something to console herself with. He felt pleased with himself at his generosity and his kind handling of the situation. These were words she could treasure. And this way he could break with her without hurting her feelings; their love would be ill-starred, their parting inevitable. He was so moved by his own kindness that he made love to her especially tenderly. Why not? It would be the last time anyway. Give her a good send-off. He left with a great show of reluctance, but once down in the street alone, he strode along smartly, feeling like he had on new shoes. The business with Inma was as good as over, and what's more, he was going to be a father! And if that wasn't proof of manhood . . . ! He stopped on impulse and bought some flowers for Conchi.

The room no longer seemed shabby and grim without him. It had a fresh charm, seeming to still ring with his recent declaration. Inma threw the window open and strolled about the room naked, bouncing a bit on the balls of her feet, arms outstretched, safe at last. Antonio loves me. Her anger was gone. Nothing else mattered. No, no, that wasn't right. Something else did matter: she had to free him. No difficult thing, really. She lit a cigarette and smoked it energetically, blowing the smoke out hard and accurately as the details of her plan took shape in her mind. Then she showered briskly in the rusting shower stall, rubbing her skin hard all over, delighted with her body, its slenderness, its hardness. She combed her wet hair straight back in a pleasingly boyish style and ran lightly down the cracked marble steps of the pensión. Outside it smelled of orange blossom. It was spring.

Twice already, Inma had provoked miscarriage in herself with the aid of an herbal infusion, and there was no reason why it should not work on Conchi. Taken a couple of times a day for a week or so, it was very efficacious. Inma hummed to herself as she brewed it up, added honey and aniseed to the other ingredients to take away the bitterness, and poured it carefully into her thermos.

When she unscrewed the top, a pleasant smell wafted out on an inviting little curl of steam. "Now, what's that, or don't I want to know?" Conchi said. "Honestly, the stuff you eat. No wonder you're nothing but a bag of bones." Conchi followed that up with a hearty laugh to prove she was "only joking" and sipped from the brimming cup Inma offered her. "Well, it tastes okay. That's something."

Inma refilled the cup often over the next days, smiling and chatting with Conchi like a little pageboy attending a queen, as Conchi played the glowing expectant mother, lording it over poor tomboyish Inma. Some of the students had already knitted booties for the baby, and Conchi was exquisite in her role as glowing mother-to-be, her plump curves now invested with meaning and importance. She basked in the attention. No one could have guessed at the secret cold lump of regret Conchi felt about this pregnancy. Too late she had come to see that a baby would keep her off the dance floor and relegate her to the background. It had been a stupid, stupid move. But Conchi smiled and preened, and Inma flattered and cooed, as all the while Inma worked coldly to end the existence of this child that neither of them wanted. And so they sat, side by side, day after day, sipping and chatting, thinking up silly names for the baby and giggling, then sipping some more of the grassy herbal tea Inma had made.

. . . . .

"Have you heard?" asked a woman with an ashen face, barring Inma's entrance to the dance academy one afternoon. Inma craned past her to look for Antonio. Not in sight. It was clear something serious had happened. There was no music playing, the dance floor was deserted, the lights were on full, people were clustered around the edges of the room in stricken postures, muttering in low voices.

"Heard what?"

"You haven't heard?" The woman's eyes darted eagerly back and forth between Inma's eyes, her horror at the ghastly news she was about to impart equaled only by her greedy joy that she would be the one to tell it. A feeling of déjà vu swept over Inma, and she became conscious of the blood throbbing in her cheeks just beneath her eyes. "It's Conchi," the woman whispered. "She's lost the baby." The news was no surprise. The surprise was the sickening lurch Inma felt in her stomach, panic that she struggled to convert into a feeling of defiant triumph.

. . . . .

"But don't you understand? A dead baby binds us together forever!" Inma listened in shock to Antonio, who was as nimble in argument as he was on his feet. "A live baby we could have shared! We could have had joint custody, anything! Lord knows enough children are raised like that. But now she may never be able to have another baby, that's what the doctors told her. All her hopes of motherhood shattered! And it's my baby—mine!—who did this to her. Who will want her now, Inma? Don't you see? If the baby had lived, it would have been another story. But now she's my responsibility forever." For a moment Inma considered punching his face, squeezing his Adam's apple until her fingers touched behind it, gripping his hair and slamming his head back against the wall, and while he wheezed for breath she'd whisper that she had killed it, she'd killed his goddamned—instead she walked away.

. . . . .

The dance students noted with approval that the tragedy brought Conchi and Antonio closer together than ever. Everyone's favorite couple had come through the ordeal united. Conchi had been wonderful as an expectant mother, but if possible, she was even more impressive in her role as the tragic but courageous woman who had lost her child. Everyone marveled at her strength and lavished praise and sympathy on her, which she accepted gracefully, as her due. They whispered to each other how brave she had been through it all.

Conchi could well be brave, as she had no more miscarried than she had been pregnant in the first place, her pregnancy being the invention of a jealous moment, a decision rashly taken, soon regretted, and easily undone. The devoted couple barely commented on Inma's sudden disappearance, which Conchi rightly took to be a sign of her final victory over her rival. Life went on as before at the dance school, with Conchi and Antonio still treating the students to the occasional tango as a special treat. And afterwards, to thunderous applause, Antonio would give his curls a boyish toss before bowing low and stretching out a hand to Conchi, who would execute a funny final twirl, everyone's favorite part. The students clapped so hard it made their palms sting. "She dances like an angel!" they said.

. . . . .

Inma sat alone in the Plaza de la Gavidia smoking a cigarette. She had been up all night in bars, met a few people, separated from them, met a few more, and finally all had gone home but she, who had drifted to this square where children played accompanied by smiling mothers or sullen nursemaids. Antonio's child would have been about this age by now, she thought, watching a plump little boy toddle after a ball. Abortion is okay, but aborting someone else's baby is not okay. After her long night, thoughts came to her in this simple, weary form.

Inma was never to know that Conchi's pregnancy had been a fabrication. She hadn't been near the dance school for over two years. Like so many other places, it had been used up and was now off limits. Inma went to new places now, saw new people, but she did so out of habit and necessity, without expectations. After all her previous misadventures, there had been the possibility of starting over with fresh people in a fresh place and doing things right this time, becoming someone new and clean and blameless. But that was over now. What she had done to Antonio's baby could never be undone. She had finally crossed the line, stepped off the edge; the black hole had opened and she was falling in. The little boy's ball rolled to her feet. She stooped to pick it up and held it out to him, but he eyed her fearfully. His mother took it from her with a curt word of thanks, and moved her child safely away. Inma supposed she must be looking a little rough. She dropped her cigarette butt, stepped on it, stood up and walked away. She didn't know where she was going, and it didn't matter. It didn't really matter anymore what happened to her.

MRS. WEBSITE'S DANCE
Ina Bouman

1

It happened every time a woman came too close to him. Horrendous images kept him from intimacy, visions which invaded his mind, releasing adrenalin, urging him to a state of war, arming him to the teeth.

It had started suddenly, about ten years ago, when he had first dared to ask a girl for a date. Why don't you take a girl out instead of always fiddling with that motorbike, his mother had nagged. And his father had taken him out to a bar for a talk. What about? Did he ever look at girls, his father had wanted to know. Was he interested in girls? Surely it was time for that kind of thing. Wasn't he a healthy young man? Or was he. . . . No Dad, I'm not gay. But did he know how . . . ? Should they go together into the city for the weekend, or perhaps would he prefer to go on his own. . . ? Dad would be happy to pay. He had declined. Sometimes he tried to get together with girls, but it always ended in the same mess. At the first inkling that there was sex in the air, he had a panic attack. He felt threatened and ran; more from his imaginings than from the girls. At night in bed, he was besieged by nightmares; enormous praying mantises, eyes bulging, dancing around each other and devouring or being devoured after mating. He saw a Black Widow spider circle her mate before striking. . . . No, it was *he* who mated with the spider, his sperm coming rough as iron filings, while eight, no twenty, hairy legs grasped his body, crushing the air out of him. He would awake screaming. Sometimes, his mother came to his room and sat on his bed in an effort to comfort him. Another nightmare, Son? Yes, Mother. Horrendous beasts again? He would push her away. Leave me alone. His erection was returning and this time, his hands gave him relief and comfort.

.   .   .   .   .

He had recently turned twenty-nine years old, but it was still the same old story whenever he showed interest in girls, in women. He reasoned that his fear wasn't unfounded. He had read up on penetration. And penetration is a risky business. Everyone knows the penis can be nipped off. Women's pelvic muscles are merciless. Countless men are rushed to hospitals every year to be freed from a woman whom they are literally stuck into.

In the Middle East, there had been a case where a man's entire genitals had been swallowed up by a vagina. Naturally this had fatal consequences for the rest of the man. As for oral sex, that was out of the question for obvious reasons.

Strange things happened with animals too. In many species, the female ate her mate. Obviously that was not something cows did, but nevertheless there were instances of bulls losing their balls inside cows.

He had decided to stop taking any kind of risk. He had his apartment, his stimulating, well-paid job at an insurance company, and his motorbike.

He was good-looking with regular features, dark hair, blue eyes. But it was his apparent shyness, according to one woman, that made him so attractive. He had scrupulously avoided her after that.

Several months later she'd stopped by his office to ask him for a date. I'm engaged to be married, he lied hastily.

I have a relationship with my motorbike, he told his colleagues. There were always a few who would cast him envious looks and murmur about delicious freedom. And behind his back, he would hear them speculate: I bet he gets all he wants. . . . And he did. His sex life was just fine. He kept it safely in his own hands.

.   .   .   .   .

It was six years since his parents had died. Heart attacks killed them. His father shortly before his mother. They'd always done everything together.

He had kept their fourteenth-floor apartment in a modern block, and after he threw out some beds and ugly pieces of furniture, he had decided to stay on. The light poured through the windows, which reached almost from floor to ceiling, and the view was breathtaking. A big sky and in the distance between the tall buildings, the dunes shimmered.

Deep down below city life went on, a congestion of stores, cafés, and here and there a few bits of greenery.

He had never been ambitious. He had his own portfolio of insurance clients and was very conscientious. His database was always up to the minute, and he was collaborating on his department's pages on the company's website.

A website designer had temporarily been assigned to his department to work on it with him. He couldn't remember her name, but in the office she was known as Mrs. Website because they said she was married to it. He found her completely unattractive, thank God, because sometimes they had to sit side by side at the same computer screen.

She did have lovely hands, but otherwise she was nondescript and seemed not to really notice him.

It was reassuring, yet strange—usually women paid him a lot of attention. If they weren't attracted by his looks, it was that shyness of his that drew them to him. This one ignored him. She just spoke a few words now and then without looking up at him. All communication went via the screen. He didn't always like her words but she had a pleasant voice, he had to admit. It had a musical quality. Although, why he thought that was a mystery to him. He had never had the slightest interest in music. Sometimes, in bed at night after he had worked beside her all day, he would think of that voice. It made him feel good, but this soon turned to a tight anxiety in his chest and he would rise to take a sleeping pill.

2

They called her Mrs. Website. At first she resented it, but the company employees were friendly and respected her contribution, so she accepted the nickname as a compliment. She loved her job. Going from one organization to the next, contributing her ingenuity and creativity. It paid well and brought variety to her life, and it was a way of meeting people.

She didn't know many people outside work, not that she minded. She didn't really like people. They were crude, insensitive, false. Either that, or time wasters who by cheap means tried to mask their own lack of purpose. Like the killer sites on the Web that were introduced to bridge waiting times with jokes and special effects. Some users loved them. But she worked for efficiency, the highway with a minimum of obstacles. That made her successful.

Her free time was spent immersed in music, in the rhythm and movements it produced in her body. She loved to get home, take off her clothes, and dance to the music she adored, wrapped in just her large white silk shawl, sometimes until deep into the night, like now. It was 3 A.M. but her head was clear as a starry night sky. Sometimes it seemed as though she could hear Orpheus playing and she was Eurydice lost in the underworld. But she always resurfaced and never neglected her work.

She was aware that she gave a cool and remote impression in the outside world. But she made no effort to be attractive or accessible. Nobody dared approach her. Including that young man who watched her.

Why was she suddenly thinking of him?

When at last she lay in her bed, at first light—she knew what it was. Of course, it was a sense of recognition. He was afraid, just as she had once been. He hadn't just locked himself away, he had also locked himself up physically. It was visible, there was no rhythm in his body. That was precisely where they differed. Before she fell asleep she decided that perhaps there was something she could do for him.

3

Where did that restlessness come from? More than at any other time in the past few months he needed to get out on his bike.

After work he got on his motorbike and rode through town to the sea. There were a few fast roads through the dunes that were packed in summer, but this crisp spring weather ensured they were quiet so he could roar along undisturbed. *Keep moving,* he thought. That's what Mrs. Website had once said. He wondered if this was what she meant.

When he returned from such a ride he wasn't truly relaxed. He often thought of Mrs. Website, seeing her stern face, pointed like a bird's. No, he wasn't attracted to her. And she wasn't to him. Did she notice him at all?

It was Friday, at about 6:30 P.M. He had been the last to work with her that day and shut down the computer while she slid her papers into her bag. An old leather bag, soft and supple, unlike the stiff attaché case his mother had bought for him many years ago.

As he turned to leave, she put her hand on his arm.

Startled, he pulled away.

She smiled at his reaction. "Please forgive me," she said. "Would you like to come for tea on Sunday?"

Taken aback, he didn't reply.

"I'll leave it to you," she said. "It's an open invitation." She gave him her card and left.

4

On Saturday his intention was not to go. By Sunday he dared not to stay away. Because what excuse could he give her by Monday? Maybe she wanted to discuss work.

She lived on a common street of not very large but respectable houses.

Each front door had a straight path leading to it, with a few square meters of front yard on either side. Mrs. Website had had hers paved over. The buzzer set off appalling tubular bell sounds which nearly frightened him off.

But before he could run, Mrs. Website, wearing a dress he recognized from the office, had opened the door and welcomed him in with a reserved smile.

Reassured, he stepped over the threshold and followed her into the living room.

To his surprise he found himself in a large, virtually empty room. There was a small table with two straight-backed chairs pushed against one wall. Next to it a rack containing records, CD's, and the stereo system. Beside the door he noticed an ornate hook with a large white silk shawl, or was it a dress, hanging from it.

The bare wooden floor was highly polished. There was only a Persian rug in front of the fire with a cushion on it. He felt her eyes on him, expecting some reaction.

"What a space!"

"It's very different upstairs," she smiled. "That's where I keep my books and where my computer rules. And it's where I sleep. Down here is where I live. Have a look around and I'll make tea."

He sat at the table and looked around, but there wasn't a lot to see. The walls were bare and blinds covered all but one window, which offered a meager view of the house across the street.

She returned and set a tray of tea and cake on the table.

"Homemade?" he asked politely.

She nodded. "Especially for you."

It was a delicious, fragrant cake.

Apparently Mrs. Website didn't want to discuss work. She argued how important it was to find sufficient counterweight in one's private life when one works with modern technology.

He agreed. "I have a motorbike."

She looked surprised. "What kind? How many cc?"

"Six-fifty-cc with twin cams."

"Wow, I guess that moves."

"It's not bad," he replied modestly. "What about you," he ventured. "What's your counterweight?"

It was the first time in years that he had dared to ask someone an open question.

"I listen to music and I dance."

"You dance?" his voice was hoarse.

He tried to hide his anxiety, but she noticed it. "Don't worry, it's similar to riding a motorbike."

She stood up and walked over to the music system to put on a tape. Soft music slowly increased in volume.

She unhooked the white silk shawl and draped it gently over her shoulders while moving to the rhythm of the music. After only a few minutes she stopped, thank God, because he was beginning to feel very nervous.

"You need space," she said firmly. "You have locked up yourself, I can see that. Go stand in the middle of the room."

He stood up, hesitated, took a few steps. She nodded encouragingly. He took one more step but could go no further.

"Two more steps. To move freely you need to experience the space."

Cautiously he made two steps to the center of the room, looked helplessly around him, wanted to go back to his chair, but then . . . saw the walls give way, ever more, felt the space around him grow and grow to enormous emptiness, while the floor beneath him seemed to sink away; it was like balancing on a cord over an immense void. He wavered, lurched . . . yelled, swung his arms wildly . . . then grabbed the hand that was extended to him.

A moment later he was back in his chair. Dizzy, his heart beating like a steam train. Far away he could hear a voice. "Don't worry, you're quite safe."

Mrs. Website's smile brought him back to reality.

Nobody had given him such frequent and reassuring smiles.

He drank the water she handed to him.

Slowly the dizziness passed. His heart slowed, the music died away, Mrs. Website had hung up her white cloth. Once more she looked the way she always did—plain, dull.

He had sat there for an hour or more before he stood up at last.

"I should be going."

She didn't protest.

In the middle of the room he found himself asking "Will you come to my place next week?"

It was out of his mouth before he realized. "If you'd like that, of course. . . ."

"I would."

On his way home he recovered. He gulped deep breaths of fresh air.

Something had happened to him. Something he hadn't experienced before. Something that almost exceeded the pleasure of speeding on his motorbike. He felt some kind of movement inside his body, around his stomach—not an unpleasant feeling.

He walked back through the park and there in the middle of it, he found himself skipping a couple of times involuntarily. Then he skipped some more, deliberately. And be hummed to himself for a moment in the elevator.

His apartment was just too full of junk, he noticed. He filled a cardboard box with surplus objects—three lamps, a vase, a stuffed squirrel, a bunch of dusty ornaments, a still life—and took the box, together with his mother's old armchair, down to the trashcans. The worn sofa cover was replaced with a light foulard.

Then he poured himself a whisky and looked around, satisfied.

His thoughts wandered to Mrs. Website. Never before had a woman expressed an interest in his motorbike.

5

It was one of the tallest blocks in this part of town. The lower floors held stores and offices.

Impressed, she looked up at the frontage, glad not to be living there herself.

At street level there was a nice atmosphere. For a moment she considered buying a good bottle of wine to take with her, but that thought alarmed her. Alcohol was far too banal and wasn't part of her way of doing things.

She felt inside her bag—there were the tape recorder, the cassettes, and her white silk shawl. And, of course, the cake, which she had baked with care and the precise dose the previous evening.

Reassured, she walked to the entrance, moving her head and shoulders as if to shake off an uncomfortable invisible load.

His voice sounded hesitant through the intercom. She had to expect some resistance. But she was used to that.

She decided to take the elevator to the tenth floor and walk the rest to feel the building's atmosphere, and to avoid running into someone in the elevator on the fourteenth floor. Best to take care in case things got out of hand. Tasting freedom for the first time can cause hefty reactions in some. Nothing is more difficult to handle.

The doors slid open slowly. Happily, the elevator was empty. She felt uncomfortable in tight spaces.

Now she needed to concentrate fully on this young man.

He had been rather shy at work that week. They hadn't worked together as much as usual. It could have been coincidence, but she got the impression that he had somehow been avoiding her a little. She smiled. Naturally. He must have been so shocked by his own spontaneous invitation.

The first thing to do was to win his trust. Then with the help of movement, dance, and rhythm—the essentials of life—she would free him from his deep-rooted fear.

On the tenth floor she stepped from the elevator.

She had as yet not seen a soul and neither did she hear a sound in the stairwell as she calmly walked up. Half the residents are ill in bed and the rest are busy e-mailing, she speculated scornfully. And all of them are alone. People should be aware that modern electronics and communication technology stifle their natural impulses. They stare at a screen instead of into the eyes of their fellow man. And they move far too little. They think they compensate for this by peddling on imitation bicycles or performing feats of strength on complicated contraptions in brightly lit halls, while fake pine scent is blown in and sloppy muzak oozes out of the speakers. In discotheques, where tense young people jump around with shaky staccato movements, they play hard thumping music.

There's no communication, whereas music and especially dance are the methods with which to communicate. Dance frees the emotions, opens the soul, provides energy, and brings people together. It's the same with animals. Don't they also use dance, as part of the mating ritual and to give expression to affection, rage, fear?

On the fourteenth floor, one of the three doors was ajar. She took a deep breath and pushed it open.

6

He was dreading it. Whatever had possessed him to invite her over? Politeness? Maybe she'll cancel, he hoped.

What was he to do with her?

Just get rid of her as soon as possible, he thought.

She had announced herself through the intercom. The tea was steeping and he had bought a cake.

She seemed to like cake.

It took a long time for her to come up. His hope lingered, maybe it had been someone else after all. It happened sometimes that a resident forgot his door key, but he was kidding himself, he had recognized her voice. Suddenly she was there in his hallway. She was dressed casually, less formal than usual, but it was the weekend. And she was wearing makeup. She smiled at him. He felt himself blushing and turned to lead the way to the living room.

"May I have a look around?"

"Of course."

He told her that he had lived here since his childhood and had decided to stay on after his parents' deaths. "But I have changed the interior a lot since then."

She stood in front of the open window. "What a wonderful view."

"Be careful," he warned, "the sills are very low."

"Were your parents never afraid you would fall out?"

"No." He didn't feel like telling her that he had never dared get anywhere close to those windows. But since his parents' deaths he seemed to suffer less from vertigo.

"I like your space," she said.

He went into the kitchen to get the tea. She followed him and took a golden yellow cake from her bag.

"I made it myself; you cut it—good thick slices."

There was something maternal about her, he decided.

He left his own cake in its wrapping.

Back in the living room, he saw Mrs. Website sitting on the couch, looking at a photograph of his motorbike.

He sat down in a chair facing her, poured the tea and took a slice of cake from his mother's pretty porcelain plate, just as she did.

Mrs. Website was definitely interested in motorbikes. He spoke of the capacity and performance of his machine, of the trips he had taken, noticing that he embellished the stories, especially exaggerating the speed at which he travelled. But she listened attentively and asked questions.

When she carefully replaced the photograph of his motorbike on the sideboard, he felt a lot more at ease. It was time to talk about her.

"How are things with your hobby?" he asked in a confidential manner.

"You mean my dancing? Are you really interested?"

He nodded, although he wasn't sure that he really was.

She stood up and took the white silk shawl from her bag.

"You had a foretaste already, do you recognize this?"

Yes, of course he recognized that piece of material. He wondered why she had brought it and feared she would dance for him. *Oh my God, here she goes,* he thought. She wrapped it gracefully around her shoulders, while panic rose in his throat. She saw it happen. Of course, she saw everything. But she just smiled calmly.

"Let us have more tea and cake."

He relaxed and they spent a few minutes discussing the view.

"Riding a motorbike is also a sort of dance," she said suddenly.

"Well, I don't know. . . ."

"And just as dangerous, if you are of a squeamish disposition."

He shrugged his shoulders, unsure.

She eyed the table between them. "If we just move this to one side, then we have a great space to sit on the floor."

"Why would I sit on the floor?"

But already, she was moving the table, freeing up the carpet in the center of the room.

"Space," she said, satisfied.

He protested feebly but let himself be talked into sitting down on the sand-colored wool.

"Just like on your bike," she said.

He squatted, knees apart.

"That feels good doesn't it? Take the throttle . . . that's fine . . . and the clutch with the other hand. All right, are you comfortable?"

He nodded with his eyes closed. This posture was familiar to him.

"Do you feel the seat under you?"

It was nonsense, but he obeyed her voice. Her voice, which seemed to come from farther and farther away, even though she was kneeling right in front of him.

"Do you feel the tension in your legs? Look in the distance, the road is clear, go for it!"

He could feel the bike tremor beneath him, he opened the accelerator and shot forward. The speed turned everything around him into a blur of light. The road was empty and endless. He accelerated further and became even lighter. His clothes were falling off him, there seemed to be a spirit dancing around him. . . . No it was her, dancing around him, wrapped in the fluttering white silk, she became translucent, he drove right over her, right through her. The silk flew off her body and now he floated above her, descended into her. And he grew larger and saw her eyes shining, deeper and ever deeper he delved through her into tantalizing space . . . while the universe opened its gigantic void, imploding and exploding like a runaway constellation.

. . . . .

He heard soft words he did not understand.

She lay beneath him on the carpet, her eyes closed. She was naked just as he was. The white silk lay beside her.

Confused, he untangled himself. She didn't move. Quickly he spread the shawl over her face and body to make her disappear.

He walked to the open window and gulped fresh air, trying to bring some kind of order to his muddled brain.

Slowly, he realized what had happened.

"I survived it." That was his first thought.

No nightmare visions threatening him, no fears strangling him. On the contrary, his body tingled with life. He felt all powerful, master of the elements, as he stared out of the window watching large clouds push past. His thoughts were free, his feelings limitless.

How long had he been standing there?

Suddenly she was there beside him.

Had he forgotten her, rejoicing in this unknown well-being? From out of the corner of his eye he saw that she was wrapped in the white silk.

"I'm still here," he heard her say.

He was silent.

Without seeing he knew her to be looking at him.

It bothered him. Her presence disturbed his euphoria. He shrugged his shoulders as if he could lose her that way. The feeling of well-being was ebbing from his body, while his irritation mounted.

Suddenly he seemed to be standing in a cold bare landscape.

"How do you feel?"

He turned his head. Her eyes startled him, they were staring into his with an intensity he did not recognize. Her mouth was half open as she smiled at him and he could see her breasts through a gap in the silk.

"Why don't you say something?"

He was trembling, wanting to run for it, but stood nailed to the spot. He had to avoid looking into those eyes at all cost, escape those breasts which scared him to death and that mouth which threatened to devour him.

In his panic he was obsessed by that one thought, he was in mortal danger but he couldn't move.

Petrified, he felt her arm against his, knew her to be watching him and heard her ask again: "Why don't you say something?"

. . . . .

How could this have happened?

Had he made some involuntary movement so that she tripped?

Or maybe he had touched her rather clumsily.

It was possible that she had become dizzy and lost her balance.

He didn't know.

But suddenly she was no longer there beside him. She had disappeared.

Just that scream, that awful long scream that seemed to go on forever and turned into the screeching of sirens that came ever closer.

Later the banging on his door.

All those cops, asking questions that he couldn't answer.

He remembered nothing.

Someone took him away from the window and gave him his clothes.

Yes, Mrs. Website had visited him. No, he had no idea what her real name was.

They had talked about his motorbike.

And what about the silk cloth and her naked body and his own nakedness? Were they lovers?

He shivered and didn't say anything.
Had they quarreled?
No.
There was only one thing he remembered: she had danced for him.

AT THE HOP
Bill and Judy Crider

One

Bo Wagner crammed another peppermint Chiclet into his mouth. It wasn't easy because he was already chewing what he estimated to be eight more of the little white bricklets of gum. He was chewing them to maintain his sanity, since he hadn't smoked a cigarette in three weeks, four days, eighteen hours, and—he glanced at the clock on his desk—forty-three minutes. He might not be able to count Chiclets, but keeping up with the time since he'd given up cigarettes forever was something else entirely.

The first week had been the hardest. Holding his coffee cup in the morning had been almost impossible for seven days. It clicked against his teeth when he tried to take a sip, and it clicked on the saucer when he set it back down. At least he didn't have the shakes anymore.

But while his hand was steadier now, he was still dreaming about smoking every single night. Not only that, he was dreaming about all the little rituals associated with smoking: tearing the little red cellophane strip from around the top of the pack, tearing away the foil, tapping the first cigarette against his watch crystal to pack the tobacco, lighting up with his silver Zippo that never failed to flame up the very first time he flicked the little ridged wheel against the flint, blowing out a satisfying plume of white smoke.

Jesus, but he needed a cigarette! He rummaged in his shirt pocket and dragged out the Chiclets pack, thumbed back the flap, and dumped a piece of gum out into his palm. He stared at it for less than a second and then shoved it into his mouth with the rest of them.

"You look like an old cow chewin' her cud," Janice Langtry told him.

Janice was Bo's writing partner, his collaborator on a highly successful series of mystery novels featuring Sam Fernando, the gentleman sleuth.

Technically, Janice did all the writing, while Bo did the plotting and the typing. He couldn't write at all. He had no grasp of grammar, no perception of punctuation, no concept of correctness.

He could, however, plot. He had devised some of the most fiendishly clever crimes of the mid–twentieth century, all fictional, of course, including the famous case where Sam Fernando proved that a man who had been shot in the head four times with four different weapons had committed suicide, thereby saving the man's wife from going to prison forever and earning her undying gratitude in the bargain.

What Bo wanted more than anything in his own life was to earn the undying gratitude of Janice Langtry, who was tall, blond, and beautiful. Also unattainable, as far as Bo Wagner was concerned, which was why he had quit smoking, as he now took the opportunity to remind her.

"It's your fault I look this way," he mumbled around the wad of chewing gum. "You told me you might go out with me if I quit smoking, so I did. But I have to do something, and chewing gum is it."

"*Might* is the operative word," Janice told him. "I didn't say I would. I didn't make any promises."

Bo sighed. Well he knew the power of might. He was everything that Janice didn't want in a man.

She wanted suave and sophisticated; he was bumbling and inept, the kind of guy who had mustard stains on his shirts. Ketchup stains, too.

She wanted cosmopolitan; he was provincial. The only time he'd been out of Texas was to visit a Boys' Town in Nuevo Laredo one time when he was in college, and he wasn't about to tell her that.

She wanted neat; he was messy. His books and papers were scattered everywhere, and while he knew where everything was—well, almost every-thing—no one else would have been able to discern a system in the way things were strewn around the desk and the floor.

She wanted mature; he was adolescent. Hey, could he help it if he admired the late, great James Dean and preferred to listen to Dion and the Belmonts on the radio rather than some classical piece by that guy Gershwin?

If life were only like the movies, he'd be in fine shape, of course. Janice would naturally fall for him, just like Katharine Hepburn always fell for Spencer Tracy. In fact, that was a perfect analogy. Hepburn was taller and classier than Tracy, but she went for him in a big way. If only Janice would go for Bo, he would be eternally happy.

It wasn't working out like that, however.

"I think it's more than the smoking," he mumbled. "I think it's because I'm getting bald."

"You are not," Janice said, inspecting the back of his head, an act that was made easier because she was standing behind him as he sat at his desk to type the manuscript of their latest book. "Well, maybe just a little."

Bo's hand shot to his head. "Where? How bad is it? Quarter-size? Half-dollar?"

Janice laughed. "I'm just teasin' you, Bo. You've got more hair than a wolf. Don't worry about it."

"It's because I'm shorter than you, then," Bo said. "But I'll tell you something: all those movie stars you like so much are shorter than I am. Alan Ladd, for example. He's five-foot-two."

"I don't believe that."

"Well, it's true. And Richard Widmark? I saw him in O'Hare Airport once. Or maybe I should say I didn't see him. He was there, all right, but there was a crowd around him, and I couldn't even see the top of his head."

"You're making that up."

"I am not. It's a well-known fact that John Wayne is only five-foot-six."

Janice laughed. "You're pathetic, Bo Wagner, you really are. Why don't you quit worryin' about your personal appearance and worry about how Sam Fernando's goin' to figure out this latest mystery you've got him mixed up in?"

Bo looked down at the old Underwood and at what was written on the page of white typing paper.

. . . . .

Sam Fernando let his gaze wander up the wide marble stairway leading to the second floor of the museum. There were three doorways on the second floor, all of them leading to completely empty rooms, rooms that were in two days to be furnished with the museum's latest exhibition, a display of the jewelry maker's art as practiced in Italy during the Renaissance. It was in one of those rooms that Geoffrey Falkerson had been murdered, a knife thrust through his heart. Yet more than two hundred people had stood in the area where Sam Fernando now stood and watched Falkerson walk up those marble stairs alone. They had seen him enter the central room on the second floor—alone. And they had heard his piercing scream as he died there—alone.

For there was no one with him in that room. Two hundred people were willing to swear that no one else had entered it and that no one else had left it. And there were no fingerprints on the knife. Furthermore, there was, as Fernando knew quite well, no exit from the second floor, no door leading outside, no door leading to the roof, no door leading from one room to the other, nothing.

It was therefore impossible for Geoffrey Falkerson to have been stabbed by anyone at all.

Sam Fernando smiled his slow, superior smile. Impossible? That was what the murderer wanted everyone to believe. If it was impossible for Falkerson to have been stabbed by anyone, then it would be impossible for anyone to discover the murderer. But nothing—nothing!—was impossible for Sam Fernando!

.   .   .   .   .

"Isn't that wonderful?" Janice said. "I just love it when Sam smiles that way."

Bo didn't love it. He hated it, in fact, though of course he would never say that to Janice. He thought Sam Fernando was a condescending snob, and if Bo could write—which he couldn't, but if he could—he'd write about a hero like Mike Hammer or Philip Marlowe or Sam Spade, someone who was rough, tough, and irresistible to the women, someone who would take Sam Fernando and his superior little smile and mop up the marble museum floor with them.

"Sometimes I get the impression that you don't like writing about Sam," Janice said as if reading his mind.

"Well, you're wrong," Bo mumbled. "I love it."

Which wasn't entirely a lie. As long as writing about the gentleman sleuth kept him and Janice in close proximity to one another, he'd do it gladly. Or if not gladly, at least not grudgingly. It paid the rent, after all, and a good deal more than that.

"I also love it when Sam figures out the answer to impossible crimes," Janice said. "You still haven't told me how he does it this time."

"I don't want to spoil the surprise."

"You'll have to tell me soon if I'm going to write it."

"Oh, all right."

But Bo didn't get a chance. Just at that moment the telephone rang.

Two

They were in Bo's office, where they always worked on the final draft, so he answered the phone. The voice on the other end sounded like several small stones being ground up in a blender, so Bo knew at once that it was Lieutenant Franklin.

"Wagner? That you?"

"Sure is, Lieutenant." Bo refrained from asking Franklin who else he thought would be answering Bo's phone. "What's going on?"

"We've had another one of those murders," Franklin said.

Bo didn't have to be told what that meant. Franklin had called Bo and

Janice a couple of times in the past when he had a case that seemed a little out of the usual line of things. Franklin seemed to think that because Janice and Bo were mystery writers, they could look at the facts in a way that the police couldn't, which made Franklin unique among the cops that Bo knew. None of the others thought an amateur could find his fanny with a flashlight.

"What is it this time?" Bo asked, which was a logical question when you considered that the last time Franklin had called, a witness had seen a headless man fleeing the scene of the crime.

"One of those locked-room things," Franklin said. "It's not something I can explain over the phone. Do you want to check it out or not?"

"Sure I do," Bo said. "Where are you?"

"At a sock hop."

"You're kidding me," Bo said.

"I never kid. This sock hop is part of an engagement party that was being held at the Regan High gym. You know where that is?"

Bo knew. "I can be there in fifteen minutes."

"Don't forget to bring your partner along."

Bo didn't have to ask what that meant, either. Franklin seemed to have gotten the idea that it was Janice who was the brains of the pair, an idea that bothered Bo somewhat, since he, after all, was the master plotter. On the other hand, he had to admit that it was Janice who had been able to come up with the logical solution to real-life "impossible" crimes they'd been involved in.

"She's right here," Bo said. "I know she'll be glad to come along."

"She's there with you? At your house?"

"That's right."

"You lucky dog. Maybe you're too busy to come to something as boring as a crime scene."

"I wish," Bo said.

"You wish what?" Janice asked when he had hung up.

"Never mind. That was Lieutenant Franklin. He has something he'd like our help with."

Janice's eyes lit up. Bo liked to think of her as a kind, sensitive, and gentle person, but he had to admit that she took an avid interest in felonious conduct. In fact, the more felonious the conduct, the more interesting she found it.

"So where are we going?" she asked.

"To a sock hop. Could that be considered a date?"

"Not unless we dance."

"Do you think—"

"Don't count on it, buster. We're going to investigate a crime, aren't we?"

"Maybe it's not a *bad* crime," Bo said.

Janice shook her head. She was wearing her blond hair in a ponytail, which Bo thought made her almost unbearably attractive.

"I have to give you credit for persistence," she said.

"Is that good?"

"I'll have to think about it," she told him.

.   .   .   .   .

They drove to the gym in Bo's '49 Mercury, his pride and joy and just the kind of car a guy should be going to the hop in if you asked Bo. He wondered if there was a live band or if they were just using records.

When they arrived at the gym, no one was dancing. A large crowd was gathered outside the doors on the sidewalk. Everyone was milling around and talking, and they were all adults, which was a little surprising. Bo didn't think of adults as attending sock hops.

Even more surprising, Bo recognized some of them from having seen their photos in the society pages. They weren't dressed the way they had been in the photos, however. The men were all wearing jeans, and many of them had on white shirts with the collars turned up. A lot of the women were wearing jeans, too, though some of them were wearing straight skirts and matching sweaters, while a couple even had on the full poodle skirts that had been popular a couple of years back.

And while everyone wore white cotton socks, no one was wearing shoes. Bo assumed that the shoes were all inside, piled where they had been removed for dancing on the gym floor. He didn't see anyone who looked like a band member.

There was a uniformed officer making sure that no one either left the scene or went back into the gym. When Bo told him that he and Janice were there to see Lieutenant Franklin, the officer sent them inside.

There was a wide entrance hallway with ticket booths on one side and a popcorn machine on the other. Bo took a deep breath. He loved the smell of fresh popcorn. Behind the popcorn machine was a trophy case, but there were only a few small trophies in it. Maybe Regan's students weren't athletically inclined, or maybe most of the school's trophies were kept elsewhere.

Beside the popcorn machine was something that Bo wouldn't have expected to see in a high-school gym: a portable bar. There were napkins and glasses sitting on the polished surface, and Bo could see the necks of liquor and beer bottles sticking up over the top of the bar.

After looking things over, Bo and Janice went through the double doors and into the gym, which like most every gym Bo had ever been in smelled like some weird mixture of sweat, disinfectant, and floor wax. Add in the popcorn smell, and it wasn't so bad, however.

The gym looked like most gyms Bo had been in, too. There was a basketball hoop at each end of the highly polished hardwood floor. Red paint marked the court boundaries, and the folding seats had been pushed back against the wall. The scoreboard was at the far end of the gym, high up on the wall.

This gym had one thing that most others didn't have, however, and that was the huge Wurlitzer jukebox right under the scoreboard. It glowed with shifting colors—purple, orange, red, and yellow—and it was playing "Come Softly to Me" by the Fleetwoods.

Bo and Janice stopped just inside the doors. Bo looked to his right and saw Franklin and several other people, including a plainclothes cop named Farmer whom Bo knew slightly, standing off to the right. Franklin noticed Bo and Janice at about the same time and waved for them to join him.

"Should we take off our shoes?" Janice asked.

Bo could see that Franklin and the other officer were wearing their shoes, which didn't surprise Bo at all. Franklin wasn't the type to let a little thing like marking up the gym floor bother him. But Bo wasn't like Franklin, and he was still harboring the secret hope that Janice might dance with him. The thought of holding her close while dancing to "Come Softly to Me" sent little chills dancing up and down his spine.

So he said, "It might be a good idea."

He slipped off his Bass Weejuns and carried them over to a pile of men's shoes. He laid them where they'd be easy to find later. There were women's shoes close by, and Janice put her black suede penny loafers down beside them. Together they walked down toward Franklin. They didn't actually have to go out on the court to meet him, but Bo was glad they'd taken off their shoes anyway.

Franklin wore a rumpled suit that looked as if it had last been pressed, if it ever had been, during the Hoover administration. He wore a short, wide tie at least ten years old. It had a large yellow fried egg painted on it. Or something that looked like a fried egg. Bo thought it might be a sunrise instead, but he didn't know much about art.

"What's up?" Bo asked.

"Murder, that's what," Franklin said.

Bo couldn't be sure, but he thought Janice's eyes got just a touch brighter at the word.

"Tell us about it," she said.

Franklin explained that the sock hop was actually an extravagant engagement party for a young couple named Allan Blaine and Cynthia Norvell.

"Society types," Franklin said. "They thought this would be a cute way to celebrate. So they rented the gym and invited a hundred and fifty or so of their closest friends."

Things had gone along just fine for the first hour or so, but then someone noticed that the groom hadn't been around for a while. No one had really missed him. They'd all been having a great time, and they'd assumed he'd been doing the same, most likely doing the dirty bop with all the maids of honor.

"Did he have a weakness for maids of honor?" Bo asked.

"I understand that he had a weakness for anything in skirts," Franklin said. "Not that anybody here tonight is wearing a skirt."

"Some of them are," said Bo, who was of the opinion that there were probably fewer maids than there were women wearing skirts.

"Okay, okay," Franklin said. "But most people are wearing jeans. Anyway, somebody noticed that Blaine was missing, but no one could find him. The first place they looked was the parking lot."

"Why the parking lot?" Bo asked.

Janice looked at him. "Think about it, Bo."

He thought about it, and the first image that came to his mind was of himself and Janice, sitting in the backseat of his Mercury in one of the darker areas of the parking lot. He had his arms around her, and her face bent toward his, her lips parted slightly—

"Bo!"

He jumped slightly, as if he were the one who'd been caught philandering.

"You don't have to think about it so hard," Janice said.

Bo blushed. "Sorry. I think I get the picture."

"I'll just bet you do. But they didn't find him in the parking lot, did they, Lieutenant?"

"No," Franklin said. "They didn't.

"Blaine's white Cadillac Fleetwood was there, however, so they assumed that he hadn't left, though he might have gone off in someone else's car.

"Some of the guys had been getting really worried by that point, but when their dates, fiancées, and wives turned up, they were a lot less worried and decided just to enjoy the dance. No one had mentioned Allan's absence to Cynthia, so at least she wouldn't be upset over anything.

"It was at about that point that someone complained about not being able to get into the men's room.

"Right over there," Franklin said, nodding his head to his left.

Bo saw an alcove with doors on both sides. On one side, the door had the word WOMEN painted on it, and on the opposite side was another door with a sign that said MEN. This door was slightly ajar. Farmer, the plain-clothesman, stood in front of the door as if guarding it. Two other men and a woman, dressed for the hop, stood off to the side.

"There's another men's room," Franklin said. "Down at the other end. But it's part of the dressing room, and it wasn't open. Anybody who had to go had to use this one."

Bo looked at Janice to see if all this talk about using the men's room was making her uncomfortable. She just looked thoughtful and didn't seem to be bothered at all.

"The door to this rest room was locked," Franklin said. "So a couple of the guys started banging on it and calling out Blaine's name. They figured he might have had too much to drink and locked himself in by mistake."

"Did he answer them?" Janice asked.

"Nope," Franklin said. "But by that time some of the men were feeling a little pressed. They'd been drinking, and they needed some relief. A lot of people were gathered around, and they kicked in the door."

"And found Blaine," Janice said.

Franklin nodded. "Right. How'd you know?"

"You told Bo it was one of those locked-room crimes." She pointed toward the rest room door. "So I guessed that was the locked room."

"Well, you guessed right. Blaine was lying on the floor by the urinals, dead as a hammer. So what we have is a dead body all by itself in a room that's locked from the inside, with no way out."

"Unless the killer flushed himself," Bo said, and was immediately sorry for being so crude in front of Janice.

"Go ahead and joke about it, Wagner," Franklin said. "But it's not very funny."

"I know," Bo said. "I apologize."

"Well, you should," Janice said.

"I asked you two to come because you've been a real help to me before when I got a weird one like this," Franklin said. "But if you're gonna make jokes about it, then maybe I made a mistake."

"I said I was sorry," Bo told him. "It won't happen again."

"All right then. You got any questions?"

"How was the door locked?" Bo asked.

"You won't figure it out that easy," Franklin said. "It wasn't one of those spring locks. It was bolted. Why don't you have a look?"

Bo started toward the door. Janice was right behind him.

He looked back. "Maybe you'd better not go," he said.

"Why not? I've seen dead people before, too."

Bo was shocked. "When?"

"None of your business." She pushed past him. "Are you coming or not?"

Farmer stood aside to let them in, and Bo glanced at the other two men and the woman who were standing there. He recognized one of the men as Gary Stafford, a rising young defense lawyer. He didn't know the other one or the teary-eyed young woman who clung to his arm.

Janice stopped to look at the lock on the door. It was a cheap bolt, and it had broken through the frame. There didn't appear to be any way it could have been locked from the outside.

Bo walked on into the rest room, which was partially shielded from the outside view by a wooden partition. The disinfectant smell was much stronger here than in the gym, the smell of sweat much less pronounced. The walls were painted green and were relatively free of graffiti except for a couple of penciled lines, one of which said JEAN PAUL SARTRE IS A FARTRE. Bo thought that was pretty classy for a high school, much less for a gym.

The rest room floors were white tile, and there were three shiny white urinals on one wall and three wooden toilet stalls on the other. Looking around, Bo was seized with an almost overpowering urge to smoke. His hand went automatically to his shirt pocket, but it found only a box of Chiclets. Bo was disgusted at the unfairness of life. He had spent a lot of time smoking in the boys' room at his own high school, and now he was reduced to chewing gum. He got out two Chiclets and stuck them in his mouth, cracking their thin shells between his teeth and chewing furiously.

In front of the urinals, Allan Blaine, dressed in jeans and a blue shirt, lay on the tile floor. His socks were white, and nearly spotless. His head lay on his arm, as if he'd pillowed it there while taking a little nap. There was no blood.

"Hit his head on the urinal," said Franklin, who had followed Bo and Janice inside. His voice echoed off the tile, and Bo thought that the rest room might be a good place for a doo-wop group to practice.

"Got drunk, fell, hit his head," Bo said, trying not to smack his gum. "Case closed."

"Maybe," Franklin said. He didn't sound convinced. "Why'd he lock the door, though?"

"Modesty," Bo said. "Some guys like privacy."

"Why didn't he just go in a stall, then?" Janice asked.

Bo didn't like to talk about these things in front of her. It just didn't seem right. He could still hear the jukebox, which was now playing a song from a couple of years back, "In the Still of the Night" by the Five Satins. Somehow that didn't seem appropriate, either.

"He wasn't shy," Franklin said. "I think we can rule that out."

Bo looked around the room. There was a window, as he supposed there had to be for ventilation. It was half-open, but the opening was very small. No one could have escaped through there. Not unless Blaine had been killed by someone who was a tad undersized.

"Any cast members from *The Wizard of Oz* here tonight?" he asked.

"Not funny, Wagner," Franklin said. "And I thought you said that wouldn't happen again. Anyway, that window opening is covered on the outside with wire mesh. You can't see it from here, but we've already checked. No one got out of here that way."

"We're gettin' off the track here," Janice said. "What we need to know is whether anybody at this sock hop had a reason to want Mr. Blaine dead."

"Just about every guy out there," Franklin said. "Blaine was quite the ladies' man. I wouldn't be surprised if he'd slept with half the women here and tried for the other half."

Bo couldn't stand it. Not only were he and Janice standing in front of the urinals in a men's room, but she and Franklin were talking about a dead man's sex life. It wasn't seemly at all.

Janice didn't seem to notice. "What about the women?"

"I'd be surprised. From what I hear, they all enjoyed his attentions quite a bit. He, uh, loved 'em and left 'em, I guess you could say, but he left 'em satisfied."

Bo knew that no woman had killed Blaine, and he didn't like all that talk about sex, not in front of Janice. Besides, Bo still thought that Blaine's death might have been just an unfortunate accident.

"Why couldn't he have just slipped on the floor?" he asked.

"He could have," Franklin said. "But he didn't. We've already had the coroner in here, and there's a fresh cut on Blaine's jaw where somebody hit him. We think there was a scuffle, and the killer knocked Blaine down. Blaine hit his head, and it killed him."

"Then it was an accident," Bo said.

"Sure it was. But an accident in the course of a fight, well, that's a little more than an accident, at least in the eyes of the law."

Bo looked up at the green ceiling. There was a long pipe running the length of the rest room, but no one could have escaped through the openings through which the pipe passed. The clearance was no more than a quarter of an inch all around the pipe.

But there was something else in the ceiling, a cutout square that probably led to an attic or a storage area. The square wasn't huge, but Bo felt that if it were removed he could slip comfortably through the opening.

Franklin noticed where Bo was looking. "We've already checked that out. There's nothing up there. It's just a way to look at the wiring and stuff.

There's dust all around the opening that hasn't been disturbed since this place was built, and that was thirty years ago."

"Who broke down the door?" Janice asked.

"That would be Thomas Ralston. He's right outside with Gary Stafford. That woman crying on his shoulder is Cynthia Norvell."

"Why don't you let me and Bo talk to them?" Janice said.

"In here?"

"Well, maybe we could go outside," Janice said, sniffing. "It might be a little less smelly out there. And we wouldn't need to disturb Mr. Blaine any longer."

Franklin looked down at the body. "I don't think we bothered him at all."

Three

Franklin had Farmer pull out one section of the bleachers, and Thomas Ralston sat there in front of Janice and Bo. The jukebox was playing an old Big Joe Turner song, "Chains of Love."

Ralston was wearing brand new Levi's, and his white socks were dark on the bottoms from his having danced in them. He was a handsome man, Bo had to admit, with a nice tan and very white, even teeth. He'd slicked his black hair back into a pretty good DA—duck's ass—for the hop. Bo had never been able to make his hair stay in place in that style, and he wondered if that was because his hair was thinning.

"Allan and I were good friends," Ralston was saying.

He had a deep, confident voice that made Bo immediately suspicious. Anyone who sounded that sure of himself undoubtedly had something to hide.

"And you can't imagine anyone who'd be angry enough with him to get into an argument with him?" Janice asked.

Ralston looked up at her. He had bedroom eyes, like Fabian, and Bo didn't like the way he was looking.

"Angry with Allan?" Ralston said. "No, I can't think of anyone. Everyone liked Allan."

"That's not what I heard," Bo said, mainly to get Ralston to look at him instead of Janice. "I heard that Allan was playing around with half the women here."

"I wouldn't know about that," Ralston said.

"You wouldn't? What about your date? Who is she?"

Ralston stood up. He was at least four inches taller than Bo.

"My date is Gail Barnett," he said, "and you'd better not bring her up again."

"Then I will," Janice said. "How well did she know Allan Blaine?"

"I've had about enough of this," Ralston said. "I don't have to talk to you people. You're not even the police."

He turned and walked away, his back stiff.

"He's got a point, you know," Bo said. "We're not the police."

"But we're working with Lieutenant Franklin," Janice reminded him. "That gives us a sort of semiofficial standing, and it means we can ask questions if we want to. Any citizen can ask questions."

"I guess we're sort of like Sam Fernando, then, except that we don't have infuriating smiles."

"Well, one of us doesn't," Janice said. "Let's talk to Mr. Stafford now."

Bo motioned to Franklin, who spoke to Stafford. Stafford was shorter than Ralston, which gratified Bo, but he was just as handsome, and just as smooth. And he appeared to be just as interested in Janice.

"I don't believe I caught your phone number when we were introduced," he said.

"I don't believe I gave it," Janice said. "Why don't you have a seat so we can talk."

Stafford sat down and crossed his legs with his ankle resting on his knee. The bottom of his white sock was quite dark.

"You like dancing?" Janice asked.

The jukebox was playing "Chantilly Lace," a song that Bo had always liked because the part about the ponytail reminded him of Janice. He hoped Stafford wouldn't jump up and start twirling her around the floor.

He didn't. He said, "I'm actually a very good dancer. Would you like to find out?"

"No, thank you. What I'd like to find out is what you know about Allan Blaine and Gail Barnett."

Stafford smiled. He was almost as infuriating as Sam Fernando.

"Nothing that everyone else doesn't know," he said.

"*We* don't know anything about them," Bo pointed out.

"Then you must not move in the same circles I do," Stafford told him, using that smile.

"Probably not," Bo said, chewing his gum a little faster. "So tell us about them."

Stafford turned his attention to Janice, who seemed to interest him much more than Bo did.

"Gail was a teaser. Do you know what that means?"

Bo balled his fist, something Sam Fernando would never do, but something that Mike Hammer would have understood. He would also have understood Bo's desire to pulp Stafford's lips against his teeth for making vulgar remarks.

But Janice didn't seem bothered at all. She said, "Why, of course I do, Mr. Stafford. But why don't you tell me anyway."

Stafford looked a bit disconcerted, as if Janice had spoiled his fun. He'd obviously expected a different reaction.

"Well, she liked to work men up, and then leave them high and dry. Except the rumor is that she didn't do that with Allan."

"Is the rumor true?" Janice asked.

"I don't know for sure, but I believe it is." Stafford smiled ruefully and shook his head. "Allan did have a way with the women."

"So I've heard. Were you with Mr. Ralston when he broke down the rest room door?"

"Yes. There were quite a few of us actually. We'd been drinking a little, you know."

"I'm sure. Can you give me the names of everyone who helped?"

Stafford looked surprised. "I'm afraid not. There were just too many of us, and some of us were in quite a rush. We all piled into the room together."

"But it was Mr. Ralston who spotted the body?"

"That's right. He rushed right over to him and started yelling. Before you knew it, half the people at the party were in there."

"I imagine that there was quite a crowd."

"You could say that, yes. Poor Cynthia. It must have been horrible for her to see Allan like that."

Bo said, "Looks like Mr. Ralston is doing a pretty good job of letting her cry on his shoulder."

"Thomas and Cynthia are old friends," Stafford said. "And I'm sure he'd resent your implication."

"I'm sure I don't much care," Bo said.

Janice put a hand on his arm. "Now Bo, don't go sayin' things that you don't really mean."

Bo started to say that he really meant every single word, but Janice gave his arm a little squeeze, so he kept his mouth shut.

"Did Thomas and Cynthia ever date?" Janice asked Stafford. "Before her engagement to Mr. Blaine, I mean?"

"For a while," Stafford said. "Maybe a year, all together, but not steadily. Why?"

"I was just wonderin'. And I suppose that Mr. Blaine had long ago given up seein' Miss Barnett."

Stafford uncrossed his legs, put his feet flat on the floor, and looked down at them as if they were interesting, which they weren't, not to Bo at any rate.

"I wouldn't know about that," Stafford said after a few seconds.

"But you'd know about the rumors," Janice said.

"Maybe."

"So what do the rumors say?" Bo asked.

He thought he saw where Janice was going, now. It was obvious. Blaine had been sneaking around on Cynthia, seeing Gail Barnett on the sly. Ralston had found out about it, confronted Blaine in the rest room, and punched him out. Unfortunately, Blaine had fallen the wrong way, struck his head on the urinal, and it was bye-bye Blaine.

The only question left was how Ralston had locked the rest room door from the inside, but Bo was sure Janice had that figured out, too. It sort of bothered him that she was the one coming up with the answers, since he was the plotter, after all, but this case was simple once you saw the dynamics of the characters involved. Given a few more minutes, he would have come to the same conclusion that Janice had reached.

Now all they had to do was figure out how to make Ralston confess. Or prove that he was the guilty party. There had to be a way, if they put their minds to it.

Bo nudged Stafford with his toe. "About those rumors," he said.

Stafford looked at Bo. "They're only rumors, you understand."

"I get it. Now tell us."

Stafford ran a hand through his hair. It was long and thick and neatly combed, but there was no DA in the back. Bo wished his hair was that thick.

"According to the rumors," Stafford said, "Gail and Allan were still carrying on a little affair. They were discreet, but someone saw them at Benteen's. Do you know where that is?"

Bo nodded. Benteen's was on the highway well north of town. Most of the customers were people who were looking for a little privacy. Or a lot.

"Well, whoever saw them must have told someone. So the word got around. I'm sure Thomas must have heard."

"How serious are Mr. Ralston and Miss Barnett?" Janice asked.

"Now that I think about it, not too serious. Do you think that—"

"I think that we don't have any more questions for you, Mr. Stafford," Janice said. "We really appreciate your help, though. Would you ask Lieutenant Franklin to send Miss Norvell over here?"

"I'd be glad to," Stafford said. "Would you give me your number?"

"I don't think so," Janice said, and he smiled like a good sport. Bo hated good sports.

As Stafford walked over to the others, the jukebox changed to "Stagger Lee" by Lloyd Price, the original version, not the one Dick Clark always played on *American Bandstand*. Bo liked both versions, but as much as he hated to admit it, the one Clark played might have been a little bit the better of the two, even if the words were too genteel.

Both of them had a great beat, though, so Bo said, "Doesn't that song make you want to dance?"

Janice looked him over. "With you?"

"Uh, yeah. I guess so."

"I'm not sure. Ask me again sometime."

The answer filled Bo with hope. Okay, so it wasn't exactly an overwhelming endorsement, but it certainly wasn't a definite no. He didn't have a chance to follow up, however, because Cynthia Norvell was on her way to the bleachers.

Bo had to admit that she was a striking woman. Long blond hair that Bo would have liked to see in a ponytail. A figure that was perfectly made for the tight Levi's she was wearing. Innocent light blue eyes washed by her crying, high cheekbones, and skin that was a smooth advertisement for whatever complexion soap she used. She was a little too tall, but that didn't detract from her beauty at all, not to Bo. He liked tall women.

"Down boy," Janice said. "If you try to take a step, you might trip over your tongue."

"Har-de-har-har," Bo said.

Cynthia Norvell introduced herself and sat down. Her shirt was whiter than white, and she'd turned the collar up in back, a little touch that just killed Bo. Her socks were white, and they and her shirt seemed to Bo like symbols of her purity. Her engagement ring sparkled under the gym lights. The diamond was huge. Bo was sure that it had cost thousands.

"I hope you don't mind answering a few questions," he said.

"Of course not." Her voice was soft and sweet, as Bo had expected it would be. "I'll do anything that would help find whoever killed Allan."

"I know this has been hard for you," Janice said. "I hope we don't cause you any more pain, but we would like to ask a few questions."

Cynthia sniffled and reach into a pocket of her jeans for a tissue. If anyone had asked him, Bo would have said there wasn't room for it in there.

She dabbed at her eyes and said, "I don't mind. I really don't."

"Were you the one who noticed that Mr. Blaine was missing?" Janice asked.

"Oh, no. I was too busy with the guests. There are so many of them, you see. I didn't know anything was wrong at all, not until I heard the yelling."

"And I suppose that you were one of the first ones in to see the bod—to see Mr. Blaine lying there on the floor."

Cynthia dabbed at her eyes again. "Yes. It was just awful to see him there like that. Just awful. I know I'll never forget it."

Her shoulders shook and she began crying in earnest. Bo wished he had a handkerchief to offer her, but he didn't. And even if he'd had one, considering the generally disgusting condition of his handkerchiefs, he would have been embarrassed to offer it to her.

She pressed the tissue to her eyes and sobbed for a few seconds while Bo stood there helplessly. Janice sat down beside her and put her arm around her shoulders.

"There, there," Janice said. "I know it must have been terrible for you, but all this will be over soon."

Cynthia's sobs slowed and then stopped. She wiped her eyes and stuffed the tissue back in her pocket.

"Yes," she said. "I'm sure it will. Lieutenant Franklin says that the two of you have been very helpful to him in the past."

Bo puffed up a little at that. "We sure have. And I think we already know who's to blame this time, too."

Cynthia's eyes widened. "You do?"

"Yes, I think we do," Janice said.

Bo was sure they did.

Four

"She's crazy," Bo said, looking from Janice to Lieutenant Franklin and then back to Janice. He really, really wanted a cigarette. "You're joking, aren't you?"

"I wouldn't joke about something like this," Janice said. "She did it, all right."

"She couldn't have," Bo said. "I mean, she's a woman. She couldn't have been in . . . there."

"Why not?" Janice asked him. "I was."

"Well, that was different."

"Hold on," Franklin said. "What I want to know is how she did it."

"That's the easy part," Janice said. "She hit him, he fell, and the urinal was in the way."

Bo couldn't believe that Janice had said *urinal*.

"But it's a men's room," he said. "She wouldn't have been in there. And if she was, how did she get out and lock that door?"

"She didn't get out," Janice said.

"Huh?"

"Let her tell it," Franklin said. "First tell us how you know it was her."

"Look at her socks," Janice said. "The bottoms are nearly snow white. She hasn't been dancing or checking on the guests. I'll bet that if you ask around, no one will have seen her since early in the party."

"Farmer," Franklin said, "get over here."

Farmer left his post by the door and came over. Franklin told him to go out and question some of the guests about Miss Norvell's whereabouts. As soon as Farmer was on his way, Janice went on with her theorizing.

"I'd say that someone at this party told Cynthia about Blaine's having an affair with a woman named Gail Barnett, Thomas Ralston's date. That Gary Stafford seems like the type. You could ask him. Cynthia got upset, but she probably didn't want to cause a scene at her own engagement party. So she thought about a nice quiet place for a talk. She might have followed Blaine into the rest room, or maybe that's where they agreed to have their discussion. Anyway, they went inside."

"Somebody would have seen her going into the men's room," Bo said.

"Not necessarily," Franklin said. "If they went into the alcove, anyone seeing them would have thought they were going into opposite doors."

"That's right," Janice said. "And when they got into the men's room, one of them, probably Cynthia, locked the door. She didn't want to be interrupted."

"I can see that, I guess," Bo said. "But what if there'd been someone in there already?"

"I'm sure she had Blaine check. Then they must have gotten into an argument. Maybe Blaine threatened her, or laughed at her, or even made a grab for her. That's why she hit him."

"Are you sure it was her?" Franklin said. "And even if you are, how are we going to prove it?"

"Check her ring," Janice said. "I'd say that's what made the cut on Blaine's face. She probably washed the ring off, but there's bound to be a trace of blood left in the setting."

Franklin looked more and more convinced, but he said, "What if we do find the blood? How do we explain the locked door?"

"She never left the rest room," Janice said. "She stayed in there, behind that partition. Maybe she was just scared because of what she'd done. Or maybe she thought about it and decided that staying there was her best chance. When the men broke down the door, they ran to the body. They never thought about looking behind the partition. Then there was a lot of confusion, and she just joined the crowd. If she started screaming and crying, would anyone have thought to wonder where she came from?"

"No," Franklin said. "They wouldn't. By golly, I think you're right. I can see how it would work."

So could Bo. He was just sorry he hadn't thought of it. A little blood on a ring wasn't going to convict Cynthia of anything, however.

"How are you going to prove she was in there?" he asked.

Janice said, "It might be impossible. But you could work up a good circumstantial case if you could prove she hadn't been seen at the party. And if you could find someone who saw her go into the rest room, it would be even better. Add to that her clean socks and the blood on the ring, if it's there, and you might convince a jury."

"It sounds like it was just an accident to me," Bo said.

"We'll let the district attorney and the grand jury decide that," Franklin told him. He smiled. "You two have done it again. Maybe I should recruit you for the force."

"You don't pay enough," Bo said.

"True. Not as much as you make writing those books, that's for sure. Well, I think I'd better go have a talk with Miss Norvell."

Bo and Janice watched him walk away. Then Bo looked out at the empty gym. On the jukebox Jimmy Clanton was singing "Just a Dream."

Bo said, "Uh, about that dance . . ."

Janice smiled, and Bo felt his heart flutter.

"If I dance with you, will you get rid of that chewin' gum?" she asked.

"Oh, yeah. Sure thing. Absolutely."

Bo floated on air toward the rest room, where the wastebasket was located, wondering if he would be able to afford an engagement ring the size of the one Cynthia Norvell was wearing.

THE DANCE OF THE APSARA
Joan Richter

As small as it was, Pochetong Airport in Phnom Penh could be hairy for someone arriving in Cambodia for the first time, so that was the excuse Mike Swann had for meeting her plane. She was coming in on Thai Air's morning flight from Bangkok, en route from New York. He stood outside of customs and spotted her right away, fair-skinned in a sea of Asian faces. Jeans, white T-shirt, and blazer. And, Jingo's eyes. That was a jolt. Lady-killer eyes, the guys used to say. Fortunately nothing else of her father had been passed along that he could see. She was beautiful. And slim as a reed. Her brown hair gleamed.

"Jill Winfield?" It was obvious she wasn't expecting him, but at the sound of her name, her eyes lit up. The flickers of gold were there.

He introduced himself, and played it close to the truth. "I've been asked by the folks at the *Cambodia Monitor* to be your local guide for the next few days."

"That's generous of them," she said, studying him uncertainly. And then a slow look of surprise came over her face. "Michael J. Swann? Pulitzer winner, National Book Award?"

That was unexpected. "Guilty," he said.

"Your novel was on my bedside table for a while last year."

"I take responsibility for only part if that. I hope it was worth it."

"I've read books that gave me sweeter dreams, but you made up for it with the ending. I liked it a lot."

The photograph on the book jacket hadn't romanticized him. Lean face, dark brows arched over serious gray eyes. His hair had some gray in it, a good-looking guy.

"Tell me, though, what have I done to rate *you?* You must owe someone at the *Monitor* a big favor."

"I wouldn't say that. The truth is I just happen to be between assignments." His answer wasn't a lie, but it left out a lot. It didn't feel right.

A porter came along and picked up her bags, and Mike led the way through the hot steamy air and the confusion of arriving and departing passengers to where he had parked his Toyota.

They were headed for the Lucky Siam, not a bad little hotel on a quiet side street, run by a Thai he knew. She told him she'd picked it out of a guidebook. He was glad she hadn't chosen the sprawling Cambodiana. It catered to business accounts and high-end tour groups. They gave Phnom Penh an overnight and then headed for the temples at Angkor.

"You've had yourself a bit of journey. How's the jet lag? Are you up for some sightseeing this afternoon?"

"I'm a bit groggy now. A shower should clear that. I'd love it, if you have time."

"I've been looking forward to it," he said and turned onto Phnom Penh's only wide boulevard, easing in behind a pedicab. He felt her stiffen when he crossed two lanes of oncoming traffic to make a left turn onto a narrow side street.

"Sorry. I should have warned you. The Cambodians haven't gotten around to traffic lights. The rule of the road is that anything goes. People are pretty polite and small cars can stop on a dime."

He pulled up in front of the Lucky Siam. Pots of tall palms framed the wide white steps of the entryway. A porter came toward the car.

"Is there anything particular on your list, or do you want to leave it to me today?"

"I'm happy with that. At some point I'd liked to go to the Killing Fields."

He took that as an indication she knew something about the country. As pretty as she was, too clean a slate would be a drag.

"That takes some stamina," he said. "Let's leave it for tomorrow, and start out easy today. How's three o'clock? I'll give you a call first."

"Thanks," she said smiling at him. "I hope you won't mind. I ask lots of questions."

He smiled. "That's okay. So do I."

· · · · ·

The publisher of the *Cambodia Monitor* and Mike had been in the Special Forces together, not something they broadcast around now. Larry had turned into a businessman and lived in Hong Kong. As expats in the same neighborhood, they gave each other a high-five once in a while. E-mail from Larry was no surprise, but this one made Mike think about hitting delete and leaving town:

> *A young woman is headed your way, daughter of our old buddy Jingo. You're not supposed to know that, and neither is anyone else. That shouldn't be hard. She's divorced, but is using her married name. Jill Winfield. I'm not sure what the story is, but she wants to work out here. It's arranged. Jingo asked that you take her under your wing for a few days. She's never been to Asia, no less Cambodia, so you've got your work cut out for you. He wants her to have a look at the Apsara Project, a community development program up north. Cambodian named Ving is supposedly in charge. That's it for now. The Senator says thanks.*

Mike stared at the screen, wondering who else still knew the Senator as Jingo. If rumors of a run for the oval office were serious, his "old buddy" might like to find out.

. . . . .

They'd saved each other's ass more than a few times, but the guy had been extra trouble. The buzzard must have settled down, and diverted all those juices into political ambition. His picture was in *Time* and *Newsweek* off and on. He had a bit of jowl. Well, a lot of years had rolled by, and the Senator was twelve years older than Swann.

He figured Jill Winfield was somewhere around twenty-five, which made her young enough to be his daughter, if he had started early, but then he hadn't started at all. He'd known Jingo had a family back home, but there was not much talk of that. Jingo was into the thrill of the moment, his mind on his own game. Jesus! It's a wonder we got out alive.

What the hell was his daughter doing out here? A job with the *Monitor* made no sense, not for her and not for the Senator. The English-language paper did pretty well covering the current mess of Cambodia, a poor country, trying to rise out of its beleaguered past. It had been ruled by France, occupied by the Japanese, bombed by the U.S. and invaded by Vietnam. Add to that the Khmer Rouge.

The *Monitor* staff was the usual foreign outpost mix—a few lonely planet types, some serious students of Asia, a few green journalism grads, and a couple of guys who had no other place to go. It was sure off the beaten track, unless you had a special reason for being out here. He wondered how Jill Winfield fit in.

. . . . .

As soon as her voice came on the end of the line, he could see her smile and those eyes, and he realized he was *really* looking forward to showing her around, and when she said she would be out in front waiting for him, he liked that too. And there she was, standing in the shade of one of the palms, in a yellow short-sleeved dress, a straw bag slung over her shoulder.

"It's hot, so we won't walk far," he said. "I should have told you to bring a hat. The sun is fierce."

"I have one in my bag. It's one of those roll-up straws. Not the Madison Avenue look but it's okay." She put it on and peered up at him from under the brim. Dark lashes fringed her eyes.

He smiled. She looked great.

He hailed a pedicab at the next corner. "This may feel a little unpro-tected," he said as they settled into the wicker seat, the driver peddling behind. "Next to hoofing it, this is the way to see the town."

It was a kick watching her take in the obvious, and then get caught up in some detail he didn't notice anymore, like the towers of mangoes and pomolos on fruit-sellers trays, defying gravity.

She couldn't get over all the rubble. "Half the buildings look as though they're falling down."

"Some are. Some just look that way. With all the foreign aid pouring in, agencies need office space and housing and big cars to chauffeur officials around. Reconstruction is in full swing."

He had asked the driver to go by the Royal Palace and the Silver Pagoda.

"Just think of all that wealth behind those walls," Jill said as they drove past the ornate structures, golden spires blinding them in the reflected light of the setting sun. "According to my guidebook, there's a life-size Buddha inside, encrusted with 9,584 diamonds. I'm sure our pedicab driver has all of his wealth in his leg muscles."

"I was counting on your fresh eye."

She laughed. "Where's home to you, when you're not here?"

"I grew up outside of Los Angeles. My parents are still there, in the same house. When I was a kid we were surrounded by acres of orchards—nec-tarines, plums, oranges. Now it's tract housing. I try to get back once a year, but I don't always make it. My mother writes, once a month. I try to match her, if it's only a post card. But if we kept score, she'd win." He waited a moment before he followed up. "And you?"

"Boston most recently. It was a natural transition. I'd gone to boarding school in New England and then Connecticut College. It has a good performing arts program. I wanted to be an actress. It turned into just fun. I decided on journalism. I worked on the *New London Day* for a while and then went on to freelancing for the *Globe*."

He decided not to press her on family.

Along about five he had the driver let them out at the Foreign Correspondents' Club. They were a little early. No one was at the bar. He chose a table in the corner.

"The FCC is a mecca for journalists passing through, and a hangout for those who live here. There's a small auditorium behind those double doors where they have cultural events and panel discussions every couple of weeks. Visiting dignitaries and politicos give speeches. Sometimes you can get a story out of it. The expat community loves it. It gives them a handle on the outside world."

His beer and her club soda came. "So what brings you out here? The *Monitor* is a good paper for what it sets out to do. Do you want to live out here?"

Jill eyed him thoughtfully. She was having such a good time, she'd almost forgotten that he wasn't playing straight with her. It was time to call him on it.

"Michael, the *Monitor* isn't expecting me for another ten days. I came out early to have a look around on my own. If I hadn't read your book and looked at that jacket photo often enough, I wouldn't have had a clue who you were, except some guy trying to pick me up. That didn't seem to fit, and it still doesn't. So what's going on?"

He almost laughed, the surge of relief was so intense, but that would send another wrong signal. Jingo, your cat is out of the bag!

"I know the publisher of the *Monitor*. Larry lives in Hong Kong. He passed along a message from your father."

"My father!" she exclaimed.

"The Senator and I knew each other a long time ago."

"He isn't even supposed to know I'm out here."

"Well, apparently he does."

She sat back and stared at him, more than bewilderment in her eyes. Anger flickered there, and he was pretty sure it wasn't entirely directed at him.

"Here's the story."

She eyed him skeptically. "I can't wait to hear this."

"Your father and I were in a special unit here in the seventies, just before Pol Pot took over. We were in some tough situations together, but when it was over we didn't stay in touch. We were too different." He decided to leave it at that for now.

"I followed his political career, and he obviously kept track of what I've been doing. It's been twenty-two years.

"Then out of the blue this e-mail came from Larry—he'd been out here with us. I guess he and your father are still tight. The word was you were coming to work for the *Monitor* and your father wanted me to take you under my wing for a few days." He shrugged. "That would have been okay. Only, there was a catch—I wasn't to let on I knew whose daughter you were." He sat back and opened his hands. "That's it."

"Oh, come on, that isn't it. You smelled a story. Get at the Senator through the daughter. You've heard the rumors—my father's talking of running for president."

He shook his head. "I can't blame you for thinking that. I'll admit to being curious, but I'm not after a story. I've hung up my reporting hat for a while. I've a book contract. I'm taking a year off. I leave here in two weeks." He could see she was wavering.

"Just to get everything out on the table, your father had another request. He wants you to have a look at the *Apsara Project*."

Genuine surprise flashed in her eyes then. She played with the ring of condensation around her glass, and then looked up. "What's that all about?"

He had a feeling she knew the answer, but he let it go.

"I have no idea what your father's interest is, but I know the project. It's a unique mental health program for this part of the world. It uses art as therapy. This particular project teaches the dance of the *apsara* to young girls suffering some form of trauma.

"The apsara is an icon in Cambodia. *Apsara* dancers performed in the courts of kings, way back in the days of the early Khmer Empire. There are stone carvings on the temples in Angkor that show them in all their various dance poses."

Jill nodded. "My father had a large book of photographs of the temples at Angkor. I was too little to know what they were all about, or to know where Cambodia was, but I loved it because he was spending time with me."

It was a memory that had always brought her pleasure. It didn't now.

Mike caught the turmoil in her eyes and imagined the sense of betrayal she was feeling. He looked away, toward the bar, to give her time. Two people had just walked in, not anyone he knew.

"My mother told me the *Apsara Project* was her private deal, that my father didn't know anything about it at all. I believed her. I should have realized it didn't make sense. She never had any connection to this part of the world. My father did. But that was years ago. He has other interests now."

She frowned. "The mental health side of it fit. That's been my mother's big thing. . . . A political wife needs to find her own issue. . . ." Her voice trailed off. The light in her eyes was fading. She looked totally exhausted.

He stood up and took her arm. "Let's call it a day and get you back to the Lucky Siam. We can chew on this some more tomorrow."

It was close to dark when they stepped outside. The stairway to the street was in shadows, hiding the huddled figure at the foot of the stairs. She was startled by a hissing whisper, "Missy, Missy . . ." A hand reached out and she almost missed her step. Mike held on to her as they walked toward the line of pedicabs.

"He's always there in the evening," Mike said as the pedicab pulled away from the curb. "His name is Joe. He works at the bike repair shop off and on. Someone drops him off. You probably couldn't see it, but he's in a basket on wheels. He's one of Cambodia's land mine victims."

"That's what I thought," she said softly.

Mike turned around then and spoke to the driver.

"That's no way to end your first day in Phnom Penh. If you can keep your eyes open a few more minutes, we'll have a quick look at the river. The Mekong and the Tonle Sap meet just over there. The fishermen are out in their boats now, and the light from their lanterns casts wonderful reflections on the water. It's a beautiful sight. It will give you sweeter dreams."

When they reached her hotel, he walked up the steps with her. She looked up at him with a sleepy smile. "Thanks for meeting my plane . . . and for the lights on the Mekong. I'll let you know about those dreams."

He lay awake for a long time, watching the shadows of the palms outside his window move across the ceiling. She was a nice kid. He wondered what Jingo was up to.

. . . . .

They did the markets the next morning. "Central first," he said. "You need to see it. It's a storehouse of goodies for the expat community: refrigerators, croissants, smoked salmon, antibiotics, TVs . . . you name it, they've got it."

"I thought Phnom Penh was a hardship post."

"Only for Cambodians."

The Russian Market was a labyrinth of local goods—fabrics, clothes, hand crafts. He showed her where the silver was—intricately patterned bracelets, necklaces, and serving spoons. Inexpensive. "Cambodian silver isn't the silver we know. It's a mixed metal of sorts. It blackens quickly and needs polishing. But the pieces can be beautiful. I sent my mother some. She said she loved them, but I'm not so sure. Polishing silver isn't her thing."

She patted his arm. "It's the thought, Michael. She loved you for that."

They had lunch at a small restaurant with outside tables shaded by pink umbrellas. The menu was in French. "I keep seeing such contrasts," she said, looking up at him. "Is it like this all over the country?"

"Not really. In the countryside everyone is poor. There are so many land mines around, farmers can't get back to planting rice."

"What makes you stay?"

He shrugged. "This is where I got started. I've bopped around most of Southeast Asia, in and out of Cambodia a lot. It's what I know. If my first job had been in Latin America, would I still be there now? Who knows? Sometimes the roll of the dice determines your life." He nodded, putting a period to his thought, and went on studying Jingo's daughter.

He had been leaving it up to her to return to their conversation of the previous evening. She did then.

"When I woke this morning I was afraid you might decide you'd had enough of the Senator and his daughter. I'm glad you didn't. As much as I hate to admit it, I'm not sure I can figure this out by myself." She smiled and a crinkle of mischief framed her eyes. "I need you. And since you promised yourself to me for a few days, I'm going to hold you to it."

He laughed. "You don't see me running, do you?"

She stared at him for a long moment and thought, *I like this guy.*

"What do you know about a man named Ving?"

He had been expecting the question.

"He's head of a community development center about three hours north of here. The *Apsara Project* was his idea. It's one of a number of programs he's working on. He's a remarkable man. I dropped in on the center a little more than a year ago, when he was just getting started. He was working out of a couple of lean-tos then.

"I'd met him in the spring of 1995. A lot of Cambodians returned home that year. It was an anniversary of sorts. Twenty years before, Pol Pot had marched into Phnom Penh and the killing had begun. Ving was a doctor. If the Khmer Rouge had known that, his life would have ended right there. He pretended he was a cobbler. Eventually he escaped through the jungle into Thailand and then found exile in the United States."

"Do you know where he gets his funding?"

"He didn't have much when I was there, but he seemed pretty optimistic. I was afraid he was in for a long wait. Then I heard the money had come through. I hope it's true. I've been meaning to pay him another visit. I didn't think I'd get around to it this time." He smiled. "But that's changed. If you like, we can drive up there tomorrow."

She didn't answer him immediately. She was having trouble sorting through her alliances. She wondered if she was naïve to feel she could trust this man.

"I don't know what this is all about and I don't know where it's going. There are things I probably shouldn't tell you, but I'm about to—if I have your word that all of this is off the record."

He reached into his pocket and took out a card. He wrote a few words on the back and signed his name. "You've got it."

She looked surprised. "You didn't have to do that."

"We didn't get off to a good start. You have every reason to wonder if you can trust me. I want you to know you can."

"Okay," she said and took a deep breath. "Ving got the funding he was waiting for . . . it came from my mother."

That was a curve. "Your mother? What's that all about?"

"About two years ago she chaired a major fundraiser in support of research in the mental health field. She got a tremendous amount of national publicity. You can guess what happened. Tons of requests came pouring in. A Cambodian woman, named Mei, sent her a proposal describing Ving's plans for a program that would use art as therapy in Cambodia. My mother met with Mei. And Mei won her over."

"So what did your mother do? Organize a fundraiser for the *Apsara Project?*"

Jill shook her head. "No. She decided to support the project herself, anonymously. She's adamant about keeping it that way. She told me about it only recently. As I said, she insisted my father didn't know."

"And you believed that?"

She sighed. "My mother has family money, so it was possible. Since it was all a fait accompli, I didn't examine how little sense it made. The mental health aspect of it fit, but the constituency was all wrong. Cambodia? My mother needs to score points domestically.

"My parents are joined at the hip when it comes to political ambition. All of my mother's outside activities have been to support my father. I don't see how the *Apsara Project* does that."

"So, she asked you to come out here and do what? Check up on Ving?"

"That was the general idea. There was some urgency about my getting out here. She didn't explain. I was at a bit of a crossroads—my marriage hadn't worked out—so I decided just to do it. Getting a job with the *Monitor* was my idea. I don't know how I feel about that now."

. . . . .

He picked her up later that afternoon and they set out for the twelve-mile drive to the Killing Fields.

"It's something I have to do," she said. "It would be disrespectful not to. It would be like going to Normandy for the wine and not visiting the battlefields."

"I'm with you on that. But no matter how much you've read and how many pictures you've seen, this is going to be rough. The Cambodians haven't softened a thing. They want everyone who comes here to know what happened."

He walked through the entry gates with her and then let her set her own pace. He didn't want to crowd her, or intrude on the emotions that were sure to rise.

Her first view of the pagoda was as it was for everyone, a simple and sedate memorial against a clear blue sky. A closer look was when shock set in. Behind its glass windows were the skulls of Pol Pot's victims. Piled layer on layer, they stared in silent accusation across a landscape of communal graves, turned into shallow craters by the sun and rain of passing years. Bones lay scattered like shells on a beach.

. . . . .

He took her to the No Problem that night. It was Rick's Café Asian style, straight out of *Casablanca*. Patrons settled into high-backed wicker chairs, sipped Singapore Slings, or whatever else they fancied, while ceiling fans stirred the hot moist air. Pierre had his own repertoire, but was always happy to oblige with "As Time Goes By."

You could count on a collection of regulars at the bar, and if you came in alone, they would lay it on about how they'd finally gotten to understand the country. Swann never entered that cloud of hot air. No one understood Cambodia. Not even the Cambodians.

He knew their entrance would get a rise. Her dress was short and made of white linen. It hugged the curve of her high breasts and showed off her slim legs and honey-gold suntan. The mirror behind the bar had given the warning, and all heads turned. He made the introductions, and guys who could be hard and crass were transformed into charmers. He gave them some room, but not for long. It was a sweet trip having her on his arm.

A spray of orchids floated in the bowl in the center of their table. The lights were low and the fans' soft whir blurred conversations other than their own. "Here we go with contrasts again," she said. "Just think of where we were this afternoon. And now this. I can't imagine wanting to be any place but here, right now."

In the soft light her eyes were the color of amber. Steady, Swann. Off limits.

He took a deep breath and reached for his wine. "It's a nice spot," he said casually. "I had a feeling you'd like it. As for contrasts, expect a few more tomorrow. The road is bad—trucks, cars, oxcarts, all trying to navigate around ruts, potholes, and assorted debris. No one drives it after dark.

There's an okay hotel run by a Frenchman, not far from Ving's. I called ahead."

Their waiter came with the first course, shrimp remoulade, over slices of avocado.

"I've guessed your secret, Michael Swann. You stay because of the food."

He laughed. "That's one good thing the French left behind. Actually, as colonizers go, they get some good marks."

"We've talked about Ving, but I forgot to ask you about Mei."

"Can't help you there. I never heard of Mei until you mentioned her."

"According to my mother, she's out here now, working with Ving."

"We'll soon find out. I called Ving early this morning to let him know we were coming. I said I was bringing along another journalist, but I didn't mention your name. I wasn't sure how you wanted to play that."

"Winfield isn't my family name, as you know. And since my mother's donation is anonymous, my family name wouldn't mean anything to Ving."

"But it would to Mei. She's met your mother, which means she knows who your father is."

"For some odd reason my mother trusts Mei. The more I think about it, the stranger it gets."

That's for sure, Mike thought. Why would the Senator's wife support a project with none of the usual benefits? And why the secrecy?

Pierre was back at the piano and the strains of "La Vie en Rose" floated towards them. Jill reached across the table and brushed the back of his hand with the tips of her fingers. "Mike, let's forget about my parents for a while. I don't want to spoil all this."

He lifted his glass. "Just one last question. How serious is your father about pursuing the nomination?"

"Major serious. He's had his eye on that prize for a long time. My mother, too. For years she's talked about their walking down Pennsylvania Avenue together. She teases him about wearing a top hat."

JINGO FOR PRESIDENT. Wouldn't that be a slogan!

She started to smile, but her lips never got to it. He waited, wondering where her thoughts were taking her. He thought he knew, but she wasn't there just yet.

"That's what this has to be all about—my father running for president. . . ." Her voice trailed off in disbelief.

"He would never discuss what he did out here. It was so off limits I didn't dare ask, even later on. The only thing he talked about was Angkor Wat and seeing the ancient temples. I loved the story—the jungle swallowing up an entire civilization and keeping it hidden for centuries. Then a French explorer just happened along and found one of the temples. For a while I had it confused with *Sleeping Beauty*. But I got it straight after a while. The pictures were amazing—gigantic heads on top of towers, a snake that went on for miles and a huge parade of elephants carved in stone. There was a double spread of dancers in the most intricate positions. That's when I first heard the word *apsara*."

She shook her head. "But that was all a long time ago. What does it have to do with now?" She leaned toward him. "Something has my parents worried. Something must have happened out here that could be damaging to my father's candidacy. That would explain how Mei got to my mother."

Mike had arrived at the same thought. It came from instinct and knowing Jingo, but he was glad she had gotten to it on her own. He thought of all the times he had been close to decking his old buddy. His hand was itching now. Senator, what the hell are you doing to your daughter?

"Mike, don't look at me that way. I don't want your pity. I want your help. I need you to tell me what happened out here. What was my father into that would make him a target for blackmail . . . drugs . . . arms dealing? Help me; I don't even know the right questions to ask."

He waited, thinking hard. Okay, Swann. Let's see how objective you can be.

"Your father didn't talk about his work, because those were the rules. They still are. What we did was covert. I'm sure that doesn't surprise you. But that's all I can say about it. I wasn't his keeper, but I'm sure he wasn't into smuggling drugs or arms. He took unnecessary risks, just for the hell of it. Your father was a handsome guy and he had a way with women."

"What do you mean he had a way with women? Are you talking sex, or something else?"

"Sex. He could never get enough of it. He loved the game."

She rolled her eyes. "Are you telling me I had a horny father, or is there a whole orphanage out here with kids that have eyes like mine?"

"Jill, there's no point in getting mad at me. I've told you as much as I know."

"God, there are times when my father can be such a jerk."

The waiter came along then with another bottle of wine. It was Jill who changed the subject after he had gone. She asked Mike about his novel. "How long were you working on it?"

"It was in my head for a few years, but when I actually sat down it took me about ten months. I'm not as far along on this next one. A few years ago I bought a cabin in the hills in southern California. That's where I'm headed after here. I'm hoping to work things out."

When they left the No Problem, Pierre had just finished playing "Moon River."

Jill slipped her hand through his arm. "Let's go look at the lights on the Mekong."

The dreaminess in her voice told him it was the wine talking. There were enough people taking advantage of her. He wasn't adding his name to the list. "Jill, it's late. We've got a lot ahead of us tomorrow."

. . . . .

On the way out of town the next morning they drove past a small farming village. The roofs on the houses were sagging, but there were vegetable patches and a few banana trees in each of the yards. It would have passed as a quiet picturesque scene, except that at the doorway to each house a dark effigy-like figure stood guard.

"What are those all about?" she asked. "They're the most frightening scarecrows I've ever seen. They have more on their minds than crows."

"The enemy has many faces in this country."

"I'm beginning to understand that."

The road had gotten worse since the last time he drove it. The ruts had multiplied and the potholes were deeper. Dust devils swirled in the dry fields and then danced across the road. The sun played its own tricks, creating mirages that dissolved and reappeared. Mike kept his eyes straight ahead.

"Is that for real?" she asked. Signs posted along the shoulder warned of land mines in the fields beyond.

"I don't suggest we check it out. Land mines are all over this country. Most places aren't marked, particularly along streams and old rice paddies. Foreign aid is out here digging them up, but it will be years, maybe never, before the land is clear. The enemy didn't leave any maps. Some of the mines they dig up don't get detonated. Now there's a market in live mines."

"Who buys them?"

"Cambodians. They put them around their houses to keep the enemy out. It's another kind of scarecrow. Then they forget where they've buried them. Someone in the family trips one and another amputee is added to the list."

"The stories don't get any better, do they?" she said.

"There are a lot of bad things still happening out here. Good things, too. They're harder to find. Ving's project is an example. . . . But to complete the land mine lecture, don't go wandering off on your own. Keep to defined roads and paths. The hell with modesty. The woods are off limits."

"I hear you." She looked out the window at the yellowed fields with their tufts of high grass, dense enough to provide modest cover, and suppressed a shudder.

. . . . .

Mike expected that Ving's new building would be one of the prefabs crop-
ping up all over the developing world, so he was startled to see the structure
that had replaced the rickety lean-tos. Made of bamboo and woven palm, it
had a sloping roof of thick thatch that sheltered verandas with half walls and
inner rooms. It was a replica of the houses built before the Khmer Rouge.

"It's beautiful!" Jill exclaimed. "Did you expect this?"

"I sure didn't. I knew it was what Ving wanted, but the chances of finding someone to put it together were pretty slim. Those were the kinds of
skills Pol Pot did a good job of snuffing out."

On the phone, Ving had asked that they come early. "I have many things
I would like to show you and much to talk about. The young *apsaras* will give
their first performance in the afternoon."

That explained the small crowd that had already gathered. Women and
children sat on the ground in a wide semicircle that followed the perimeter
of the yard, hugging the shade of the giant fig trees that edged the sur-
rounding forest.

"There's Ving now," Mike said as he returned the wave of the man who
had come out onto the veranda of the new building. He was dressed in a
loose-fitting light blue shirt and trousers. There was an air of tranquility
about him. When he reached them he brought his hands together in the traditional greeting. "Welcome. I am honored that you have both made the
journey today."

"Ving, it's good to see you," Mike said. "I'd like you to meet Jill Winfield.
She arrived in Phnom Penh just a few days ago to work on the *Cambodia
Monitor.*"

"You are both most welcome. You have chosen a special day. Our new
building is finished and, as I told Michael, the young *apsaras* will give a performance this afternoon." He motioned then to a young woman standing off
to the side, and spoke in Khmer. "Lok speaks only a little English," he said
to Jill, "but she will take you to refresh yourself."

Lok led her to a screened-off area, shaded by trees. The facilities were
primitive but clean, and in a few minutes Jill rejoined the men on a side
veranda where a breeze stirred the hot, moist air. Ving poured tea, and Lok
reappeared with a bowl of seasoned rice and vegetables and small individual
bowls. Ving explained they were the polished halves of coconut shells.

"You would be amazed at how much can be derived from a coconut
palm. We use all our natural resources wherever possible. If we can pluck
something free from the forest, we do. This building, as you can see, is made
of our natural materials. It is very cost effective. Finding someone who knew
the old skills was the challenge."

"I'd sure like to know how you managed that," Mike said.

"I sent word to the local villages. An old man came to see me. He said he had some memory of the way our houses were built and thought he could work out the puzzle, but he was not strong enough to do the hard labor. I knew some farmers whose land had been taken from them by mines. They had become depressed by their idleness. I persuaded them to let the old man be their teacher."

A mischievous gleam came into Ving's dark eyes. "I'll admit, it was a bit of a gamble, as you would say in your country, but their endeavors proved more than satisfactory and beneficial to everyone. They have become a team now and have gone on to do similar work, smaller houses than this. You will see one shortly."

"It's certainly a beautiful building, Ving, but what it represents is a major achievement. You should be very pleased."

"I will not deny that I am," Ving replied and then glanced at Jill. "Much of what we are doing now were only ideas when Michael visited here last. For the entire time I lived in your country I had the idea to return to Cambodia and work with the mentally wounded. There are so many here who suffer the post stress of the Khmer Rouge. Art as therapy is common in the United States, but it is not known here. It intrigued me. As you know, Pol Pot targeted the educated, so there are few left who have the memory of our traditional arts and crafts. The program I proposed had two goals: retrieve our lost skills and heal the mentally ill. The *Apsara Project* is the cornerstone of that effort.

"There is someone I should like you to meet. She knows you are here, and she is waiting for us. Mei is responsible for the progress of our young *apsaras*. Like myself, she found exile in the United States. Toward the end of her stay she took it upon herself to seek funds for our efforts here. I know nothing of the magic she worked, except that she found a benefactor."

Magic. Jill heard the word, and thought it an interesting choice. Without a doubt there was an unusual aspect to Mei's influence over her mother.

"But there are some things you should know about Mei before I take you to see her. What I say may sound disloyal to someone on whom I have learned to rely. But it would not be fair to you to keep silent." A ripple of emotion passed over his face.

"By now the entire world knows of the atrocities Pol Pot committed here, but some Cambodians still have the need to repeat their tragic stories. I do not fault them, but it is not my way. When Michael and I met two years ago I had already made the decision to no longer speak of how my wife died. The details are too strong. When spoken, they render people impotent. The man Ving disappears.

"Mei is different. She is compelled to speak of her tragic story. My wife

137

and Mei were sisters. The three of us were together when my wife died. There is no forgetting. There is only healing.

"I thought that our work and time would help to heal Mei's wounds. It seemed so when she was in the United States, but it is different now. She has returned to longing for things that cannot be. There are times when she thinks with great clarity and then others when she slips into fantasy. It is difficult to predict what she will say, or do."

As Jill and Michael followed Ving out into the sun-drenched yard, they exchanged questioning glances, each thinking about what they had just heard, Jill reminded of how little her mother had told her about Mei.

At the edge of the forest, Ving paused. "It is not far, but be sure to follow in my footsteps and do not stray off the path."

Mike's warning reverberated in Jill's ears.

They came to a clearing and a small building of the same style as the one they had just left. Off to the side was a circular enclosure, with a raised thatched roof. The sound of singing drifted toward them.

A soft smile appeared on Ving's face. "What you hear are the voices of the young *apsaras*. They sing now to give strength to their voices. When they came to us, some could not speak at all. Others spoke no higher than a whisper and their words were few. Mei's approach was not to bring attention to their disability, but to distract them from it. She began by telling them stories. Using a lantern, she cast shadows with her hands, creating animal images that entertained them and made them laugh. Laughter was a new experience for them. One day one of the girls put her hand alongside Mei's and began imitating the motions of her hands and fingers. From there, Mei went on to introduce them to the dance of the *apsara*.

"The enclosure is their school room and dance studio. The small house is where Mei lives. They were both built by the new building team."

Ving raised his voice then and called out, a few words in Khmer.

From behind the half wall of the veranda of the small house the figure of a woman appeared and moved along the passageway. When she stepped into the sunlight, it was with the composure of someone accustomed to the stage. She was not young, but she had the aura of studied beauty. Her jet hair was wound into a coil and rested on her head like a crown. The skirt of her dark green dress skimmed the ground. She walked slowly, leaning on a cane.

Mei acknowledged Ving's introductions, inclining her head in a graceful bow, and then motioned toward the veranda. "Please," she said, "It is much cooler out of the sun." She led them under the overhang of thatch to where four chairs were arranged around a low table. The air was humid and still, but the direct rays of the sun were gone.

"I should like to add my welcome to Ving's," Mei said when they were seated. "The young *apsaras* have been the focus of my attention, but Ving has other programs in place that follow the same model—art as therapy in combination with the revival of our old traditions.

"The making of baskets and weaving is art. As is fishing, planting, and the keeping of bees. So, too, is building a house such as this." With a graceful movement of her hands, she embraced the space in which they were seated.

"It is amazing what you have accomplished in so short a time," Michael said, directing his words first to Ving, but carefully including Mei.

"Ving has spoken of your visit here some time ago. I am sure it would give him great pleasure to show you a few of the other projects." She turned then and smiled at Jill. "You have come a long distance. I would like us to have some time together."

Although Jill was surprised by the suggestion, she felt no ill ease at the idea of being left alone with Mei. For that matter, she was rather intrigued.

"You will be going to the hives, I am sure," Mei said as the men rose. "Ving, I would be pleased if you brought me some honey."

"Ah yes, you asked me yesterday, and I did not remember. Today I will not forget."

Mei turned to follow their departure, giving Jill a chance to study her profile and wonder why her mother had never mentioned how beautiful the Cambodian woman was.

Mei's gaze lingered, long after the men were out of sight, and Jill began to wonder if Mei had forgotten that she was there.

When she finally turned, Jill was startled by the change in her expression. A distant look had replaced the cool directness that had been present before. Her eyes seemed unfocused and when she spoke it was with a lilting cadence.

"I have dreamt that you would come. I saw you when you arrived. When Lok took you to refresh yourself, I was nearby. I have seen you before. Many times. Yours is a face that comes to me in my dreams. I knew a man with eyes like yours. . . ."

Jill stared at the Cambodian woman, stunned by the words that had flowed from her mouth. They seemed to hang in the hot, still air.

"You are wondering about me. . . . I was an *apsara* when the Khmer Rouge came. Pol Pot took my legs from me, but he did not take my memories or the dance my hands can still do."

In a studied motion, her hands rose from her lap. One gesture flowed into another, detailing sequences of the *apsara*'s secret story.

"My sister was an *apsara*, too," she said when she had brought her hands to rest.

"Kaa was Ving's wife. They marched us from Phnom Penh into the forest, with no shoes on our feet and only grass to eat. They tied us in a circle of trees, so we could know each other's pain as well as our own. They tortured us until we begged for death. It was Kaa and her child who died. They slashed open her belly and ran off with her child."

Jill recoiled from the horrific image, feeling as though her own blood had drained away. She thought of what Ving had said. "The words are too strong. They render people impotent."

"The man I loved had eyes like yours. I have dreamt that you would come. . . . I have longed to see the child I might have had. . . ."

Mei was staring at her, but she wasn't seeing her at all. Jill spoke quietly, as if to a sleepwalker who should not be startled awake.

"Mei, this man you knew who had eyes like mine, what was his name?"

"I did not know his full name. I learned it later. But it is not the name I knew him by, so it is gone from me. I know him only by the name I whisper in my dreams. Jingo." She brought her palms together and bowed her head.

In the next moment she looked up, her face washed of its daze. Her voice was firm and clear.

"They will be back soon. We must hurry." She rose, leaning on her cane. "I told Ving I would introduce you to the young *apsaras*. There is not much time."

. . . . .

Eight young girls, dressed like dolls for the grandest of parties, welcomed Jill with the deepest of bows.

She returned their greeting with a smile and then turned to Mei. "The girls are beautiful. Their costumes are lovely. Will you tell them that for me?"

Mei spoke in Khmer and the girls bowed once again. Then at Mei's prompt one of the girls stepped forward, her small hand extended to meet Mei's outstretched palm.

"Kaa was the first to put her hand alongside mine. I saw it as my sister's hand and I gave her my sister's name."

Ving's voice reached them then. Mei spoke hurriedly to the dancers and turned to Jill. "They have come for you. You must join them. It is almost time for the *apsaras* to perform."

The feeling of relief was almost overwhelming when she stepped outside and saw Michael and Ving waiting for her. She saw the look of concern in Michael's eyes, but it was Ving who spoke.

"So you have seen our young *apsaras*."

"They are lovely. Mei has taught them well." There was a tremor in her voice that both men heard.

"I will walk you to where the path ends. Lok will meet you there and take you the rest of the way.

When they reached the end of the path, Ving turned to Jill. "I had hoped that your time with Mei would not bring you pain, but I fear that is not the case. I assume she told you the tragic story we share."

Jill nodded. "Yes, she did."

"I had hoped to spare you, but there are times when hope is a feeble defense. The story Mei tells is not as it happened. I am not sure why she has reconstructed it as she has. It is no less harsh or more so than what happened. It is true that my wife died a cruel death, but there was no child in her body. It was Mei who lost a child.

"Everyone was malnourished. Starving. The child just slipped from Mei's body, without life. She still mourns that loss. People came in and out of our lives we never saw again. I never knew the man she loved."

He turned to Michael then. "So now you have heard more about me than I ever wished to say. But I am not afraid to have you know. You have seen my fishponds and our beehives, and much of what is happening here. Soon you will see the *apsaras* dance. I have no fear that you will not continue to see Ving." He pressed his palms together. "I see Lok coming now."

He turned and started back down the path.

As Jill looked after the pale blue figure receding into the forest shadows, the tears she hadn't shed at the Killing Fields flowed from her, gathering with them all the sorrows and betrayals that had touched her young life. Mike drew her toward him and held her close, absorbing the rise and fall of her sobbing breasts. He stroked her hair.

· · · · ·

A red carpet was spread on the ground in front of Ving's new building. Lok led them to a place in the shade where two chairs had been set aside. Mei and Ving soon appeared and took their seats off to the side, positioned close enough so Mei could give the dancers their cues.

A hush fell over the crowd when the young *apsaras* appeared. Their costumes were complete with small pointed crowns. They greeted the audience with graceful bows and then with the slowest of movements began the dance. With the positioning first of a hand and then a foot, a ribbon of motion flowed through their young bodies. Their gestures followed the ancient choreography of the old Khmer Empire, designed to appease the gods. They gave life to the stone figures carved on the temples in Angkor.

As Jill watched the young *apsaras*, she saw the book of her childhood open on her father's lap. A tremor flowed through her and she felt the sting of tears burning at the back of her eyes.

· · · · ·

They sat in the flickering light of a kerosene lamp in the hotel's small court-yard. Dinner had been an omelet, fresh vegetables, bread, and cheese. A bottle of water and a flask of brandy were on the table now, compliments of the proprietor. They were the hotel's only guests. Night had fallen a long time ago.

"I feel like I've been talking forever," Jill said. "You must be tired of it by now."

He shook his head and smiled at her. "I signed on for this, remember? My time hasn't run out yet."

She had thought it would be so easy, that the words would just pour out of her in a torrent, but they stayed locked inside her. She didn't want to talk about it. She didn't want to repeat the words Mei had said, or interpret what they meant, not to herself, not to anyone. She wanted to pretend it hadn't happened.

But eventually the words began to form, tumbling from her mouth in jagged phrases that needed re-explaining, gradually smoothing into an unselfconscious flow that went on for a long time. She decided she had said it all, except for one small detail.

She leaned into the pool of flickering light and looked across at Mike. "Before we went to the Killing Fields you warned me that no matter how much I'd read or how many pictures I'd seen, it was going to be rough. You were right, of course. There are some things you can't prepare for.

"There is something about my experience with Mei that reminds me of that. I knew so little about her when I arrived in Cambodia. Only her name, really. Then Ving told us about her work with the young apsaras . . . and warned us about her growing instability.

"But she had such a take-charge attitude when we arrived that I forgot Ving's warnings. They didn't seem to pertain to the woman he introduced us to. But as soon as you and Ving left, a change came over her. She went into a sort of trance. It was all there, full-blown, just as Ving described."

She shook her head. "But even if I had held on to Ving's caution, I wouldn't have been prepared for the things she said."

Mike waited, not sure she was finished. Mei's graphic story would give her nightmares for a long time. But he had a feeling there was something else she hadn't gotten to.

"I keep thinking back to why I came out here. I thought seeing Mei would give me some answers. It hasn't, not yet. But it's taken care of one thing. Mei is too unstable to be a threat, if she ever was one. I can take that home with me."

In the flickering light sadness filled her eyes. "There's no pleasure in that."

. . . . .

They were surprised to find Ving waiting for them in the courtyard the next morning.

"I have come to wish you a good journey. But I have something to tell you . . . about Mei.

"If you remember, she asked me for honey, and I brought it to her, wrapped in a palm leaf. When you cut honey, sometimes there is a bee still inside. I made sure there was none, because for Mei the sting of a bee could be fatal. She knew that.

"It was her custom at the end of the day to sit on the veranda until sleep seemed not far off. She did this last evening. She took the packet of honey with her and opened the palm leaf wrapping, knowing the bees would come. Lok and I found her early this morning."

His eyes sought Jill's. "You are new to Cambodia. Our history is strewn with many sorrows. Some are greater than others. Life had become a torment for Mei. Her passing should not make you sad for too long. She would not want it to."

. . . . .

Mike picked Jill up at the Lucky Siam the next morning and drove her to Pochetong airport for her flight home.

"You're sure I can't persuade you to come with me to Angkor? You've come this far. It's a shame to miss the temples firsthand."

"I need to settle some things. And then get on with my own life. Maybe I'll come back here another time, without the family baggage. There are stories out here that need to be told. Remember you said I had a fresh eye? I want to think about that."

"Come visit me in California," he said. "I'll be doing some thinking, too." He reached into his shirt pocket and handed her an envelope. "Here are the particulars, even a map. I won't be hard to find."

"You're a nice guy, Michael J. Swann. I'm not all that anxious to say goodbye to you. I may not know my way around Cambodia, but California isn't that hard."

She glanced away and then looked back at him. "Just one last question. . . ."

He smiled. "A *last* question?"

"Well, for now anyway."

"Okay, I'm ready. I hope it's not too hard."

"Did my father have a code name?"

He'd been waiting for something like this. He'd known there was something she hadn't said. Now he knew what it was.

"You've read enough spy novels to know the answer to that."

"What was it?"

He shook his head. "Jill, I can't tell you that, not even now."

"Was it Jingo?"

He looked at her for a long moment. "It's not that I never called him that. Jingo was a name we had for guys who thought they were hot stuff. There were often plenty of them around."

DEATH OF A DAMN MOOSE
Barbara Burnett Smith

Eight shining little faces beamed out from the videotape, and even in the sterile surroundings of the Friendswood Police department, for just an instant, I enjoyed watching.

All the little girls tipped to the right, although not in unison. Then they began to twirl and curtsy, each in her own fashion. A smile started across my face, halted abruptly by Miss Autumn's voice in the background of the tape, "Together, girls! Twirl and curtsy together!"

Lieutenant Gray shifted in his chair.

I focused on the tape as Shelby, my granddaughter, with the shining dark hair and huge violet eyes, did a brisk little curtsy then grinned smugly. Shelby loves to dance and is convinced that everyone loves to watch her dance. Since only doting relatives have seen her, she is accurate.

Her best friend, Ariana, giggled as she whirled around, grabbed Shelby's hand to steady herself, and performed a wobbly but endearing little bow.

The camera panned from the girls on the huge old stage to the applauding audience. For this rehearsal there were three moms, two dads, one grandmother (me) and a few scruffy siblings. Some were enthusiastic; others were distracted as if they were already mentally on the road to the next event—soccer game, church camp, or birthday party. The camera bobbled, and then Miss Autumn was full screen. I felt a terrible tightness in my throat, knowing what had happened to her only a few minutes after this was filmed.

Autumn Barkle is "The Danzoos" as Shelby calls her. I'm sure Miss Autumn preferred the French pronunciation, but Shelby is barely four.

I had expected an older woman when my daughter-in-law, Martie, told me about the dance teacher. Miss Autumn had sounded like a cross between an aging courtesan and a mean nun. Instead she was tall with streaky blonde hair and wore dance clothes covered with filmy scarves, because while Autumn Barkle still moved with the elegance of a dancer, her body had bulges that didn't belong.

I have been told that she danced in New York for a few years before she was accidentally pushed down a flight of subway stairs. Her anklebone never healed properly and it ended her career.

After that she came back to Texas, supporting herself by teaching little girls to dance.

The camera focused for a moment on the audience; then, as Miss Autumn's voice became more intrusive the camera moved to her again.

"Julianne, I have told you before, you must stop grinning. And Ariana, you may not grab Shelby's hand when you twirl. Do you understand?"

"Uh, uh . . ."

"What, Ariana? Please, answer me properly."

The little voice sank even lower, and the beams left all the faces. "Uh, yes, Miss Autumn."

At that point, I could have killed Miss Autumn myself.

"Good." Miss Autumn turned and picked up her water bottle. The cap fell off and, with a move of sheer grace, she scooped it up from the floor. Even I, who had only spoken to her a few times, knew that she drank only mineral water during rehearsals.

A week before Shelby and Ariana had wanted to know what mineral water tasted like so I bought them a bottle. After one sip, Shelby had said, "Gross. Like a pig's eye."

"A what?" I'd asked.

"You know, a pig's eye. This," she held out the bottle, "tastes like a pig's eye smells."

After some additional conversation I determined she meant a pig sty, and since I don't like mineral water either, I could only agree.

"Now," Miss Autumn went on, her voice clear on the tape, "I would like the girls to wait in the green room while I have a short meeting with the parents about tomorrow's recital."

Before the girls moved, one young mother jumped forward. It was Emma's mother, with her purple-red hair, green nails and four earrings on each ear. "What about the girls in the front—" It was futile jockeying for the two positions in front of the line.

Miss Autumn said, "I thought I made it clear last week that they are set. Brittany and Katie will be in front."

Emma screamed. Even hearing it secondhand on the tape I felt myself flinch. Not that the scream signified anything; Emma simply screams. She screams when she sees each girl at rehearsal, she screams when she trips, she screams when she laughs, and she screams when you tell her you have a headache, as I once did.

Emma's mommy, as usual, ignored the child. In my opinion the woman had taken far too many happy pills and too few birth control pills. Maybe she likes the screaming, or considers it a form of healthy self-expression, like purple hair.

"But Emma's grandparents are coming all the way from—"

Miss Autumn turned away, saying over her shoulder, "It's not a matter of discussion. Oh, and girls, " she said, stopping them before they could clear the stage, "I want you to rest before the recital. You are to arrive tomorrow ready to dance beautifully. Do you understand?"

They answered more in chorus than they danced, "Yes, Miss Autumn."

"Good. Nice work, girls." They scattered, although in surprisingly dig-nified fashion for four-year-olds, except for Emma, who screamed when she bumped into Katie.

Miss Autumn ignored them. In a graceful move, she smoothed the silk scarf around her hips. I remember thinking at the time that it was a sensual gesture, and I had wondered if the mothers considered her competition.

"Here is a list of arrival times for the girls," she'd said, placing the bottle on a seat as she reached for a pile of papers. "Bring their costumes and some books, so that they can entertain themselves while waiting for makeup." She passed out copies and within a minute a protest began.

"An hour before the recital?" Emma's mother demanded, fingering her purple hair. "And Emma isn't even the lead?"

"What am I supposed to do while she's here?" Kayla's mother asked. Kayla's mother is a tiny, dull-looking blonde, who usually wears jeans and Roper boots. Prior to that her voice had always been soft and uncertain, although I heard it clearly then, and heard the edge in it, too. "We can't sit in the car, you know!"

"Are you kidding about this?" Julianne's mother demanded. Her tall slen-der body shook with indignation, or perhaps it was charging adrenaline. She seems to live with her car keys in one hand and a cell phone in the other. "I don't even want her to think about the recital until it's time. She has to be at her best. And I have two other kids."

"There is a park nearby for your other children. Or where the parents can wait." Miss Autumn picked up her water bottle, but again, didn't drink from it. I willed her to put it down, which, of course, she didn't.

"Look, this is nuts." The voice of Allison's father was overly loud, although he couldn't be seen, since he was behind the camera filming. "Allison threw up this morning because she was so nervous. We want her to be relaxed tomorrow."

"The girls are to eat lightly before the performance, that way they will not be ill." Miss Autumn flashed a purposeful look toward the camera, and presumably at Allison's father. She gestured with her water. "You selected this class because you wanted the best for your daughters and tomorrow is a very big part of that. At the time of enrollment you all agreed to abide by a set of standards."

It is a grandmother's prerogative to spoil her grandchildren, so I had paid for Shelby's dance lessons. It meant I had signed the contract, but I didn't remember there being fine print.

Miss Autumn went on, "There will be many agents in the audience looking for talented little girls, which is why it's so important that everyone make a good impression.

"We will have stylists to do hair and makeup. I assure you, I have done everything I can, and all you have to do is take pictures and sign contracts." I assumed that was to be an amusing closing line, although no one even smiled.

I was watching the tape with extra attention now, like a dog on point. I knew what was coming.

Miss Autumn took a large swallow of water and turned a mottled red. A horrible rasp came from her throat then faded into a gurgle.

The images on the tape jerked sideways as the camera was placed on a seat. I could only see torsos—adults began running, some toward Autumn, some away. Voices assumed that urgent lets-all-be-calm-tone that is anything but calm.

The tape continued for a few more minutes, but it was hard to make sense of anything because of the angle and the confusion. People were on their cell phones—some calling 911, others calling spouses to pick up children, and someone phoned a friend who was a doctor. In the end it had done no good. Miss Autumn had mercifully died very quickly, and a patrol officer had arrived at the same time as EMS. He had politely held us hostage until we had been allowed to drive to the police station just around the corner from the old theatre.

At that point we had been separated until, one by one, each was questioned. The parents with children present had gone first. And finally, now, it was my turn. I was last, since my daughter-in-law had come immediately to get Shelby.

"Convenient that there was a videotape of the rehearsal," I said.

"Yes. I'm hoping it brought everything back into focus for you. Did it help, Mrs. Peters?"

"Yes."

Sitting outside, waiting my turn, the afternoon had taken on a surreal quality. The police department was beige and modern with aluminum windows; it smelled of burned coffee. I could have been waiting for a doctor, a dentist, or an insurance agent. Now all of that was background and I was firmly focused on the ornate but faded old theatre.

I felt as gray as Miss Autumn had looked when they took her body away.

Autumn Barkle had died from strychnine in her mineral water. Someone had put it there. Someone at the rehearsal. Since I couldn't believe a four-year-old would do such a thing, it had to be one of the three mothers or two fathers. I knew it wasn't the grandmother.

"Did you know Autumn Barkle before your granddaughter, uh, what's her name?" He shuffled papers.

"Shelby," I said.

"Shelby started taking lessons from her?"

"No. I'd never even heard of her."

"Shelby's parents picked out the class?"

"No. I gave her the lessons as a birthday present." Part of the deal was that I would also drive her to the lessons. I didn't mind; in fact, it gave me time with Shelby and that was part of my intention.

"Tell me about this rehearsal," the lieutenant said. "What happened before the tape starts? Begin with your arrival."

"Our arrival? Well, we went in the rear door into the backstage area. Miss Autumn, uh, Autumn Barkle, was there talking with uh, uh." I shook my head. "I'm sorry. I don't really know these people. I don't even know their names—I only know the man as Kayla's daddy." He was a young Mel Gibson type, who seemed to know and charm everyone.

The lieutenant's smile was grim, not a bit charming. "It's okay. We'll call them by their kid's names. So, was Kayla's daddy alone?"

It sounded ridiculous, but there seemed no other way. "No, no. He was with Miss Autumn. Oh, wait, I understand. You mean his wife. Well, she was there, yes." She was the tiny, dishwater-blonde woman who'd complained about sitting in the car before the recital. I hadn't noticed where she was when we came in, but then, Kayla's mother was rarely more than a pale shadow to her husband.

They seemed an odd match, her in her jeans and boots, him with his charismatic smile, but maybe they were perfect for each other. Unlike the other parents, they were usually together at the rehearsals.

"Was she with her husband backstage?"

"No, I don't really know where she was."

"Did you hear any of the conversation between the adults?"

"No, it's a good ten feet from the door to the stage and we had to maneuver around a couple of heavy curtains. I only heard the little girls."

"Then what happened?"

"I spoke to Miss Autumn and Kayla's daddy. Just a hello. About then the back door opened and Emma and her mother came in. Emma's mother . . . I don't know her name," I apologized again, "tried to get Miss Autumn alone, but she wasn't successful."

"Was Miss Autumn rude?"

"No. She just cut her off and said something like, 'we'll talk later.' Something like that."

"How did Emma's mother react?"

"Well, first she gave Miss Autumn a cold look, they were eye to eye, they're both tall. Then she swung around and walked toward the front of the stage. To get to the seats in the audience." I let my voice trail off.

"What did she say?" he asked. He added a small smile that was almost apologetic. "Someone else overheard her. I just want to confirm it."

"Oh. I see. Well, she said, 'Up yours, bitch.' Under her breath, of course."

"And then what happened?"

"Allison's father came in—"

"Front door or back?"

"Front. At least, he was below the stage when I saw him. He had the video camera, and he wanted to know if he could tape the rehearsal. Miss Autumn said he could."

The lieutenant glanced over at the tape recorder, which was silently chronicling everything we were saying, then at a notebook with a page of deceptively simple notes.

"He had three of the girls with him," I added. "People trade off driving, as I imagine you've found out. He sat down out front to work on the camera. I followed him, and that's when I saw Kayla's mom."

"Where was Miss Autumn by this time?"

"Backstage. There's a light booth and she was turning on lights and closing some doors to dressing rooms. I couldn't actually see her, but I could see the lights shifting and hear the doors. I wasn't really paying attention."

He raised one eyebrow, as if to question that. "I was watching Shelby," I said.

"Your granddaughter."

"She was coaching Ariana, and they were just so cute." I imitated Shelby as best I could, "'You know you're very good at this when you try, Ariana. You could be a danzoos.' They're all worth watching."

Even the lieutenant smiled. "I have a three-year-old granddaughter myself." Then he turned serious. "Mrs. Peters, I'll be straight with you. The parents I've talked to have either been distracted or biased. Most of them live in the same neighborhood and their kids have gone to preschool and every other kind of class together. They aren't going to say a word against their friends and I guess I don't blame them. But Autumn Barkle was murdered, and I need help."

"I see." Apparently I was the cleanup batter, wrapping it all up and bringing it home.

"This wasn't your usual friendly, little neighborhood dance class, was it?"

"Well . . ."

"The girls are being groomed for something bigger. Some of the parents were hoping to get their children into commercials and such. Is that correct?"

Martie and I had jokingly called it *Fame at Four*. It didn't seem amusing now. "Yes. That's my understanding."

"Is that why you put your granddaughter in the class?"

"No! Shelby's friend, one of her friends—Ariana? No, I think it was Kayla, was taking lessons from Miss Autumn, so Shelby wanted to take them, too. We have no expectations of her—she's a little girl. . . ." I faltered at his look of disbelief.

But it was true. The dance class was only special because Shelby's friends were in it. A simple reason. A kid reason.

Did he believe someone had killed because a four-year-old wasn't getting to dance at the front of the stage during the recital? Because their child might not be noticed and picked out of the crowd by a talent agent?

It wasn't possible.

"Lieutenant," I said, "little kids like to be with their friends and Shelby wanted to be with hers in this class. That's it. Her parents wouldn't sign her with an agent, even if one wanted her."

He shrugged, dismissing either my protests or the entire topic, then said, "Before the rehearsal did you see the bottle of water that Autumn Barkle was carrying?"

"What?"

"Autumn Barkle's water bottle. Did you see it?"

"Oh. Yes. I did." Autumn Barkle had carried an oversized, leather purse that always had amazing things stuffed in it. Rehearsal schedules, sample costumes, snacks, etc. This particular day her purse, a sweater, and her water bottle had been on a seat in the side section of the front row.

I explained that to the lieutenant and he said, "New bottle or one that was already open?"

"I don't know, but it was full. Very full."

He nodded, his eyes squinting as if against the light. Eventually he said, "You know it was strychnine. It's a terrible way to die."

"I saw." I went cold with the memory. "It was horrible, and when the EMS tried to help her the spasms got worse." I didn't want to replay that memory—not now or ever. "What I don't understand is how someone could get strychnine. Isn't it illegal? Or something?"

"It's definitely something, but almost anyone can get it. It's still used for predator control, and it's legal to buy from a pharmacy. You just have to sign for it. Or you might find it at an old barn sale or on a ranch. There's lots of it still around." I shuddered and he continued, "Did you see anyone touch that bottle of water?"

I shook my head no.

He stood and held out his hand. "Thank you, Mrs. Peters. We'll be talking to you again in a few days. And we'll be talking with your granddaughter, of course."

"Shelby?" I stopped. "That's ridiculous! She's barely four years old. You can't be serious about upsetting her with questions—"

"Mrs. Peters, we have specially trained investigators who will talk to all the little girls," he said. "You have to understand that one of them might have seen something important. Don't worry, we won't upset them."

"How can you be sure—how do you know you won't . . ." I was going to say something about scarring them for life, but then I remembered what they'd already seen, or heard, from a distance. "What trained investigators?"

"They work with abused children. They're very good at what they do. Unfortunately," he grew even grimmer, "just when I need them one is out having a baby. The other is on a plane coming in from Washington, D.C., except she's stuck in Atlanta with a delayed flight. She's supposed to be here by six-thirty."

"Maybe you'll have it figured out by then."

He gave me a doubtful look before telling me about signing a statement, and other details I didn't hear. Finally I was free to go.

. . . . .

Rather than drive straight home, I went to my son and daughter-in-law's house. I needed to talk to someone, and since they were involved, at least peripherally, they seemed the most natural choice.

My son, W.D., let me in the front door and gave me a hug. "How are you doing, Mom? You look terrible."

"Thank you; I'm glad to know that. It wasn't a nice day. How's Shelby?"

"She's fine." He ushered me in and took my purse, setting it on the fireplace hearth. "A little quiet, but she didn't really see anything, since Martie got there so fast and brought her home."

"Where is everyone?" I noticed the keys in his hand. "And where are you going?"

"Neighborhood watch meeting. I'm chairman." He lifted his head toward the stairs, "Tyler! Your grandmother is here."

My eight-year-old grandson came flying down the stairs and almost knocked me over with an exuberant hug. "Hi, Grams. Want to watch TV upstairs with me?"

"No, thank you. Maybe later."

"Okay! Bye." Another hug and he was headed back up the stairs.

My son shook his head. "I don't know how he got that way."

"He's just like you used to be. Only calmer."

"Now there's a guilt trip." He kissed my cheek. "Tell Martie to feed you and give you something to drink. See you in a couple of hours." And then he was gone, too.

I turned to find Martie standing in the kitchen doorway, watching me with concern on her face. "Come on in and talk to me," she said. "You look exhausted. Are you hungry? I've got lasagna and salad. How about a glass of wine?"

"Only if it's red. I'm not drinking anything that I can see through."

She smiled as I seated myself at the kitchen table. It's a nice kitchen, big, like you find in most of the newer homes, but still warm and friendly with golden oak cupboards and wallpaper of soft blues and greens. The kids' artwork covered the refrigerator and an angel made of old barn wood was hung on the wall behind me. My son had made the angel.

"What a terrible, terrible day," I said. "Especially for Autumn Barkle."

Martie put a fresh placemat and a glass of wine in front of me. "I'll nuke the lasagna—"

"Let me have some of this first," I said, raising the glass and taking a drink. "I don't want the effect dulled by food."

She nodded, but filled a plate anyway. "So what happened? Were the police okay with you? Jim Gray goes to our church and we don't really know him, but he's always seemed like a nice man." She was talking about the lieutenant. I couldn't imagine him in church. "Did they say what killed her?" She slid the plate in the microwave and turned it on. "Or do you want to talk about it?"

I lifted my palms. "I don't mind. I just don't know very much. Someone put strychnine in Miss Autumn's mineral water."

"Strychnine! Oh, God. That's ugly."

"Very. And it had to be someone at the rehearsal. At least, he made it sound that way."

"Really?" She sat down beside me. "Who was at the rehearsal today? I saw Alan Webster—"

"Who?" I explained that I only knew the parents by their kid's names.

"Allison's dad. About five-eleven, real slender. He's a runner."

Of the two men, I placed him easily. "The one with the camera." Not the young Mel Gibson. "He was there, along with Emma's mother, Julianne's mother, and both of Kayla's parents." I sipped more wine and thought about the group and the rehearsal. "Allison's father was very concerned about her getting nervous and throwing up tomorrow, but the video didn't bother her."

"He started filming her during the birth and I don't think he's ever stopped. She probably doesn't even notice. He adores his daughter."

Enough to kill for her?

Martie went on. "They're building that huge new house over on the other side of the highway. It's going to be monstrous; I think someone told me it was almost seven thousand square feet. Remember, I showed you that acreage with all the trees?"

"I remember. They've had to clear part of the land, but there's still a creek, right?"

"Right."

And when you clear land like that, you have problems with animals being displaced. Rats, snakes, and all types of predators. If you were the conscientious type who worried about your four-year-old, you might put poison out in special traps that were people-proof. They have such things, and quite often strychnine is used in them.

Although—Allison's father had looked like a very nice man.

"Martie," I said, "he could get poison. The lieutenant said that anyone can buy it for control of wild animals, which I'm sure they have with the construction. And Allison isn't in the front row of the dancers. Is he the type who might get mad and—"

"Over a dance recital?"

"There were going to be agents in the audience tomorrow. Would that matter to him?"

She laughed. "He owns a computer software firm and they did an IPO during the height of the craze. He's rich. Really rich. If he wanted Allison to have an agent, he'd buy her one. Remember when the market crashed, or dropped six hundred points, or whatever it did?" I nodded that I did. "He told me that he'd lost several million dollars. And he was laughing about it! He said something like, 'I needed the write-off.'"

"It didn't stop the construction on their house?"

"Didn't even slow it down."

"Oh." So, he didn't need Miss Autumn or her dance class. In some respects that put Allison's dad out of the running, but then what did I know? "What about Julianne's mother?" I thought of the woman who always arrived late, her keys jangling, her cell phone usually attached to her ear. She certainly seemed aggressive enough.

"A real estate broker. Single mom, always on the go, but then with three kids to support and no husband, I guess she has to be."

"That's hard. Is there a weekend dad who takes the kids periodically?"

"Not these days. He remarried and moved to Canada, and he doesn't even send child support. Can you imagine that? I know she wanted Julianne to start acting. She was telling me last week how much you could make on a commercial that runs nationally." The microwave dinged and Martie got up to retrieve my plate of lasagna, decided it wasn't done, and put it back in. She forgot to turn on the oven, but I didn't say anything, since I wasn't really hungry.

"Where do they live?" I asked.

"About a mile from here. In that new subdivision. Well, it's not new, but newer." And there was additional construction going on in that area. More predators? More strychnine?

Martie and W.D. had chosen their home carefully. Beyond certain size requirements, they'd looked for large trees and quiet streets so the kids could ride their bikes. The home they'd found was a little older, and was about a mile from most of their friends, such as Kayla's parents, Julianne's mother, and Allison's family.

"What about Emma's mother?" She of the purple hair, who wanted Emma to dance in the front row. "Does she live near the others?"

"I think so, but I don't really know her. She's sort of intense, you know? Another of those computer whizzes."

"Another rich one?"

Martie thought about it for a minute. "No. Not yet, at least."

"That leaves Kayla's parents. He is something to look at—"

"And he knows it."

"Really? Does his wife seem insignificant to you? Not just in size, but in personality?"

"Well, she's different. You don't know her," Martie said. "She used to be a barrel racer; put her on a horse and she's like superwoman. She really lets the horse know who's in charge."

Shelby drifted in.

"How's it going?" I asked her.

"Okay. I was playing Nintendo and I loosed. Do you like losing?"

"No, but it happens sometimes. Come here." She came over and climbed up on my lap. "I'm sorry your recital is canceled."

She shrugged. "It's okay. Mommy says I can wear my costume and dance in the living room. Maybe I can dance at the nursing home for Nana, too. Me and Ariana and Katie."

"That's good."

"Nana will like that. But, I'm kind of sad because Miss Autumn had death."

"So you know that," I said. I glanced over at Martie who was watching silently. "Do you know what death is?"

Shelby nodded, her dark violet eyes full of wisdom. "It means you can't move anymore. Then they put you in a shoebox and then they put you in the ground."

"And how do you know that?"

"Because that's what they did with Zachary's turtle."

"Sounds pretty accurate to me," I said.

"Except," Martie added, "they don't put people in shoeboxes. They put them in places called cemeteries and then the people go to heaven to be with God and the angels. And their friends."

"But not Zachary's turtle," Shelby said. "We dug him up and he was still death, and he had bugs on him. He didn't go anyplace." She turned to her mom. "Can I have some orange juice?"

Which put an end to that discussion.

While Martie poured the juice I explained about Lt. Gray wanting to have the girls questioned. "He mentioned a professional who'd come in. A counselor, I think he said. Does that bother you?"

"No, not really. If Jim says it's all right, I trust him."

"Oh, and he thinks that everyone is covering for everyone else. Because all the parents are friends."

"You have to stay at the table and drink this," she said to Shelby, handing over the glass. I helped Shelby into a chair beside me, as Martie added, "That's a simplification. Just because we all know each other doesn't mean we're friends. Emma's mother is like the stage mother from hell, uh, heck."

"I heard you," Shelby said. To me she said, "Mommy is not s'posed to say that word, but she does. Mommies do."

"Oh, really?" I said.

"Yes. I know another mother who does; I can't tell you who. But," she looked thrilled to repeat this, "she said 'damn moose.' Damn is a bad word, and she said that Miss Autumn was a damn moose."

"No, no, not quite. Danseuse. It means the best dancer, or something like that. In French."

"No, he said Dan-zoos, but she said DAMN MOOSE. And he got mad, because he said it wasn't fair, and he *accidentally* fell asleep with Miss Autumn. He didn't mean to fall asleep. It wasn't fair."

I almost got whiplash from jerking my head around to face Shelby. "Who said this? When?"

She sipped orange juice placidly. "I can't tell you."

"You have to tell—"

Martie was in action before I finished the sentence. "Shelby, put down that juice and get in the car. Now." She was grabbing for her purse. "Tyler! Get your sandals; turn off the TV; we're leaving this minute. You may bring the Gameboy."

I jumped up, too. I'm not as well trained as the kids, and I'm sure the commands weren't directed at me, but Martie obviously had this whole thing figured out. I wasn't going to miss whatever came next.

By the time I found my purse and got to the car, Shelby was buckled in the back seat, the garage door was open, and Martie was starting the engine of the minivan.

"Where are we going?" I asked as I slammed the door and the van began to move.

"Police. I want Shelby to tell this to someone official."

"He said a counselor was coming from Atlanta right about . . ." I glanced at my watch, "right about now."

"Perfect."

Martie was focused totally on her driving, which was a very good thing, but I still had to know if my translation of Shelby's words was accurate.

I dropped my voice. "When Shelby said it wasn't fair, the word she actually overheard was 'affair.' Am I right?"

"That's what I think. Although how he could claim to 'accidentally' fall asleep with Miss Autumn—"

Shelby piped up from the backseat. "I accidentally fall asleep in cars sometimes."

"You," Tyler said, "accidentally fall asleep all the time, but that's because you're a baby."

"I'm not a baby—" Shelby tried to swing at him, but Martie reached back and caught her arm with a practiced move that an Olympian would admire. She also did it without taking her eyes off the road. "No hitting, and Tyler, she is not a baby." To me she said, "There is only one father in the group who 'accidentally' falls asleep. If you know what I mean."

"I know," I said, waiting to hear which one.

"And there is only one woman who used to live on a ranch. With predators, so she could probably get the strychnine. And that same woman is the only one petite enough to consider Miss Autumn a 'damn moose.'"

"I know who it is," I said, thinking about the Mel Gibson cutie and his shadowy wife. "Are you sure?"

"Pretty sure, but Jim Gray will have to prove it." She gave me a quick glance. "Do you know who I'm talking about?"

I took a breath. "I sure do. Kayla's mommy killed the damn moose."

The End

JOOKIN' 'N' JIVIN'
Linda Kerslake

The silky sounds of "Chattanooga Choo Choo" filled the air of the activity room at the retirement home, drawing the residents in like fish to bait. A young couple stumbled through the steps, counting out loud, staring at their feet. The audience gathered around, bobbing their balding heads and tapping arthritic toes to the beat.

"You're getting it," encouraged Ellie Grow as she adjusted her glasses. Her grandson, Josh, had begged for her help with his history final. His teacher, angered by recent budget cuts in the arts, had concocted an interesting final project. First, he paired the students off, then let them draw a slip from a top hat. Each slip had the name of a dance on it, and they were to learn the dance, give a demonstration, and do an essay on American history during that era. Josh and his partner, Kara, drew Swing and World War II.

"I can't believe you used to dance this stuff, Grandma," said Josh as he collapsed into a salmon pink molded-shell chair.

"Oh, we could go all night! Once you get the basic steps down pat, it gets fun."

"But the competition's Tuesday! We're gonna get creamed!" He shook his head, his humiliation evident.

"Sondra Longston's mom hired a seamstress to do her gown for the Virginia reel," added Kara.

"Oh, fiddlesticks," replied Ellie, "Don't worry about that. We'll find Josh a zoot suit and flashy tie and doll you up in a slinky rayon number. And we've got some experts on Swing right here." Glancing around the room, she spotted Clyde Benson by the candy machine. "Clyde, come here a minute. We've got a problem."

A retired detective for a nearby police department, Clyde could never resist trying to solve a problem. He stuffed the remainder of his Snickers in his mouth and joined them at their table.

"The kids are giving a dance demonstration on Tuesday, and we need your help," she said as she reached over and wiped a smudge of chocolate from the corner of his mouth. "You know better than to eat those things," she admonished. Leaning toward the kids, she explained, "He's borderline diabetic."

They looked at him with a mixture of pity and disgust.

"So what kind of help do you need?" he asked, picking a nut from between two of his remaining teeth.

"Grandma, I'm not sure this guy can help us."

"Now hush. Clyde, you were quite the Swing dancer, weren't you?"

"Took fourth in a competition at the Polamar Ballroom in L.A. just before the war."

Josh rolled his eyes, then glanced sideways at Kara. No way!

"They need a little help with their basic steps, and then the breakaways. Just a few hints. And some ideas on costumes."

The two males eyed each other like roosters circling for a cock fight. Clyde saw an arrogant child with bleach-tipped hair in somebody else's jeans, and Josh saw a whiskery old fart with coffee stains dribbled down his shirt who smelled used. Ellie saw a solution.

"Tell us what you know about Swing. Get us "In the Mood," she giggled.

"Swing has its roots in jazz, and began years before the war, in Harlem. . . ."

"Cut with the history lesson, Gramps."

"Josh! Where are your manners?"

"Sorry, Grandma, but this we can get from a book." He rose, reaching for his jacket.

"You want to learn Swing? Real Swing? Or you just want to do some steps?" Clyde fired back.

Josh paused, locking eyes with the man. He saw a wrinkled face with eyebrows escaping over black-framed glasses, but looking deeper, he saw a sparkle in the man's eyes that made him sit back down, replacing his jacket on the back of the chair.

"We want to be good. We want to win."

"I can't promise you'll win. But I can promise you'll lose if you don't understand the dance."

"Okay. We're listening."

"Swing isn't really a type of music; it's a way of playing music, something you feel, something you do."

"I don't get it."

Clyde chuckled.

"Most people don't. Artie Shaw once said, 'Swing is a verb, not an adjective.' It's also the name given to an era when jazz music swept the nation, a nation on the brink of war, and it became a symbol of the American lifestyle."

Clyde told about the relationship between jazz and Swing, and about the early bands that ushered in the era known as Swing. He named the legends: Louie and the Count, Billie and Ella, Benny Goodman and the Duke. Songs like "Ain't Misbehavin'," "Little Brown Jug," "Kalamazoo." Then he told of the clubs and ballrooms: The Cotton Club, the Apollo, the Club Alabam.

Suddenly, the excited flush in his cheeks drained away.

"Clyde, what is it?" asked Ellie.

"The Savoy, too."

"That's right! Most of us only dreamed of going there. *Downbeat Magazine* featured it all the time. Did you really dance there?"

"I can't talk about it." He stood and moved back to the candy machine, fishing in his pocket for more change. He looked like he needed a stiff drink, but unable to get one, he'd take sugar. Josh and Kara looked at Ellie, but she just shrugged. One by one, they followed him across the room.

"Please, Mr. Benson," said Josh, "we'd like to hear more. It's kinda interesting, ya know, not like regular history."

Clyde ripped open his second Snickers, but Ellie kept silent this time. They all sat down at a round Formica table. The dance music had played out, and a soft Billie Holiday tune spun its magic on their mood.

"It's not something I care to remember. Not that we had a choice," he added quickly, then bit into the bar. His forehead creased, then he went on.

"We'd just received our orders to ship out, and we had a seventy-two-hour furlough in New York. Me and Vinny Manelli. We'd just finished basic training. Before we left, we wanted to see the real hot-spot. The place it all began. We were hoping to catch one of the big bands. We hopped on the A train, the one running to Harlem. . . ." Clyde's eyes glazed over, and he appeared to be transported back to his leave in New York.

. . . . .

The summer air is thick with the fear of war, and we just want to get away. We get off at 125th Street and walk a block down to the Apollo, sharing our last Lucky Strike between us. We'd been drinking dinner. Highballs. Back home, we're too young to drink, but we're not too young to get our brains blown out for our country. We don't talk about it, but it's there. In our minds. Trying to remember what we enlisted for. What's worth dying for . . . so young.

Music pumps down every street, out of jook joints, packed with dancers. Anyone who can pays the cover for the ballrooms—the rest go jookin'. The closer we get to the Apollo, the faster we walk. You can't hear this music and not move. It vibrates the air, the pavement you walk on. You can smell it. We pay the cover and slide into two empty chairs off to the side, close to the front. They're having amateur competition. A five-piece band with a screaming horn's playing their rendition of "It Don't Mean a Thing if It Ain't Got That Swing." We order drinks and buy a fresh packet of cigarettes from the hostess. Just as we settle in, the song ends to a decent round of applause.

After a few minutes, the spotlight comes back on, creating a cameo on two knock-out babes, the singers. Canaries, they call 'em. The one on the right, she's a shade taller. They look almost identical to me, real pretty, but not to Vinny. He says, check out the one on the right. One look at his face, I know he's a goner.

They sing this slow song first, and the audience is restless. They don't want romance. They want the beat. To go wild. To feel the heat. To forget.

So when they're done, the tall one, she turns to the drummer, a lanky black guy in high-waisted trousers and spectator shoes, black and white. He grabs her wrist, pulls her close, whispers something in her ear. She jerks her arm back, rubs her wrist. The beat picks up and they launch into "The Boogie Woogie Bugle Boy of Company B." The crowd starts clapping, people get up, they dance around tables. The place is hoppin'. Beer sloshes down the neck of my uniform, but I don't care.

Can these gals ever sing, and what a sight! Red rayon dresses that cling to their breasts and flare from the hips, with skirts that swing wildly. Large lips painted red spew out words in perfect tandem. Sculpted black hair pulled back with a white gardenia I can almost smell. I know Vinny can. The tall one zeros in on Vinny.

The song ends, the light dies. Vinny grabs my arm. We try to get backstage, but the bouncer's impressive—hopefully he's on our side of the war. We get stamped, then go outside. He runs around the side of the building, then down the alley. I follow. We wait by the stage door, smoking. Smelling the rotten cantaloupe and onions from the grocer's garbage down the way. Rats scratch. He paces. I'm ready to go back, then the door opens. A single bulb shines a bluish halo on her black hair. The gardenia looks fake, her lips purple. Vinny steps forward.

"I liked your show."

"Thanks. You got another one of those?" He rips the pack getting one out.

She smiles. Perfect white teeth.

"Now, you got a light?"

He grins. I know he's blushing but it's too dark to tell. I take a few steps backward, but they don't notice. They're laughing now. I wonder about the other singer, the shorter one. A sister? But I remember Betty back home. My Betty. I walk on. I wonder if Vinny remembers his girl, but it doesn't look like it. I turn around and glance back.

I hear her say "I'm Wilma May." She's leaning toward him. Inside, a new band has started up, playing "Stormy Weather." I get to the corner. Vinny and Wilma are dancing by now. The cigarettes are gone, so is the small talk.

I turn the corner.

For three nights we come to the Apollo to catch her early show. She's trying to break into singing. Then we go over to the Savoy where she works as a dancer. After that, Vinny and her, they head off, and I'm on my own. On the third night, I'm inside waiting for him again. He's outside with her.

I'm on a stool at the bar. The band playing is okay, and after another highball, they sound better. Then Vinny is at my side. I ask where's Wilma. He says she can't come in here. I wonder why. He says they're going over to the Savoy for some dancing. I say go ahead— I'll join you later. I'm tired of being the third wheel. He leaves, and the drummer in the spectators watches him go from the corner of the stage. I don't think anything of it.

Two highballs later, I'm revved and feel like dancing, even though I stumble to the door. I think, it's time to find Vinny. It's almost 3 a.m. Out in front there's a taxi full of GIs. They're headed to the Savoy. Heard a rumor Ellington's back in town. I pile in. They're shipping out tomorrow too, out for a last fling like Vinny and me. This skinny little guy with a grin full of teeth hands me a flask. One for the road.

We get to the Savoy, and I navigate the stairs by holding on to the railing, trying to act straight. It's a swank joint. Red carpet, no less. The ballroom is huge, at least two hundred feet long with two bandstands against the long wall. The house band, the Savoy Sultans, is playing a song I don't recognize, and the dance floor is packed. Everybody's doing the Lindy Hop. The drummer from the Apollo walks by. I follow his gaze. I spot Vinny, but he's too far away to hear my shout. I skirt the edge of the hardwood floor, working my way over to him.

He's on the dance floor, really jivin'. Some hep steps. She's one of Whitey's Lindy Hoppers and she's taught him a lot in a few days. And nights. They look great together, he's tall and lean, she's thin but curvy. He's tanned, she's a shade darker. Whitey himself is watching them closely, watching every move Vinny makes like a cat watches a mouse. The song ends. Just as I get close, they head off down a hallway marked "Exit."

"Hey sailor, can you dance?" asks a flirty brunette, bouncing on her tip-toes.

I can dance, but not this through-the-air-and-between-the-legs crap.

"Later, doll," I tell her. She moves on to the next guy in uniform. Dames! I look up and Vinny and Wilma are gone. I start down the hallway, but I'm blocked by the drummer. He says that's for performers only. I turn away; he follows them. I backtrack out the main entrance, then around the back side. This place is huge. I keep going, using the music as a guide. I see a loading dock, where they unload the equipment. I start toward it, calling his name. I hear voices, angry ones, then a woman's voice pleading. The light is dim. I can make out three people on the dock. The two men are shoving, one takes a punch. I start to run forward.

The light is bad, but I remember seeing the spectators, shining like whitewalls on a Chrysler Airflow in the moonlight. And the gardenia. In her hair. He grabs Vinny, they fall to the dock. She pulls his arm. There's a pop that echoes off the brick walls. Funny, it's just a small bang, not like the bolt-action rifles we've been training with. A flash just bigger than a candle's flame. Then it goes out.

Nobody moves. I wonder who got shot.

Slowly, two bodies move away from the one that remains still. The spectators don't move. He's limp. I lurch forward onto the dock, picking up the gun, wondering who fired it. It's a small, pearl-handled one, easy to conceal. Vinny starts to rouse. He looks up at me, and then to her, then at the drummer, now quiet. He crawls over to her, draping an arm around her. They stand.

The shot's attracted some attention from the second floor.

"Hey, you with the gun! Hold it right there." It's Whitey. He starts for the stairs.

I realize he means me. None of us know what to do. Suddenly, she grabs the gun from me.

"Get outta here," she whispers, her brown eyes sparkling with tears. "I can cover this."

"No!" says Vinny. "We're not leaving you like this."

"We broke the rules, sugar. They'll make you pay. Now go! This is Harlem. I'm one of their own. I'll be okay."

Until that moment, I hadn't known she was black. She's one of those light ones, like Billie Holiday, the shade of coffee, with lots of sweet cream.

What she says suddenly makes sense to me. I hear footsteps pounding down the staircase, getting closer.

"Come on. There's nothing we can do here." I pull at Vinny's arm. This looks bad. My prints are on the gun.

"Vinny, come on! The ship's about to sail. We'll be AWOL!"

This gets through to Vinny, and he bends, touching her lips with his finger. "Go," she says. "Now." She plucks the gardenia from her ebony hair, crushing it into the palm of his hand. I see pain in his eyes as he turns.

Then we race down the alley, looking for a way out. We hail a cab that's just dropped off some all-nighters at the Cotton Club, and head for the ship. The sun threatens to break the day before we get onboard, but it holds off until we're up the ramp. We barely have time to clean up before we set sail.

. . . . .

Clyde leaned back, drained from the telling of his tale. Ellie's eyes were wide, and she reached out a hand to cover his shaking one.

"We didn't have a choice." He recoiled his hand.

"Who shot him?" asked Josh.

"I figure he was trying to shoot Vinny, and the gun turned on him when she grabbed his arm." Then he stood, avoiding their eyes. Shaking his head, he left.

"That was hard for him to tell," said Ellie.

"He made it all seem so real."

"They were difficult years, Josh. The war changed all of our lives."

"Grandma, what did she mean about breaking the rules?"

"Things were different in those days, honey. The blacks kept more to themselves, and the whites liked it that way. The employees of the Savoy could dance with whites, but they couldn't be involved with them. They weren't supposed to mix. That's another reason the drummer got so mad."

"Like segregation?"

"Right, and there were serious repercussions if you broke the rules."

"He sure made it all come alive. I felt like I was there."

"Well, maybe it served a purpose, his telling it all again like that."

They agreed on a time Saturday for a final lesson, and Ellie promised to talk Clyde into showing them some steps.

. . . . .

When Saturday came, Clyde made himself scarce. Ellie worked with the kids, reviewing the basic steps and showing them the pretzel, the cuddle, and the tandem, or back Charleston. They worked out a routine with several swingouts, then took a break.

"I can't believe you used to do this, Grandma!"

"I wasn't always this old, Josh."

A can of cold Pepsi clunked its way out of the machine, and Josh popped the tab, chugging half of it. As he lowered the can, he saw Clyde enter the room, headed for the candy machine.

"Mr. Benson! Did you see us dance?"

"No, I just got here."

"Watch this!" He grabbed Kara's hand, half-dragging her back onto the dance floor. Ellie started the music, and their song, "In the Mood," flowed from the speakers. They danced the routine, carefully counting steps and remembering every turn. Turning with smiles, they expected praise from Clyde.

"Your turns on the pretzel are still rough, and your footwork needs practice. Do it until you feel it, and you don't have to think about it, then you're Swingin'. And when you do the cuddle step, bring her right in to your side, your right hand behind her back, right on her hip. She won't bite, will you, doll?" He coached them through a few times, then left them to practice. Josh was disappointed to see him go. They worked for another half-hour, and Clyde returned, carrying a blue serge suit.

"Get this old thing cleaned and wear it. It's just been hanging around."

"Oh, Clyde, is that what I think it is?" asked Ellie. "Is that an old zoot suit?"

"Sure is. My lucky one. Just like Cab Calloway's."

"And you were griping about my jeans?" snickered Josh. He held up the suit and gave a whistle. The long jacket had over-sized lapels, and a swing chain dangled down from the pocket. The pants were comical in proportion, high-waisted and baggy, meant to drape the dancer. They cuffed at the ankles. A wide tie with red polka dots and yellow dashes completed the ensemble.

Ellie hurried over to a box she'd brought in, lifting out a red rayon dress with a fitted bodice and a pleated skirt.

"This is a Marc Jacobs," she said, as if that needed no explanation. "The pleats really let you move!" She held it up to Kara. "I think it's just about a perfect fit, kiddo!" She handed her a pair of Bakelite earrings and some black suede wedgies. "All you need is a white gardenia, and you could step back in time."

"A white gardenia . . ." said Clyde as he thought of the one still pressed in Vinny's tattered Bible, marking the twenty-third psalm.

"I'm sorry, what did you say Clyde?" asked Ellie as she strapped a shoe on Kara's slender foot.

"The gardenia. She gave Vinny her gardenia that last night. The night we sailed."

"What ever happened to her?" asked Josh.

"I don't know, son. I promised Vinny I would try to find out, but I never could."

"You mean Vinny never tried? I thought he was really hooked on her."

"He couldn't. See, he died two months later."

"What happened?"

"We sailed for England. The bay at Southampton was swarming with warships, coming and going. We stayed there ten days for more training, then we were sent to northern Italy. Ol' Vinny was thrilled. Finally getting to see the homeland. We were sent out on recon."

"What's that?" asked Kara.

"Reconnaissance. A fact-gathering mission. We were to report on a bridge they considered useless, but it would prove vital for the Allies. We were out one night, and got spotted by a German patrol. They were supposed to be way north of us, near the eastern front."

"What happened?" asked Josh.

"They spotted us from the bridge, down on the bank. I dove in, swam under water. When I came up, everything was silent. I waited until dawn, and I found Vinny, washed up downstream. He was barely breathing. 'Hold on buddy,' I said, 'I'll get help.' He just smiled. He knew it was over. Even in the anemic light, I could see the reddish water around him, the flow of blood slowed some by the cold, but not enough. That's when he asked me to check on her, if I made it back. To help her out of that mess we left her in. I thought he was nuts, falling so hard for a gal he'd only known a few days, but the way things turned out, I was real glad he had."

"Well, you said you tried to find her," offered Josh.

"Right. I tried. But when I got back, nobody remembered a singer named Wilma May. I'd been shot up pretty bad in a battle just before the big invasion. Missed D-Day. After three surgeries and months of rehab in London, I finally made it back to New York. I tried all the clubs, and the cabaret entertainer's union. Couldn't even find Whitey. By then he was out in Hollywood doing movies. I tried. I really did."

"You did your best," said Ellie, but she could tell he wasn't comforted.

The kids packed up what to them were costumes, and turned to say good-bye.

"Will you be coming to the competition Tuesday, Grandma?"

"I wouldn't miss it, honey!"

"What about you, Mr. Benson?"

"Clyde. The name's Clyde. Mr. Benson was my dad."

"Okay, Clyde. What about it?"

"We'll see. I might be busy." He hurried off in search of his long-forgotten candy bar.

. . . . .

Rain poured down Tuesday. Clyde couldn't think of an excuse so he accompanied Ellie to the school gym. Parents and friends packed the bleachers, so they sandwiched in between two boys with partially shaved heads and pierced noses. Josh and Kara would dance last, so they settled in to endure the program until then. Muggy air slowly circled around them as large ceiling fans persuaded it to move.

"These damn things haven't gotten any softer," said Clyde as he shifted cheeks on the bleachers.

"Just be glad you have all that padding."

"Can we stop at the diner on the way home? This is lemon meringue pie day."

"That's where you get your padding. Now hush."

. . . . .

The first team represented the colonial era and performed the Virginia reel. Ellie's nose went up as she examined the ball gown sewn for Sondra Longston by the seamstress. The fabric was definitely too shiny.

The next notable performance came from the pair doing the Twist, representing the Sixties. They got a vivacious round of applause from the parents.

A team of four flappers with beaded headbands and chemises doing the Charleston preceded Josh, and they almost brought down the house.

"The kids will have to really shine to outdo them!" whispered Ellie.

"Is this thing over soon?" asked Clyde. "I've got to pee."

"Shush!"

The boys on either side chuckled.

The music of the Big Band Era boomed from the speakers, and the audience sat up straighter. Josh and Kara came dancing onto the stage in perfect step to Glenn Miller's song. Their first swingout went into a turn for Kara that made her red skirt flair out then twist shut like an umbrella around her slender legs. She was feeling the dance so much she instinctively added swivels to her steps, something Ellie had not shown her.

"Well, look at that!" uttered Ellie proudly.

Josh led her into a backward Boogie, a series of kicks and claps with a lot of hip movement. The crowd hooted and cheered, clapping in time to the music. Clyde nodded his approval at their smooth pretzel, and actually whistled when Josh snuggled her into a cuddle at his side. Then they did a "mess around," stepping in time to the music around a circle on the stage. For a finale, they did an aerial, one created by Frankie Manning in the forties, the over-the-back. Josh and Kara linked arms back-to-back, he bent over and she rolled right off his back. The song ended to a tremendous roar of applause and stomping.

When they were officially named the champions, they bowed, and Josh took the microphone.

"Learning this dance was like, really cool, but the best part was when Mr. Ben—I mean, Clyde, told us about his part in the war. He told us about his friend that died overseas, and a promise he made to him that he was never able to keep."

"What the heck . . ." muttered Clyde, his eyes darting around. "That stuff's private."

"Kara and I, we got on the Internet, and we tracked down Frankie Manning in New York. He told us how to reach that old friend of yours, so we called her, and had a car wash to raise the money to fly her out here. Clyde, we'd like you to come up here now. And you too, Mrs. Crawford."

"Crawford? Did he say Crawford? I don't know no Craw—"

He stopped talking because a graceful black woman with a white gardenia in her gray hair was approaching the stage. Her hips had a familiar sway. Numbly, Clyde made his way forward, searching her gnarled face for that striking woman of years ago. He found her in the luminous brown eyes, once again filled with tears.

"I tried to find you. No one knew a Wilma May," stuttered Clyde.

"Ah, sugar, we weren't properly introduced. It's Willamae. Willamae Clark, then after the war, I married my Norman. Norman Crawford, the other love of my life. But I never forgot our Vinny. No sir. We didn't have much time, but he was special, and he made me feel that way, like a real lady."

The audience couldn't hear the conversation; to them it was the reunion of two old friends from long ago, and they applauded.

"But what about that mess, with the drummer?" Clyde whispered.

"Oh, he'd been my lover-man for a year before that, beat me up real bad twice, just fer flirtin'. I couldn't get away from him. He gave me this." She stuck her lower lip out and pointed to a thick, pink scar.

"Did they press charges?"

"Lands, no! That good-fer-nuthin', jive-talkin' fool. The police were as glad as me he was gone. Last musician I ever dated. Married me my sweet Norman, a cab driver."

A questioned nipped at the heel of Clyde's mind.

"Whose gun was it, Willamae?" asked Clyde, remembering the small pearl handle, so delicate.

"Why, sugar, you know it had to be his," she said, winking one big brown, watery eye.

DANCE WITH DEATH
Carmen Jarrera

I didn't want to go, Officer, I really didn't want to go to that school for tango. But you have to understand that it was difficult for me to say no to Maria. I loved her too much. She was an amazing woman . . . beautiful, intelligent, full of life, and she had a strong, patient character. But once an idea to do something new came into her head, it would completely take her over, carry her away, fill her with passion. That's the way she was.

Like when she wanted to join a ceramics course and she filled the house with clay vases, or when she signed up for a silk painting class and went around in all these variously painted shawls, or else when she specialized in fine pastrymaking and made me put on five kilos in a month. . . .

It wasn't that I didn't understand, Officer. Since she'd lost her job she'd become restless. . . . No, luckily we've never had money problems because I earn quite well but, being such an energetic woman, she was bored. The days, all alone in the house, were long. She had to fill them somehow.

I was a gentle sort of guy and, what's more, I adored her. By and large anything she did was all right by me, and also all those courses meant that Maria could enjoy herself, get enthusiastic about something, and make new friends, and I was happy for her. At the very most I had to show a greater interest in a painted shawl or a well-risen pastry base than I actually felt, but then these are the little sacrifices you're happy to make when you love someone. Like I said, I was pleased that her courses had given her an outlet for her understandable desire to keep busy.

The school for tango though, Officer, was a completely different story.

Maria was absolutely determined that I should enroll as well. She said it made no sense for her to learn on her own because what would she do afterwards? Whom would she be able to dance it with? We had to learn together and then, ah yes, then we could really enjoy ourselves, no more of this going to the cinema or eating pizza with friends. She was bored with the same old routine, she was still young and full of life and wanted some fun. That's what she used to say.

I began to worry slightly because when your wife keeps on saying that she's bored with her life, any loving husband needs to watch out. It means there are problems up ahead, if not worse. Bear this in mind for yourself, Officer, if you have a wife. And I for one did not want any problems, let alone my wife becoming dissatisfied. Dissatisfaction leads you to look elsewhere, and I loved her too much. I couldn't risk her setting her sights on someone else and maybe leaving me. And then what would happen to me?

And I have to say that this tango craze had been going on for such a long time. It had become a real fixation. Did you see how many tango records there are at home? And you have no idea how many films, how many tango displays I've had to go to, with Maria next to me, trembling, losing herself completely in the performers, asking me throughout how it was possible for me not to feel involved, not to feel the passion, the sensuality, the voluptuousness of the dance. . . .

And yet Maria knew full well that I had never liked dancing. Any kind of dancing, ever. I was convinced that I wasn't the right sort of person to be a dancer, that I didn't even have the right physique. And then, over the years I'd put on a bit of weight and begun to lose my hair. . . . Yes, I know that these things seem silly but, anyway, at the time that's what I used to think. Maria knew this, she shouldn't have pushed me the way she did.

But she kept on insisting, wanting me to become a *tanguista*, as they say in Spanish.

I didn't say no to be pigheaded or because I didn't want to please her. I always gave in to her, whatever she wanted. Maria knew that she could ask me to revarnish the whole house, spend hours and hours out shopping, move furniture. She knew that she could ask me anything, *anything* but to dance. I couldn't do it, I felt stupid, awkward. . . .

Let alone the tango! The dancers always seemed to move in fits and starts like marionettes, with those strange steps and absurd pirouettes that ended suddenly, leaving them frozen like statues in poses obviously meant to be sensual, but which I, in all honesty, found downright ridiculous.

But Maria insisted, begged, sulked. . . . She was so sweet when she sulked, Officer. . . . She became completely irresistible.

Anyway, it so happened that one evening I gave in and said yes. You should have seen her, she jumped with joy, just like a little girl. She told me I was the best man in the whole world, that I made her happy, that she loved me so much. . . . She hugged me, she kissed me, and we ended up making love on the sofa without even bothering to draw the curtains. . . . It was the first time since before we'd been married that we'd made love like that. It was wonderful. Maria was wonderful, that evening was wonderful.

And so it was for her love that I started to go to tango school. And I worked hard at it, believe me, because when I decide to do something I want to do it well. I even studied the history behind the dance. Its development over time. Did you know that it was invented in Buenos Aires and that to begin with it was only danced in brothels? It was a dance for gangsters, very much looked down upon by the respectable until, as these things happen, it took hold all over the world.

To begin with it was agony. I didn't know where to put my feet. I always messed up the steps, but then, slowly, I began to learn, and I understood that Maria was right, it was a very sensual dance.

And do you know why, Officer? Because the roles, in tango, are completely defined. The man is the man, the woman is the woman. The man is the one who leads, always. He's the one who commands, who draws the woman to him, who pushes her away, who bends her over, who spins her round, who throws her to the ground. In other words, a real macho.

The woman has simply to follow his steps, his movements. Just follow. Let herself be guided. Let herself go.

And this is why women love it so much. Have you ever thought about it? No? Just think about it and you'll see that I'm right. You see, women would never admit it because they're so keen on being free and independent, but deep, deep down, honestly, they're attracted to being dominated. It took me a while, but then I got it. In the tango women once again experience that primitive feeling of being dominated by a man, and they can do it without risking anything, without losing face. Because they have the excuse that they're only dancing. Think about it, Officer, just think about it.

What did you say? I'm going off the point? No, if you really want to understand how it happened then what I'm saying is important. Please let me tell you in my own way.

So, as I was saying, I began to learn the tango. The other students were all in couples, Maria was right on that point, you have to work well together. Some were middle-aged, others were younger, and everyone, at least at the beginning, was as clumsy as I was. But the teacher was a very patient lady, very kind, and slowly we began to make progress. Maria, needless to say, was the best.

Every evening, after supper, we used to dance for a little while, just to practice. Every now and then I'd make a mistake and Maria would correct me but even so things were going well. She was happy and would look at me with the shining eyes of a woman well pleased with her man.

I quite surprised myself. Pleasantly surprised, I might say. I was now able to dance quite well, whereas up until a few months ago I would never have believed it possible to put two steps together without standing on someone's toes, and I had developed a liking for it.

But more important, I felt—how can I put it? Different, stronger, more masterful, more confident . . . another man, really. The truth is that the tango was changing me.

I've already told you the history of the roles of the woman and the man in this dance, haven't I? The leading character is always the man, even in the song lines, which are beautiful, full of strong emotions. It's the man who loves, who suffers, who reacts, who dreams. The woman only exists through what he is feeling. Fascinating, don't you think?

Anyway, I thought about it a lot and I found the explanation, Officer. I understood what was happening to me. What happened was that through dancing it, through interpreting the spirit of the strong, domineering man, in the end I was becoming macho myself. It was as if the outer veneer of good manners and politeness of my breeding was slowly wearing away, allowing a different man to emerge, a man who was more sincere, less toler-ant . . . in other words a more primitive, more real man.

I can see you're perplexed, Officer. You don't believe me, do you? And yet I can assure you that's what happened. Even Maria noticed and was amused. She said that I'd become a real *tanguista*. She used to tease me and we'd laugh about it. At the beginning, anyway.

Then the course came to an end and we began to go to the dance halls. By now I'd become very good and was able to perform all the moves. I could lead well, so well in fact that women began to line up to dance with me and Maria had to manage with partners who were not so good. She didn't like this too much but didn't show it.

Anyway, it didn't matter much to me anymore what Maria liked. I could dance the tango with or without her. I liked it, it was in my blood. It had transformed my character. And this, naturally, was reflected in my day-to-day life.

Maria did and didn't understand my transformation. She kept telling me to stop fooling around, that she didn't find it funny anymore. She began to point out that I no longer said "please" or "thank you," and then, as she got more resentful, that I'd become rude, that I no longer opened the car door for her, that I no longer gave her a lift to the shops, that I never went shop-ping with her, that I treated her badly even in front of her friends.

I didn't listen to her anymore, I didn't understand what she wanted. I only knew that Maria and her complaints were getting more and more annoying. She really got on my nerves, and I didn't waste any time telling her so. But she never let up, like I told you, she was stubborn, and she became more and more nasty.

Only when we were dancing were we sometimes able to reestablish a certain harmony, for the rest of the time it was a continual battle.

Every day, every hour, every moment.

It went on like this for a long time, getting worse and worse. Until one evening Maria was so irritating that I hit her. I can't tell you what she managed to pull out of her mouth!

A woman should never speak to her man like that. Never. So I hit her again, harder this time, enough to swing her head from one side to the other. She deserved it, believe me, Officer, she really did. And then to punish her, to make her really understand who was the boss, I took away her credit card. I used to leave her money on the table, each morning, for the shopping. Counted out. If she wanted anything extra she had to ask me for it.

From that moment, Officer, that woman succeeded in making my life hell. Real hell. She even refused to make love . . . but I forced her, oh yes, I forced her all right, even if it took a good beating.

I put up with that life for months, Officer, because I can take a lot, believe me.

Then there was the tango competition, in the hall where we always used to go, and I was sure that we would win. And what does Maria do? What does she do? At the last minute she says she doesn't want to come. And why? Because she's got a black eye and she's embarrassed. A *tanguista's* woman is embarrassed about having a black eye! Have you ever heard anything so stupid? She should have been proud of it! It was proof that she was a real man's woman!

There was a problem. Either she hadn't understood a thing, I mean not a thing, about tango, or else she wanted to taunt me. I don't know which one's worse, but it was clear that that woman needed a lesson. I began to hit her harder. And harder.

Did I mean to kill her? What kind of a question is that? Then I've been wasting my time talking to you, Officer. You obviously haven't been listening. The fact is that Maria had got out of hand. I only wanted her to stay in her place. That she behave, you know, like a woman should behave. Nothing else.

Is that so hard to understand?

THE MECHANIQUE AFFAIR
Ruth Cavin

"Kari, the world is lusting for my memoirs and you expect me to take time from creation to go to some damn dance camp?"

Only Mick McGuire would call a summer rehearsal site for one of the most prestigious modern dance companies in America a "dance camp," conjuring up visions of nine-year-old girls in little skirts and totally unnecessary bra tops tapping out the time step.

I'd driven up to Mick's country house on the Maine coast, where he actually *was* writing his memoirs, a string of anecdotes, in his case, following his bizarre path through the last sixty-some years. A little round gnome of a guy, Mick grew up on the pretty mean streets of New York's west Thirties, and in spite of wearing an air of wide-eyed naïveté, he is as savvy as they come.

Mick has been a subway conductor, a (part-time) volleyball coach at a posh boy's prep school, the owner and director of a summer theater on Lake Erie (one season), and an editor of paperback books. Currently he's an ice-skating instructor. Through all that, he has been one of America's leading dance critics. (He judges the occasional dog show as well, but he insists there's no connection.) He's got two ex-wives, one male ex-lover and his long-time (also male) partner, Jobie, who had just gone down to his studio in the nearby woods to paint his exquisite small watercolors and entertain The Dog. The Dog is a springer spaniel, and if you think "springer" should be pronounced "schpringer" and is a proper name of German derivation, you have never seen a small brown and white dog with long floppy ears and the back legs of a kangaroo suddenly leap three feet in the air to clear a bush by the side of the road.

"Mick, don't lie! You know you'd love to be the first critic to get a look at Peter's crazy new work in progress. Nobody outside the company has seen the thing, and they all think it's way different from anything even Peter Butcher has ever done." I didn't add to Mick that I was afraid it could turn out to be way different from anything anyone was ever going to *want* to see, either. Which worried me big time. I love Peter, and I couldn't bear it if he was going to make a fool of himself. I wanted Mick's opinion of "Danse Mechanique," which was the name Peter had given his creation.

I had my own reasons as well. My grandmother once told me that in his morning prayers, an orthodox Jewish man thanks God for not having made him a woman. (Boy oh boy!) In *my* morning prayers I thank whatever muse runs these things for the existence of Peter Butcher. Because I'm hardly your competing-with-the-sylph type, being five-ten, broad shouldered, and although far from fat, let's say Solid and Substantial. There aren't a lot of dance companies, even modern dance companies (ballet? Forget it.) that want female dancers like that. But Peter takes them, along with other out-of-spec types if he senses talent there, and he manages to get real beauty and art from all of them. As soon as I pass Harmony 101, I'm writing a cantata called, "Eat Your Liver, Mr. Balanchine."

This new dance, though, was so far out, so bizarre an idea, that no matter how gifted the choreography or how good the dancers, it was hard to see how it could amount to anything coherent at the end of the day.

"Is it?" Mick asked me.

"Is what?"

"Way different from and so on?"

"Yes it is. That it certainly is. And Peter would probably kill me if I brought anyone down there but you. He really respects you and your opinions."

"I am armored against flattery, Kari. It is still 'no.'"

I'd have to play my trump card—the truth.

"Here's the thing, Mick. I want you to come even more than Peter does. Because I'm really worried about him. He's gotten paranoid. He thinks someone is stalking him, trying to see the elements of the new dance so they can steal it and spring it on the public before he does. You know—I wouldn't put it past someone like Hal Dale or Jason Everly or Hortense Roland, people whose own choreography is so dreary. But it's all in Peter's head. And once he heard that you were close by, he's convinced that you can find out who it is."

"Me? When did I become a detective?"

"It was when you discovered who had put the glue in the toe shoes Maria Whiteside had broken in for the premiere of her new ballet." (Hearing about it, modern dancers had rolled their eyes and said "Ballet!" as though moderate mayhem wasn't just as likely to occur among those of the barefoot persuasion.)

Mick's finding the culprit that time could hardly compare with the work of real detectives (or even TV ones) with their magnifying glasses and DNA collectors, but to Peter, to whom the world looks a bit different than it does to the rest of us, it made Mick a latter-day Sherlock Holmes, easily able to find and deal with the spy who was lurking about in Peter's imagination. I knew very well Mick was dying to see "Mechanique," so I wasn't surprised when, after the required number of false grumbles and fake blushes, he said yes.

We were working at an old Maine farmhouse farther down the coast. It had been taken over by a dance community that ran out of money a year later. The property was available for rental and suited us well. The barn had been fitted out with a lovely splinter-free hardwood floor—just as well, since Peter's dancers spent a lot of time down on it. There was a "floor" set into the ground outside under the trees, too, where we could work in the open air. There was a small lake on the other side of a wooded area on the property, and when it got really hot, the house provided a lot of electric fans, except you couldn't run them all at once or you blew the fuses.

As we drove up to the farm, the dancers were rehearsing out of doors. Catching sight of the car, Peter yelled "Break!" and ran over to us. He pumped Mick's hand as though the little critic had just brought him news of a MacArthur grant.

"Mick! She got you to come! Bless you!"

"Bless Kari. I'm putty in her hands."

By this time the company had gathered around us, greeting us with "Hey, Mick" and "How're you doing, maestro?" Dancers love Mick McGuire. He's fun to be with, but primarily they respect his extraordinary understanding of their art—Mick could put into words what they felt about it but usually couldn't say. Where he got that understanding no one knew—not even Mick himself. God knows he was no dancer.

That night, Imelda the Treasure, our cook, had made fish cakes with the local grocery's fresh-caught haddock. After we'd scarfed them all up, Peter took Mick aside and explained "the problem." Mick looked for all the world as though he was hearing it for the first time and believed every word. When they rejoined us where we sat around the main room gossiping and drinking coffee, I heard Peter say "Then you're going to do it, right Mick?" And the saddest part of that is that the tension that had been palpable in him for weeks seemed to have lifted a little.

The next morning Mick showed up in the barn just as we were assembling for practice; the sun was still low in the sky. He looked around for a moment, suddenly stiffened, came trotting over to me and grabbed my arm. With his face close to my ear, in a whisper that for sheer emotion could qualify as a shriek, demanded "Why is she wearing those?"

"Wearing what?" I really knew exactly what he was talking about. I'd been waiting for this.

He pointed to LaRoue, one of our young female dancers. "She's wearing toe shoes," he said, his voice quivering.

"Mick, when we're in costume, she'll be wearing a tutu, too. So will some of the others," I told him, trying to keep from sounding grim. "It's all part of the new dance."

"In a Peter Butcher company? Has he lost his mind? Kari, what in the name of Terpsichore is going on?"

"You'll see," I promised.

At that point an awful combination of noises—clanging and clashing and screeching and clattering—broke through the air. Mick jumped.

"It's music for the new piece, Mick," I yelled over the clamor. "You'll see. Hang in there." He gave me a baleful look.

The racket was cut off; Peter said, "OK, people, let's go," and we took our places, LaRoue and three other women dancers in ballet shoes on one side, eight of us on the other. The cacophony started up again, we moved to it while the ballerinas stood in classic poses. Then the sound stopped, we froze, and the soothing strains of the second act of Tchaikovsky's "Swan Lake" were heard. The ballerinas went into a pas de quatre unlike anything Piotr's music had ever spawned, more than topping the all-male version someone had dreamed up a few years ago. It was ballet, but it was Peter Butcher's ballet—not a parody, not a comment on tradition, simply a dance that demanded the classic ballet movements while somehow being entirely its own.

The rehearsal went on with the usual starts and stops of every rehearsal. Sometimes we repeated the back and forth sequence between the so-different styles, but many times both groups were dancing at once and the dissonant music (I suppose you have to call it music if someone had made a CD out of it) crashed and banged in its effort to drown out its melodic enemy, the Tchaikovsky.

When we broke, Mick was as worked up as I've ever seen him. "What in hell does Butcher think he's doing?" he demanded of me. "That's the most misbegotten thing anyone ever cooked up! It's going to be laughed off the stage! It will ruin him!" And that, of course, is what had been haunting *me*.

"And speaking of music, where did he find a recording of 'Mechanique'?"

"You know it?" I said, surprised.

"Of course. It was hot stuff in the twenties. Then about thirty years ago some professor found it and people started writing learned criticism, calling it the voice of the New Age—the twenties New Age, that is, not the sixties one."

The next section was made up of dancing that was startlingly original but definitely in the classic Butcher language. But it was danced to the Swan Lake music. The ballerinas had a matching session to the "Mechanique" recording a few minutes later.

Mick was fuming. "He's gone completely out of his mind," he told me grimly when we were eating lunch. He scooped up some of the fish chowder that was Imelda's contribution to everyone's good humor and stuck the spoon fiercely in his mouth. His expression underwent a sudden change. "Who made this?" he demanded. "This and those fish cakes last night?" When I told him, he insisted on trotting out to the kitchen there and then, with me trying vainly to keep him from getting under Imelda's large bare feet.

That was the last I saw of him until later in the day, when I went into the kitchen to fill my water bottle. There sat Mick, all cares forgot, discussing cast iron frying pans with Imelda.

. . . . .

In the days that followed, it appeared that Mick was clearly not only content to stay on, but was enjoying himself immensely. There was strain on Peter's part—not only was his "spy" worrying him, but he had obviously been hoping for Mick's enthusiastic praise for his baby. Alas, none was forthcoming.

Mick made a lot of phone calls from his cell phone, always seeking some out of the way spot to do it and keeping his talks conspiratorially low-spoken. Occasionally he'd run into town on some unexplained errand. I could only guess that he was trying to look as though he was earning his keep; I really had no idea what he was doing, but I love the little guy and was happy to have him with us. I did accost him once or twice about his search for a nonexistent villain. He just looked wise and said "Nonexistent? Don't be too certain."

Most rehearsal time was devoted to "Mechanique." The dancers danced, dubiously, Peter wore his worried look, every now and then demanding of Mick whether he was "getting anywhere," and Mick would reassure him that he was making progress. The little critic obviously enjoyed cozying up to various members of the company, both dancers and staff. He and Imelda exchanged recipes, cooked together, and ate together—Mick had given up the dining hall entirely for an honored seat at the kitchen table. He made friends with Sophie, one of Peter's first dancers, now in her fifties, who took care of the accounts and spent long sessions in combat with the man who handled the recordings. (Most modern dance companies aren't able to cover the cost of an orchestra even during their performances and have to go with recorded music.)

About ten days after Mick came, we were doing a run-through of "Mechanique" outdoors. I was resting on the grass while a female dancer in toe shoes and a male dancer in bare feet went through an odd pas de deux, when Mick appeared and flopped down beside me.

"Guess where Janelle comes from!" Mick demanded.

It was a hot day for Maine, I had just had a hard workout, and I hadn't the energy for guessing games. Janelle was new to the company; I had no idea where she came from and didn't much care.

"You been for a walk?"

"Uh-huh. Go on, guess."

"Where?"

"You can't guess?"

"Dayton, Ohio?"

"Nobody comes from Dayton, Ohio."

"The Wright brothers did."

"The ones who make the cough drops?"

"Come on, Mick. That's the Smith Brothers. The Wright brothers make the airplanes. Or made them. Or made one."

"Well, anyhow, you're wrong. She comes from Pittsburgh!"

"Seems just as remote as Dayton, Ohio, to me."

"That's because you're an insular New Yorker. Pittsburgh is where I come from."

"I thought you're from that place where Andy Warhol grew up—assuming he did grow up."

"Just down the road from Pittsburgh. How did this discussion go astray? I was telling you about Janelle. She and I have a lot to talk about."

"Good. What about Peter's stalker? Getting anywhere with that?"

Before he could answer there was a tremendous noise of breaking branches. It flashed through my mind that Peter had gone even loonier and had decided to add a Birnam Wood/Dunsinane touch to the mix.

Everyone froze.

Something had crashed to the ground from one of the huge oaks bordering the area where the dancers had been working. We all ran to look.

It was a small thin man with a hairline mustache and very black longish hair in a ponytail. He lay on the ground gasping. He was clutching what looked like a video camera.

"My God," cried little Wah Ming. "Is he dead?"

"Aha!" That was Peter, triumphant, gleaming with the satisfaction of having been right all along. He turned to the rest of us bunched up under the tree. "I told you! You wouldn't believe me!"

"Hey!" Don yelled. The little man had jumped up and was racing away, hugging his camera to his breast. A clutch of dancers ran after him, even one of the girls in her toe shoes, but the photographer had reached the road and jumped into a beaten-up green van. Off it sped as we stood and swore—all except Peter, who was still so delighted to have been proven right that he couldn't think of anything else. And Mick, who was watching the action with an air of polite interest.

The rest of the day was dedicated to endless and fruitless discussion of what to do about the intruder, in which, I noticed, Mick did not take part. He had asked Sophie for a local phone book, written down something he found there, and disappeared until dinner.

That evening while we were eating the phone rang. Don got up to answer it and yelled into the kitchen "Mick, it's for you."

Mick made no attempt to keep us from hearing, although most of what he said was in the nature of "Oh, yeah? . . . Great. . . . I see, OK." He took a pad from his pocket, wrote something on it, said "Not a word. I owe you, Dennis, old buddy. Thanks a lot," and hung up. He turned to the assembled company, beaming.

"It's OK. Everything is OK. Leave it to me," he assured us. "Kari, can you drive me to the bus tomorrow morning? I've got to go to Portland."

"I'll drive you to Portland," I said.

"No, no, no!" The notion seemed to alarm him. "Won't hear of it. You've got to rehearse. I'll have plenty of time."

"Plenty of time for what?"

"Well, I was curious about that van parked outside the farm this afternoon, and I remembered the license number because it reminded me of Great Uncle Patrick." Nobody took it upon himself to ask why it reminded him of Great Uncle Patrick.

"Dennis—that's Imelda's son-in-law—he's a state cop. We've gotten friendly. He did me a real favor—he ran the number, but don't say anything about it; he could get into trouble. Now I know where to find the guy's studio. Don't you worry, Peter, everything is going to be taken care of. When whoever hired that video artist comes to pick up his tapes, I'll get him."

"How?" I asked.

"Ve haff our vays," was all he would say.

Peter obviously didn't know whether to be frantic or elated. It was Sophie who had the practical question. "What if he sends a messenger?"

"Then I'll follow the messenger," Mick assured her. "Don't you worry, Peter; it'll be taken care of."

Mick took off for Portland the next morning, and the rest of us bated our breath and waited to hear from him. Three days later he called.

"All taken care of," he told Peter. "Not to worry."

. . . . .

Back at the farm, Peter decided that we wouldn't do "Mechanique" this fall season; we'd save it for the spring. I wondered if the absence of any enthusiastic comment from Mick had given him doubts. Or was he just regaining his own perspective? We worked very very hard on a lovely new dance that he created and that he had intended to put in the spring program instead of "Mechanique."

. . . . .

Summer ended. We went on tour—to Los Angeles and San Francisco, but also to smaller cities. We were immersed in our own little universe of traveling, packing, unpacking, good performance, disappointing performance, local reviews, etc. Until one day at breakfast in the hotel coffee shop Sophie, who was avidly reading the *New York Times* she had found in the gift shop, gave a shriek.

"Look!" she cried, and then refused to let us look until she'd read it to us.

It was a review of a dance concert in Greenwich Village by the Jason Everly Dance Company. Everly, a rather sleazy guy, had been a not-very-good dancer and now was a bad choreographer. Peter had had a big blowup with him a couple of years earlier over a dancer who had quit Everly and come to our company.

The dance being reviewed was called "Mish-Mosh Pit," and the *Times* critic pronounced it the worst piece of rubbish she had ever seen. "'Everly has come up with a cheap idea that is nothing but a ludicrous attempt to show off,'" Sophie read, "'although all it really does is cheapen him, his company, and the whole art of dance. It is worse than junk, it is garbage. It turned this viewer's stomach.' And listen to this: 'It must have taken Everly years to find the worst possible combination of two styles of dance and two kinds of music—if you can count that racket from the twenties as music. Art this is not, dance this is not, entertainment this is not. I cannot say what it is in a family newspaper. Everly should close down his company and seek out a good psychiatrist with an iron constitution.'"

"It's 'Mechanique'!" Peter breathed. "Mick didn't stop him after all! What did he tell me? 'It's all taken care of.'" Suddenly he grinned widely, satisfaction all over him. "And I know how he took care of it. Do you know what he did? That man saved my hide!"

. . . . .

I called Mick that evening after the performance.

"There never was a stalker, was there, Mick?"

He giggled. "Not until I hired one," he said. Then he got serious. "Kari, understand this. I'm very fond of your Peter Butcher, and I think he's not only extraordinarily gifted, but the choreographer working today who has the most to contribute to the art we all love. Once I'd seen the cliff he was about to go over, I simply had to get the tape made and give it to Everly. I couldn't have allowed that to happen to Peter."

YOU CAN JUMP
Mat Coward

So many people die. That's the main thing I've learned from life; so many people seem to die. And when they're not busy dying, they generally pass the time being unhappy, or else making other people unhappy, or else getting drunk and dancing and throwing up.

Which puts getting drunk and dancing and throwing up in a whole new light, when you think about it.

· · · · ·

I was never much of a dancer, to be honest, except for very briefly, when I was seventeen. I lacked the ability to just let go and let it happen. But my mate Andy danced. I'm not saying he was a *good* dancer, necessarily; not saying he had any particular talent for it. That wasn't the point: he enjoyed dancing, so he did it. Andy had a true punk rock soul, by which I mean that he didn't give a toss what other people thought of him. As long as what he was doing was right by his lights, then that was all he needed to know. And if you didn't like it, then that was your problem, not his.

For a while, in the late summer or early autumn of 1977, there was a sign in the window of one of the West End venues—the Vortex, possibly—that showed a picture of a punk rocker in all his glory (bondage trousers, ripped leather jacket, safety pins, spiky hair) and written underneath was the message: "If You Don't Look Like This, Fuck Off." The police eventually made the club take it down. I think there might even have been a threat of prosecution. I thought it was brilliant, hilarious. It was tribal and aggressive and punky and it said *Go to hell* to the entire Establishment—to anyone who wasn't us. Andy thought it was stupid.

"If they want to wear a uniform," he said, "why don't they join the army?" Next time we went to a punk gig, Andy wore a sports jacket and tie.

The dance that everyone associates with punk wasn't really a dance at all. Pogoing didn't involve learning any steps; it didn't require an ability to keep time, or to coordinate with a partner. That was the point of it, really. If you could jump up and down, you could pogo. If you could jump up and down even though your trouser legs were linked at the ankles by a short length of khaki fabric, or black mock leather, then you could *really* pogo. Not that it would have mattered; those were not competitive days, punk was not a competitive scene. To be better at pogoing than someone else—or rather, to have tried to be better—would have been to miss the idea entirely. Can you jump up and down? So, you can pogo. I even remember seeing two kids in wheelchairs at one gig, bumping their wheels up against the side of the stage, pogoing away with the rest of us. Even if you *can't* jump up and down, you can pogo.

Slamming and choking are not as well remembered today, but were just as important at the time, and both were a little more involved than pogoing, a little more demanding. Slamming required timing. As you hurled your body at your mate—or he hurled his at you—at distances ranging from a few feet to a few inches, depending on whether the floor was illegally over-crowded or catastrophically overcrowded, if you didn't time it right you could end up with all sorts of trouble. Not that anyone ever did get injured, as far as I know. Those were wild times, and in wild times the wild children are protected. Today, people live more safely, and children are killed every-where.

The choke (I'm not sure if we actually called it that, or even if we called it anything; 1977 was more a time of doing than of branding) was a frenzied dance, even more so than the pogo or the slam. There was a strange sense of thrill to choking a total stranger; how would he react?

To an uninitiated onlooker, seeing two teenagers gripping each other about the throat and shaking each other back and forth, while simultane-ously leaping into the air, bouncing on the rubber soles of their French kick-ers, it must have looked like a fight to the death. It is this one image of the punk era—of my friend Andy strangling Jamie Holmes, holding on and tightening his wrists even after Jamie's hands had dropped to his sides—that stayed in my mind over the years more than any other.

. . . . .

I hired a room for the reunion above a suitably dingy pub near Waterloo.

That wasn't as easy as it sounds; dingy pubs were not so plentiful in 1997 as they had been twenty years earlier.

I got there first, to set up. I had a few homemade tapes of the classics: Elvis Costello, The Clash, The Pistols, Wreckless Eric, Eddie and the Hot Rods. There was a small bar in the functions room, staffed by a friendly teenage girl. She asked me what it was, a stag night? A works do? I told her. She was delighted.

"Oh, wow! I love all that old punk stuff, it's so naff isn't it? So camp? Like, you know, so *seventies*."

I wondered when irony had become the only acceptable response to anything; when, precisely, people had decided that it just wasn't safe to actually *feel* anything anymore.

The girl passed me the clingfilmed plates of sandwiches I'd ordered, and I distributed them around the room. I stuck a few treasured old posters to the walls: creased fold-outs of the Pistols in their pomp; red-and-white handbills advertising gigs at the Marquee or the Other Cinema.

I drank a quick half and smoked half a cigarette. I was nervous. The fact was, I hadn't kept in close touch with any of the old crowd. I'd seen Andy maybe once or twice a year for a quick drink in town; most of the others I'd seen even less than that. The last time we were all together in the same room was . . . well, shit, *forever* ago.

"Can you keep an eye on things for a moment? I just need to change."

"Sure," said the barmaid. "No problem."

I took my holdall into the Gents, locked myself in a cubicle, and took off my jeans and jacket and shirt. I put on my Army surplus straights held together with an old bike padlock and chain, and a black t-shirt, faded to grey. I took off my slip-ons and replaced them with French kickers. I hadn't needed to visit a barber—my hair, these days, being short enough by nature—but I did spike up what remained of it with a comb and a blob of gel; I'd have used Brylcreem, or perhaps sugar water, back then.

"Oh, wow!" said the barmaid when I emerged. "Where did you get all that fantastic stuff?"

"I don't know. Just stuff I never threw away."

"Wow, you mean it's *authentic*! Hey, you know, that stuff might be worth something."

"I don't know. I wouldn't think so."

She looked at me more closely. "But shouldn't the t-shirt be, like, ripped?"

I just shook my head, smiled; I couldn't be bothered to explain. A ripped t-shirt was one that *got* ripped; a t-shirt ripped on purpose was for posers.

Well, I was dressed. The posters were up. The tapes were standing by.

The sandwiches were sweating. Everything was ready. I'd invited seven blokes, those I still had fairly recent addresses for, and asked them to invite anyone else they thought of. How many would turn up? Just me? Or, just me and Andy . . . I didn't fancy that. That would be even worse.

The first bloke to arrive wasn't a bloke. It was Anne. I must have looked as astonished as I felt (perhaps even—though I hoped not—as *horrified* as I felt), because she laughed and said "Hi, Steve. Hope you don't mind? I know I wasn't really invited, but . . ."

She obviously had been invited, I thought, because otherwise how would she have known about it? But who had invited her, I couldn't imagine.

"Of course not, Anne, I'm delighted to see you. It's—you look wonderful." She did. She was dressed up like Gaye Advert, black leather jacket and tight PVC trousers. Long black hair, and black eye makeup. She looked stunning.

We kissed awkwardly. You didn't kiss when you met people in the old days; that's something of the modern age, of who we've become.

To my relief—and Anne's, no doubt—the door banged again, and three men walked in. I recognized one of them (Chaz, he'd been in the Hammersmith squat with me and Andy), but I didn't know his companions. All three had dyed hair: green, with yellow highlights. It looked as if someone had been sick on their heads—someone with a streaming cold, at that—which I suppose was the idea.

Chaz introduced his nephews. Now I came to look at them, they were a good bit younger than him—nearer the barmaid's age. I was annoyed: this wasn't supposed to be a fancy dress party, for heaven's sake. But I tried not to show my annoyance, not even to myself. After all, it was only a reunion, not a sacred rite.

More people drifted in over the next half-hour or so. Old friends, old acquaintances, wives and girlfriends, friends of friends. Almost everyone had made some effort with their clothes, though the results were astonishingly varied. It seemed to me (though I don't pretend my memory's any better than anyone else's), that most of them were dressed according to 1990s ideas of what 1977 looked like.

I reckoned I was the only one wearing his own original clothes from back then—and I wasn't sure what that said about me. The worst word a modern kid can use about anyone is "sad," which seems to mean something like "enthusiastic." But the barmaid had said I looked fantastic, hadn't she? Well, no . . . she'd said my clothes were fantastic.

In the end, there were more people present than I'd feared might be the case: must have been close to twenty-five, which was about right for the occasion. A few I didn't know. A few, to be honest, I didn't remember, or barely. Rob was there; I was glad to see him, we'd been good mates. He hadn't lived in the squat, but he had got me a job in a pub near Whitehall, which had become our HQ. He was wearing straight black jeans and a long, thin tie and he was completely bald, smooth as a shaved egg. I'd pretty much lost contact with Rob sometime in the late 80s, but when you've been close to someone when you were seventeen, the years don't matter that much.

"How you doing?" I asked him, and he just shrugged and said *Oh, you know, mustn't grumble*, and then we talked about old times instead. Which—fair enough—was the reason we were there. I noticed he could hardly take his eyes off Anne. I wasn't sure if that was because he shared my shock at her presence, or just because she looked so sexy.

I was pretty busy acting like a host, so I didn't notice Andy had arrived until he tapped me on the back while I was turning over a cassette and said: "Wotcher, Stevey-boy. Good turnout."

His hair was slightly longer than was fashionable; he was wearing blue jeans, a sports jacket, and a smart denim shirt. We went up to the bar to get him a drink. While I ordered, Andy looked around him, smiling. "I see Anne made it," he said.

For the second time that night Anne caused my jaw to drop open. "You knew she was coming?" I handed him his pint.

"Cheers. Yeah, I invited her."

"*You* invited her?"

"Sure. Who wants to spend the evening at a stag do?"

"No, right. No, I'm glad she's here. I just—I didn't even know you were still in touch."

"Why wouldn't we be, Stevey? We were married, you know, albeit briefly."

A hand fell on his shoulder from behind, and Chaz said: "Andy, mate— is that you? Oh man, great to see you. Great!"

"Chaz." Andy put down his beer, and they shook hands. I got the impression Chaz was trying to do some black-kid thing with fingers and thumbs, but if he was it crumbled inside Andy's firm, conventional grip.

Chaz fingered one of Andy's lapels. "But mate, shame on you—you're not dressed up."

"Never mind, Chaz. You're punk enough for both of us. Nice hair."

Chaz ran his fingers through his Day-Glo spikes. "Oh, yeah. Well, no harm in a little nostalgia, right?"

Andy shrugged. "Sure."

"You don't agree?" Chaz smiled in the fixed way people do when they're not going to have a fight, but they're not going to let it go, either.

"I just think being nostalgic for punk is maybe a contradiction in terms."

"Sort of un-punk?" I said. I felt I knew what he meant.

"If you like. Besides, life is better now than it was then. We had a revolution and it worked—so why look back?"

"Surprised you turned up, then," said Chaz. "Still—great to see you." He moved further down the bar, and began waving a tenner to attract the barmaid's attention.

"Always was a bit of a poser," I said.

"Bloke's entitled to his point of view. They're *his* memories. Tell you what, I should have come in my work gear." Andy worked as a nurse in a busy casualty department. "Head to toe in blood and vomit—he'd have liked that."

"So. Why did you come, if you're not into All Our Yesterdays?"

He clinked his glass against mine. "See some old mates. It's good to keep in touch. No, all I'm saying is, punk wasn't a fashion, something that can be reproduced by wearing the right clothes or dyeing your hair. It was about how you walked, stood, the expression on your face, your tone of voice. Your outlook."

"Fair point," I said. But I couldn't help wondering if there was another reason why Andy didn't feel nostalgic about 1977; because that was the year he killed a kid with his bare hands.

. . . . .

When I first arrived at the squat, all I knew about punks was what I'd seen on the news, or read in the *Daily Mirror*. They couldn't play their instruments, they looked like freaks, they had no respect for anything, and they were violent. When Andy persuaded me to go to my first punk rock gig I was nervous, frankly. Excited but nervous.

I never knew Andy's full story; his accent was from somewhere up in the Midlands, maybe Wolverhampton, but it soon faded, and he ended up speaking the kind of universal sub-Cockney that was youth's Esperanto. He never admitted to a surname, not in those days, and he never offered much in the way of biography, except to say that he'd come down to London for the music, and because back home everything and everyone was "dead." I took this to mean that, like the rest of us, he wanted a few laughs before he got old and died. Obviously, there was something he wasn't talking about: a violent dad, maybe, or a juvenile criminal conviction. It wasn't a mystery that I found interesting enough to pursue. I was simply glad that he wanted to be mates with me, this quiet, rather serious-minded, grown-up man (he was nineteen, I was seventeen), who always knew where things were happening, and shared his knowledge without condescension. As a new boy in the big city, I felt safe in his company. In part this was because there was, behind his wry eyes and hidden in his understanding smile, an unmistakeable glint of danger. The first time I met him, I remember thinking: "You wouldn't want to be his enemy."

My own story was a simple one. Born in Kent, didn't much take to school, moved to London as soon as I could. I got on OK with my parents; even phoned them every now and then. I wasn't a runaway—I was just a teenager who'd moved to London. Where else was there to be, if you were young in the summer of '77?

Andy, Jamie, and Rob were already regular attendees at various of London's mushrooming punk venues. They'd seen all the bands I'd heard of, and many that I hadn't. Chaz used to tag along as well, although I don't think he really had any close friends at the squat. He was in some ways the opposite of Andy: he tried to be a mystery man, and failed. Jamie's summing-up of him was blunt, typically Glaswegian, and generally accepted: "He's a middle-class tosser, thinks wearing anarchy symbols makes him cool, but he's harmless enough."

If I'd been on my own at that first gig, I would never have got into the dancing. In fact, if I'd been on my own, I'd quite likely have turned tail the moment I passed through the weapons search in the corridor, and walked through the doors into a living definition of claustrophobia.

There were a few hundred kids there, mostly boys, and their collective *thrum* of newness and rebellion was something the press reports could never have prepared me for. It was alien and frightening and my stomach walls were squirting cold-hot liquid at each other . . . and as my heartbeat and my breathing gradually attuned themselves to this new world, I began to think that maybe I'd come home.

Between us and the small stage there were rows of tip-back chairs, and there was hardly room to get into the place, let alone to move around. Drinking from the plastic beer glasses was difficult enough, hemmed in by elbows and hips; rolling a cigarette would have required a dexterity far beyond my skills.

The lights went down, Jimmy Pursey yelled *One two three four!* and Sham 69 leapt into—I don't know, I don't remember exactly. It could have been "What Have We Got," though I seem to remember they used that as a closer, so maybe it was "They Don't Understand." Whatever it was, it was big and strong and hard and relentless, and I'd never in my life heard music so driving, so physical. The guitar chords raced each other up the hall and tore holes in my body.

"Come on," Andy shouted in my ear. "Let's go down the front."

I'd have preferred to stay put, not too far from the illuminated exit sign. Apart from anything, getting to the front would involve fighting through an almost solid mass of leaping, screaming flesh. But the others set off toward the stage, and I had either to follow them or lose them.

You couldn't actually stand in the space immediately in front of the stage. It was too crowded for that; the only way that many people could all occupy such a small floor simultaneously was by jumping up and down, taking turns to annex the vertical so that your neighbours could occupy the horizontal. In 1977, choreography wasn't an art or a science, it was a force of nature.

That's how the pogo was born, I would guess; from teenagers full of uncontrollable energy, responding to music that could never be listened to static, played in venues designed for audiences half the size. That—and the sheer speed of the beat. The conduits of information between brain and limbs weren't up to a job like this. By the time the message had travelled from head to knees, the beat had gone—and you were already too late to catch the next one. Just jump up and down: that's all there was time for.

I'd never done it before, or even seen it done, but it seemed as if my legs were veterans of the pogo while my brain was still back at the box office queuing for a ticket.

I jumped, jerking my body upwards from the hips, twisting and writhing at the point where my ascent peaked, forcing out an extra inch of flight, then using my landing to shoot me back up. It sounds effortful, but really I seemed to be hovering more than jumping. A teenager is a kind of furnace, who burns his childhood inside his belly for fuel.

My glasses flew off my nose. I caught them and shoved them in my pocket. Andy grabbed me round the throat and began to shake me.

Oh, Christ, I thought. *Here's the violence.*

His eyes were pure danger now, all rage and no wry. I didn't want to do it, but I had no choice—to save myself, I put my own hands around his throat, trying to hold him at arm's length. It was only as his mouth split into a wild smile, and then as he goggled his eyes and lolled his tongue, making believe he was choking, that I realized: my neck didn't hurt. I could breathe normally. I relaxed my own fingers, suddenly embarrassed and afraid at the force with which they'd been digging into him.

Locked together, we took it in turns to jump and kick our legs out, leaving our weight momentarily on the other guy's shoulders. We caromed around the floor, bouncing off other people, knocking them sprawling, sweat flying from our hair, and at the song's peremptory end, we spun away from each other, ending up on our arses amid a million legs.

I wondered how that was possible: how did we have enough space to fall over? I looked at Andy's laughing face and saw the answer: we'd made our own space.

The singer was swearing at the people who were still standing at the bar, clutching pints. "Tossers! Why ain't you dancing? This lot down here, they're the ones that count. They're the only ones we're playing for!"

And he pointed at me and my mates. We were the ones they were playing for. If you've ever been seventeen, you'll know how good that felt.

. . . . .

About half an hour after the last tape had finished, no one at the reunion had bothered to turn it over—including me. It wasn't that sort of evening. There wasn't going to be any pogoing tonight, let alone throttling.

By ten o'clock there were only half a dozen of us left, sitting round a couple of the tables, chatting, drinking moderately. Andy and Anne seemed relaxed, courteous with each other, though they didn't have much to say to each other. Chaz had left early, with his nephews—to go on to a seventies disco that one of them ran. Chaz at least had the decency to look a little embarrassed when his nephew let that slip. They offered us free tickets, but no one took them up. I might have been arrested for assault if anybody had.

Nobody had mentioned Jamie all night. I hadn't expected anyone would. For all I knew, I was the only one who remembered him.

I looked around at my old punk rock comrades: a nurse, a computer guy, a plumber. Anne was a housewife, with two children at school. Having spent twenty years doing crap jobs, I was halfway through a non-graduate-entry teacher training course. I was proud of that; didn't like to say so, didn't seem very punk to say it, but I was a not very academic bloke who'd left school a few days before my sixteenth birthday. I wanted to be a teacher because almost all the teachers I ever had were sadists or morons or defeatists.

The conversation at first was of the catching-up type you'd expect, and then, as the alcohol did its gentle work, we moved on to soul-searching. Rob and Andy held the floor mostly, while the rest of us listened and nodded and contributed the occasional affectionate insult. I gathered from what they said that the two of them had seen quite a bit of each other over the years, though I'd never had them down as big pals, particularly, in the old days.

Rob was the punkiest of us, so it seemed, despite his bald dome and the fact that he was on orange juice. He'd never had a steady job, never been married, still went to gigs, still lived the punk life. "Unlike you load of BOFs," he said, and we all laughed at Anne, who had to have the phrase *Boring Old Fart* explained to her.

Andy was as I remembered him; calm and quiet, serious but always amused. Never a shouter, but never one to say something just to make people comfortable. "For the record, Andy," I told him, "I reckon you're the only authentic-looking ex-punk here."

He gave me a puzzled frown, though I'm sure he knew what I meant.

I gestured at his sports jacket and clean jeans. "Well, that's what real ex-punks look like when they're knocking forty, isn't it?"

Amid the jeers and cries of "Never trust anyone over thirty," Andy said: "I'm not an ex-punk. I'm a punk. I always was punk, and I always will be."

Someone said: "In *those* shoes?"

"DIY," said Andy, and we all fell quiet, ready to hear something worthwhile. "Do-it-yourself, use the materials at hand to make the world a place you want to inhabit, that was punk. And you can do that all your life. I don't just mean music—any aspect of life. Give you an example. I'm a good cook, you know? Dab-hand with the old wok, maestro of the flung-together stir-fry. But I've never read a recipe in my life."

. . . . .

Anne and Andy met in an all-night snack bar not far from Big Ben. She was working there, he was eating there. He asked her out and she said, "Yeah, why not?" It was 2 A.M. Their first date, later that morning, consisted of having sex in an empty car park. For the second date, she took him to the pictures.

She was never into punk, which would have made her all but invisible to the rest of us except that she was too pretty to be invisible. The announcement of their wedding came as a shock; getting married wasn't a very punk thing to do. As wedding announcements go, it wasn't very formal. One evening, Anne came into the pub where I was working and asked me if Andy had been in yet.

"Not yet. You supposed to be meeting him here?"

She shrugged. "Yeah, you know. Talk about the wedding and that."

"What, you're going to a wedding?" I gave my lips a little twist as I released the words, like a bowler putting on spin. We didn't go to weddings, our sort. Funerals, maybe, they might be quite cool. But not *weddings*!

"Yeah," said Anne. "So are you—you've got to be a witness."

"What witness?"

"At the registry. Yeah? You and one of the others. Jamie, maybe. Me and Andy, we need two witnesses, when we get married. You've got to have two, it's the law. I don't know why. In case one of them's lying or something, I don't know."

It was mostly Andy's friends at the registry office. A cousin of Anne's did attend, wearing a hat, but she cleared off as soon as she decently could, and that was it for family on either side.

After the ceremony, about half a dozen of us went off to somewhere in the country, on a train. A cottage in Kent, or somewhere, owned by some

old hippies that Anne knew. They'd lent her the place for a sort of combination wedding party and honeymoon.

Speed was the true punk drug—a fast, urban buzz, harmonizing with the
fast, loud guitars of the music—but for that occasion it didn't seem appropriate, so we compromised our principles and stuck with dope and cider. My
only big memory of our rural sojourn is of staying up all night—the weather
was very hot, must have been high summer—and at one point, sitting outside the house on the front step of the cottage watching the sun come up.
Feeling tired, but completely awake. Shivering slightly from the brief period
of chill that comes at the dawn of even the hottest day. Pulling my jacket
across my chest, and putting my hands deep in the pockets: we'd all worn
hired suits to the wedding, as a laugh. (Oh, God—is *punk* responsible for
irony?)

Then, about six in the morning, going into the little house, seeing a pile
of people snoring and farting on the living-room floor, going up to use the
bog, looking out of the landing window and seeing Anne and Jamie kissing
in the back garden. She was wearing his jacket, and she had one hand behind
his head, a cigarette between the fingers.

It was a very short marriage. I never said anything to Andy, so I can only
assume that Anne did, or Jamie maybe, or perhaps Andy himself looked out
of a window and saw what I saw. At any rate, by the time we headed back to
London that evening, they were no longer a married couple in any but the
legal sense.

. . . . .

These days, the 1970s is packaged as a fashionable, cherishable decade, the
greatest flowering of a sweetly naïve kind of cool. That's not how those of
us who were there remember it. Before punk rock, with its snarling singers
and its rude graphics, the mid-70s were cold and grey, unfriendly, and above
all, *boring*.

Let me tell you about punk music, about what it meant to us. Or to me,
at least. It wasn't about anarchy—we weren't anarchists, you have to study
to be an anarchist. It was simpler than that: for the first time, or at least the
first time for white kids since skiffle, pop music became something you could
do instead of just something you consumed.

Just before punk detonated, you could buy a Yes concept album and listen to it—and that was it, that was your part of the process finished. Punk
was as different as it could have been. If you liked the noise, you just *became*
punk. Thousands of kids formed bands about ten minutes after hearing their
first punk single. People used to say "But they can't play their instruments,"
not realizing that that was the whole point! Music isn't as hard as people

make out—that's something all the young punks discovered, as bluesmen thirty or forty years earlier had discovered.

All you needed was two chords on the guitar, a bassist who could count up to four by tapping his feet, and someone who could shout loud enough to be heard over the drums—the technical, musicological term for this latter Herbert being "lead vocalist."

The lyrics; that was the easiest bit of all. You just said what was going on in your life, in your head: "I'm bored. Working is crap. School is crap. I want excitement. I'm scared." Same with the dancing. You can jump up and down, can't you? Fine, then you're dancing—so get down to the front and dance.

You didn't even need to be in a band to be part of punk. If you wanted to be part of it, believed you were part of it, acted like you were part of it, you were part of it. If you felt punk, you were punk, whether you were the editor of a Roneo'd fanzine in the heart of punkland, or a school kid in rural Wales. There was no distance between the band and the crowd; they were just the same as us, except they'd managed to get hold of an amp from somewhere, and we hadn't, or hadn't yet, or didn't want to. In 1977, all the bands were garage bands.

If you wanted to be a punk, the only thing that could stop you was death.

. . . . .

The night Jamie died, about a fortnight after the wedding, we'd been to see an all-girl group in the cellar of a pub near Kings Cross. By then, just about every space in London was putting on gigs, live music was alive again for the first time in ages.

This particular place was even less suitable as a venue for a music club than most: the sound was dreadful, the heat was unbearable, and the beer was warmer than the air. We were having a great time; me, Andy, Rob, and Jamie. Anne had been there—not with anyone as far as I could tell, just hanging around, almost as if the wedding, and the break-up with Andy had never happened. But it wasn't really her sort of place, and she left well before the end, saying she'd meet us later at a pub down the road.

"I'm going outside," Rob told me, though I understood him mainly by sign language. "Get some air."

"Right," I said, thinking I might follow him, but just then the band went into a number that was even faster than the stuff they'd been playing so far, and I decided to have one last jump around the floor.

Andy and Jamie were already on the floor, slamming into each other, ricocheting off strangers. One of Jamie's slams pretty near knocked Andy off his feet, and I felt a flash of unease; neither of them was smiling. I pogoed over to them, with the vague idea of doing some kind of peace-keeping, but I was too late. They had their hands around each other's throats, and even if no one else in the place noticed it, I could tell they weren't dancing.

I couldn't get to them through the crowd, so I just had to watch as Jamie's mouth worked—to take in air, or to expel curses, or both—and as his fingers lost their hold on Andy's neck, and dropped to his sides. Andy was smiling. Jamie's teeth danced and his bones rattled, and Andy smiled.

. . . . .

Two guys I didn't know very well were at the bar getting a round in, and Rob was lost in conversation with Anne, when Andy put his arm along the back of my chair, leaned forward, and spoke directly into my ear.

"I didn't kill Jamie, you know."

I couldn't quite manage to say *"What?"* so I just looked at him.

"All these years it's been bothering you, Stevey-boy, and you've never said anything, and I thought tonight might be the time to get it sorted."

"All right."

"Not now, obviously. Later—when everyone else has pissed off. I'll stay behind, help you to pack up. All right?"

"All right," I said, and was surprised I managed to say that much.

. . . . .

One long, distorting chord ended the set, and a bunch of punks rushed the stage. The girls in the band beat them off with kung fu kicks and spittle.

The lights came up, and Andy dropped Jamie—dropped him, I mean, like you'd drop a bag of rubbish into a swing-bin. I caught Andy's eye. He just shook his head, and marched off toward the exit.

"You all right, mate?" Jamie was slumped against a big speaker, holding his throat with one hand and rubbing at his ribs with the other. I reached out a hand to help him up.

"Just sod off, Steve," he said. So I did. I deliberately didn't catch up with Andy.

The next morning, Jamie was found dead in an alley, in amongst the dustbins of a Chinese restaurant, a few yards from the club we'd been in. It said in the *Evening Standard* that he'd been throttled.

Most people remember pogoing as the punk dance, but to me, the choke has far greater symbolic resonance. It epitomizes so much of that era: the desire to break with the past, the need to shock, the way everything was a laugh, even though everything was deadly serious, the pretend violence. Except, of course, that violence never is pretend.

. . . . .

Rob was the last to leave the reunion, apart from the two of us. He drained his final orange juice, smacked his lips as if it had been best ale, and got up to go. We'd already told the barmaid to get off home, not to worry about the cleaning up.

"Well, lads," he said. "That was a quick twenty years. Not bad, but a bit quick."

Twenty years, I thought. *Bloody hell.* "Let's make the next twenty count more, yeah? I mean, I really wish we'd kept in touch better. You know? This time, let's do it, not just say it." I held out my hand for a handshake. I really meant what I was saying. How had I virtually lost touch with someone who used to be such a mate?

Rob blinked, and his cheeks crinkled. He put his arms around me, and I could feel his bald scalp against my ear and his dry lips pressed for a short second against my neck.

I was amazed. I'd never have expected to see him act so emotional, especially when he hadn't been drinking. It took me a moment to recover, but when I did, I patted his back, squeezed his shoulder. "Look after yourself, Rob. Keep the faith, eh?"

Andy didn't wait to be asked. He enfolded Rob in a solid embrace, and said "I'll phone you."

We sipped at our drinks when he'd gone and smoked a couple of cigarettes, and then I said: "So?"

Andy nodded. "I want to thank you for organizing tonight, Steve. It's been good for me."

"Despite the nostalgia?"

"Reminded me what it's all about."

"Which was?"

"Is," he said. "What it is all about. Breaking up the established order. Bringing music back to the kids."

"Yeah, but did it work?" By 1978, people were saying punk was just another fashion. You'd see trendies wearing expensive bondage gear. Genuinely individual, rebel New Wave bands were being turned down by major labels for being "not punk enough," despite the fact that the real punk rockers had always admired, and worked with musicians from all sorts of different styles. "I mean, look at the kids nowadays—"

"Look at the kids nowadays," said Andy, and we both laughed.

"Yeah, I know, it's what every generation says. But don't you reckon? We set out to murder boredom, but boredom's become a lifestyle option. It's all satellite TV and computer games and music that would have sounded tame half a century ago! Even the drugs are boring. You've got kids of nineteen talking about careers, for Christ's sake. They either put up with boredom, or they actively *treasure* it—because life's so dangerous and horrible that a bit of boredom is a relief."

"Sure," he said. "But their children won't. I'll bet you. You can't keep the kids quiet forever. One tame generation, maybe, then it'll turn again. Seventy-year-old punks and their grandchildren'll be out to all hours smashing up clubs and getting arrested. Don't you worry, Stevey: boy bands and tribute bands contain within themselves the seeds of their own destruction."

I hoped he was right, and listening to him tell it, I was far from sure he wasn't. I drained my glass and said: "If it wasn't you, who was it?"

. . . . .

For me—for all of us, I would guess—the punk summer disintegrated the day we heard about Jamie's death and everybody split up. The way we lived, the way we thought, it was only natural that we'd run rather than talk to cops, innocent or guilty.

The punk explosion was more or less dead by that autumn, in any case. Which was no bad thing. Previous youth movements had made the mistake of thinking they were going to go on forever; we believed the exact opposite right from the start. We didn't despise people for selling out, we despised them for pretending not to sell out.

I found another squat for a while, then a bedsit, and eventually I got a council flat near my parents. I took a job in a local factory and helped my mum look after my dad while he was dying.

I never went to the police with what I knew, the half-strangling I'd seen in that club. I never mentioned it to anyone, and never confronted Andy with it, after we'd met up again by chance three or four years later.

At the time, my silence was instinctive, but as Rat Scabies once said "You can't help growing up." So, after twenty years of growing up, I held a punk reunion above a pub near Waterloo, and they all came.

. . . . .

"It was Rob," said Andy, and I knew at once that it was true.

"Why?"

"Rob's never gone into details, and I've never demanded any, but my belief is that when Rob left the club, he went to meet Anne at that pub. He made a pass at her, she turned him down. He headed back toward the club, met Jamie coming out, and—well, you know, old Jamie could have quite a sharp tongue on him."

"You think they had a row?"

"More likely Jamie figured out where Rob had been, what he'd been up to, and taunted him about it. Rob went for him, and of course Jamie was in a weakened state, because of . . ." He spread his fingers, like a manual shrug.

"You and him, choking each other on the dance floor."

"You thought I'd killed him because of him and Anne. Well, Stevey-boy, I almost did."

"I know. I thought you had, for a moment."

"But I didn't." Andy stubbed out his cigarette, and his face looked as serious—and yet as happy—as I had ever seen it. "It just came to me, from nowhere. Lack of oxygen to the brain, maybe, I don't know. But I had a sudden realization—that I didn't have to be like that anymore. I was a *punk*: I could be what I wanted. I was a self-made man, made of safety pins and glue."

"Who else knows?"

"Not Anne," he said. "She probably still thinks it was me. Or maybe she doesn't. She's never talked about it. For her, it's something that happened in the past, and therefore something that doesn't exist."

"How do you mean?"

"You never saw her wearing punk gear before tonight, did you? She was more into disco back then. As far as she's concerned, you're a kid, then you grow up, and whatever happened when you were a kid doesn't count when you're grown up. If she didn't think that, she'd never have agreed to come tonight."

"Just you and Rob?"

Andy smiled. "And Chaz."

"You're joking!"

"Chaz knew. He was there when Rob told me. He knew, and he's never said a word."

"Just like Anne."

"Except that with him, what happened when we were young is nostalgia. Same result; the past isn't real."

"And you?" I asked the inevitable question. "Why didn't you ever say anything?"

"What good would have it done? Rob was just unlucky."

"*Unlucky* to have killed a mate?"

"Sure. Millions of lads fight over birds and booze, all over the planet, every day of every year. A boy doesn't deserve to have his life destroyed for a bit of bad luck—not if he's fundamentally a good man."

"And Rob is?"

"I've kept an eye on him, over the years. If he'd disappointed me, I might have acted differently."

"But what's he done that's so great? What's he done with his life?"

"He's stuck to being who he thinks he ought to be. You can't ask more than that of a man."

"So why tell me now?"

Andy paused, as if waiting for me to catch up, and then said: "He asked me to."

"Rob did? Why?" But even as I put the question, I saw the answer. "Oh, God . . ."

"Yeah. He won't be around for the next reunion, I'm afraid."

"Oh my God." Bald Rob with his orange juice and his dry kiss.

"He wanted you to know, because he wishes he'd told you years ago. Because he's never stopped thinking of you as a friend."

The weight of twenty years wasted on occasional acquaintanceship, where there might have been constant friendship, almost crushed the air from my lungs. Rob, Andy—even Chaz and Anne, maybe, who could say? It wasn't going to happen again. "Andy. You said that when you were strangling Jamie in the club, and you stopped, it was because you realized you didn't have to be like that *anymore*."

"Yeah. That's something else I came here to tell you. Before I moved to London, all those years ago, I killed a man."

"Why? I mean—who?"

He shook his head. "Doesn't matter. It was a—a *friend* of my mother's. Point is, I'm giving you my secret for the same reason Rob gave you his." He leaned forward, locked onto my eyes. "You understand?"

"Sure. Yes, I do."

"Good. I was thinking, maybe you could come round and meet my family sometime?"

"Yes. I'd like to."

"You've never met my wife. My little daughter." He laughed. "The flat that eats my wages up, paying off the mortgage. You've never met my life. And I'd like you to, because it's a good life."

"Redemption through punk rock," I said.

He shook his head, lit another cigarette. "If you like. I don't know about redemption, but . . . I don't know if I told you, I'm a union rep. I led a strike last Christmas. They wanted to reduce the number of emergency beds at our hospital, and we weren't having it."

"What happened?"

"We won." His face glowed. "We were fierce and full of rage and acting unafraid, and they backed down and we won. You see what we were doing, Steve? You know what we were doing?"

I nodded. I did know. "You were jumping up and down."

"*Right*, Stevey-boy! We were pogoing in their faces and gobbing on their shiny shoes and shouting in their ears and shocking them with our war paint. The fact that half of us couldn't have *actually* pogoed if our lives depended on it, because our old knees are too knackered, and the other half were too young to have ever *heard* of pogoing didn't matter. We were punk, and that's why we won."

. . . . .

Let me tell you about punk rock. For an exhilarating few months, the kids controlled the music. The business, the media, they had no influence over what was happening. They recovered quickly, of course, and re-established the status quo, and they learned from it—they determined never to let things get out of hand again.

They learned from it; but so did we.

"No future" was the big slogan back then, and it's only taken me half a lifetime to figure out what it means. The future never arrives, and the past never departs, and what matters in between isn't *how* you dance—it's *why* you dance. And the day you realize that is the day you go punk.

We're still out there, us old punk rockers. We don't bother with the safety pins anymore, or the bondage trousers, or the gobbing. But you'll know us when you see us. We're the ones jumping up and down.

TANGO WAS HER LIFE
John Lutz

It was a poor country.

The bus that drove them from the port where their cruise ship _Fiesta Grande_ was docked bucked and rocked over unpaved roads, hugging the flanks of thickly wooded mountains. It was hot in the ancient gray bus. The tops of the windows were open to allow only a humid breeze as warm as the outside air. If the larger sections below were open, dust stirred and made the air in the bus almost unbreathable. On top of that, the bus driver had warned them ominously in Spanish-burdened English that sometimes the tires threw rocks up that bounced from the mountain sides and would strike their bare arms or faces with the force of bullets.

"Bullets," Aggie Armright said beside Mary Beth. "Don't you think he's exaggerating a bit?"

"It's a romantic country," Mary Beth said. "Exaggeration is a part of romance."

Aggie, a fellow schoolteacher and longtime friend of Mary Beth's, glanced sideways at her and smiled. "And you're a romantic."

Mary Beth returned the smile. "An unabashed and unapologetic one." How could one not be a romantic, here in a country to which the tango had traveled north from Argentina, and lately become important as a tourist attraction? It was an extension of the growing worldwide popularity of ballroom dancing.

Though both women were the same age, forty-five, Mary Beth looked younger than Aggie. Where Aggie was bone thin with a long nose and jaw,

Mary Beth was rather shapely and had a heart-shaped face that reflected a trusting and generous nature. Aggie's eyes were dark and narrow and cynical. Mary Beth's were soft blue and wide and, though somewhat disillusioned from over twenty years of teaching middle-school children in impoverished neighborhoods, wide open and on the lookout for a smile.

"Sweeping dirt from a dirt porch," Aggie observed, as the bus passed a row of leaning shanties that appeared ready to collapse in a heap. She was referring to a heavyset woman in a flower-print dress who was diligently wielding a broom on the hard earth area beneath a sagging porch roof. "What's the point?"

"Pride, I suspect," Mary Beth said.

She noticed that the houses' tin roofs were secured with nails driven through upside-down bottle caps, depending on the cork to provide a seal to keep out the rain. In front of some of the shanties were small children seated on the sunbaked ground or on boxes, staring dully at the passing bus. An old man with a white beard sat smoking a pipe, not bothering to glance at the rumbling, rattling vehicle.

"I don't see pride in their eyes," Aggie said. "Or hope."

"The woman with the broom," Mary Beth reminded her.

The bus lurched around a corner. Packages and carry-ons dropped from the metal racks above the seats. A man carrying a live chicken in a cage cleverly made of bent twigs fell from his seat onto the floor. A few gray feathers drifted aimlessly in the dusty air.

Mary Beth watched as the other passengers regarded the man silently. No one moved to help him as he stiffly regained his balance and slid back into his seat, the caged chicken beside him.

"A poor country and cruel," Aggie said.

"Finalmente!" the driver called. "Finally we are almost there, my buenos amigos."

"Schtick for the tourists," Aggie said in disgust.

"El hotel, amigos!"

After the bus ride, Mary Beth hadn't expected much. But the hotel was worth the driver's enthusiasm. The bus jounced onto smooth pavement, then slowed as it glided between rows of palm trees bordering a long driveway edged with brilliant tropical blooms. With a squeal and hiss of air brakes, it stopped beneath the roof of a large white portico before the hotel entrance. The vehicle's accordion doors folded open.

"The Hotel Hermoso!" proclaimed the dusty and heavily perspiring driver. "Your casa, amigos!"

The passengers got to their feet and began filing from the bus. Most of them tipped the driver, who stood at the front of the bus and grinned and nodded at them. Aggie glared at him and walked past. Mary Beth tipped for both of them. The driver widened his grin and nodded vigorously. Off to the side, a tall, slender man in his thirties, with wavy black hair and dark eyes that were liquid and vulnerable, smiled his approval. Mary Beth remembered seeing him at the dock when they came down the *Fiesta Grande's* gangplank. This was how bullfighters should look, she had told herself. And tango dancers.

Tango dancing was why Mary Beth had come here, and why she would stay here after Aggie had left on the *Fiesta Grande.* Mary Beth would take the commuter plane and catch up with the ship later at Tortola, off the coast of Venezuela.

After retiring from teaching two years ago, Mary Beth had decided to take ballroom dance lessons in order to meet people and develop more of a social life. She had always been shy, and now was the time to broaden her life, to force herself out of her comfort zone.

It hadn't taken her long to learn to dance and dance well. She was a natural, her instructor David at Just Dancing assured her. And it was true. Dancing with David, Mary Beth entered competitions and won medals and trophies. She had won nothing in her years of teaching. Her best dance, the dance she came to love, was the tango. In it the man dominated, taking long, stalking steps, never quite straightening his legs, while the woman followed his strong lead. The partners moved in a slight curve across the dance floor as Mary Beth at first had to spell out the dance mentally, T-A-N-G-O, with a sweeping side step to her right on the G, then closing her feet slowly on the O. Soon she no longer had to spell to keep time as she danced, and the steps became more intricate and she mastered the abrupt head movements with pivots and changes of direction. Her partner led now with his entire torso rather than his arms and shoulders, his right thigh sometimes tight between her legs as he drove her backward, then led her into swivels and contra checks, precise and elegant open fans that ended with the rejoining of their bodies.

It was a romantic dance but with a partner she paid and who was married to a friend. Commerce and romance were a mismatch.

But Mary Beth had become addicted to tango. She learned more about it, about how in this country it was becoming among some people virtually a religion. A romantic religion. In a poor country it was people's lives. In a poor country Mary Beth would seek the riches and fulfillments of romance. In a poor country she would dance the tango.

Eager bellhops scurried for the luggage, which they loaded onto wicker carts festooned with pineapples. Mary Beth and Aggie registered at the long marble desk and took an elevator to the fourth-floor room they would share.

While Aggie investigated to make sure the plumbing was in order in the tile bathroom, Mary Beth opened the drapes.

She was astounded by the beauty of the hotel's manicured grounds. Curving pathways wended among palm trees and colorful shrubbery. The trunks of the palms were painted white, as was an array of statuary. There was a bar and restaurant, and a gleaming outdoor dance floor beneath a thatched pavilion roof. Closer to the shore of a wide blue lake bordered by a distant green jungle were a series of smaller thatch-roofed structures. At the edge of the lake was a long dock where pleasure boats and smaller dinghies were tied up. As Mary Beth watched, a man in a white suit and a woman with a long dress climbed into one of the smaller boats. The man cast the line and settled down to row, while the woman sat gracefully with her back to Mary Beth.

"Looking at our friend?" Aggie said beside her.

At first Mary Beth didn't understand, then she saw the tall, slender man from when the *Fiesta Grande* had docked. He was standing motionless with his fists on his hips, staring out at the lake. The breeze ruffled his dark hair that was worn slightly too long at the back of his neck. He was wearing white slacks and a sleeveless white shirt. His arms were tanned and muscular.

"A beautiful sight," Aggie said.

"The lake," Mary Beth said.

Aggie smiled. "You could drown in it."

Mary Beth shook her head. "You think too much in terms of the half-full glass."

"You can't drown in a glass."

"Very sage," Mary Beth said with a grin. "Let's unpack then go down to the bar. I want to drown in some exotic drink with a parasol in it."

. . . . .

That night there was a dance beneath the pavilion roof. Colored paper lanterns bathed everything in soft hues. A white-coated band played soft Latin music. Most people were at the long buffet, but a few couples were doing a slow rumba at the edge of the dance floor.

Mary Beth was wearing the pale blue dress she'd bought on St. Thomas, white high-heeled pumps, a necklace of white shells about her neck. Aggie had on dark slacks and a sleeveless silk blouse. Often when Mary Beth traveled, in order to discourage men's advances she wore her dead mother's plain gold wedding band. Now she removed it and placed it in her evening bag.

By the time Mary Beth and Aggie had finished their shrimp cocktails there were more couples on the dance floor. A plump man in khaki slacks and a bright tropical shirt steered a path to the table. Mary Beth held her breath. He asked Aggie to dance. Aggie glanced at Mary Beth, surprised, as she smiled graciously and stood up. Mary Beth watched them join the other couples on the floor, doing a simple box step to fox trot music.

"They will soon be playing music too fast to dance to properly," a voice said near Mary Beth.

She glanced up, astounded to see the slim, handsome man from the dock. He was wearing a tailored cream-colored suit, pale blue shirt and darker blue tie. He extended his hand.

She was unexpectedly paralyzed. "You're asking me to dance?"

He smiled. "Of course. The other men are afraid to approach you."

She stood up, laughing. "I doubt that."

He held her hand and led her onto the dance floor, then into a simple two step. She knew immediately by his lead that he could dance well. He stood discreetly away from her so there was space between their bodies, leading only with arms and shoulders.

"You dance very skillfully," he said.

"I've had lessons. I think you've had some, too."

He smiled with perfect white teeth, like a model in a fantasy perfume ad, she thought. "In this country," he said, "everyone learns to dance."

"The tango?"

"Especially the tango."

He opened up slightly, taking larger steps and leading her counter-clockwise around the outer edges of the dance floor. Mary Beth had no trouble following his lead. Aggie and her partner danced past. Aggie did a double take that brought a smile to Mary Beth's face.

"You enjoy the dance," the man said in his slight Spanish accent. He danced well enough that it was easy to carry on a conversation as they moved over the floor.

"Very much," she said, thinking not of the dance they were doing but of the tango. The dance of male dominance and romance, when a woman was swept away by passion. It required a degree of trust, she told herself.

"I am Enrico." He had the faintest of scents, pleasant but masculine.

"Mary Beth Adams."

"An American on vacation?"

She laughed. "You must already have guessed that."

"I guessed your dour friend was an American on vacation, but not you. Perhaps you were her whimsical French friend. We get many French people as turistas."

"It's a beautiful country."

"France?"

He knew better. "Of course not," she said, smiling. "I meant your country."

He nodded somberly, his liquid dark eyes heavily lidded. "In places it is beautiful."

"You seem sad."

"I want to help my country. That's why I go to the university to study engineering. I know I seem old for that, but my uncle in Barbados left me a small inheritance. I decided to use it not only for myself, but for others."

"You don't seem old at all," she said. "You're still in your thirties."

"Like you. You are a professional woman like so many Americans?"

"Yes. A teacher." No need to correct him on her age.

"Ah! You see. We have something in common. We both want to help people."

"I suppose that's true," Mary Beth said. She decided not to tell him she'd taken early retirement, another burnout in a vocation that took its toll at an earlier and earlier age.

The music stopped and he smiled and stood back from her. "Thank you."

She couldn't answer because of the lump in her throat as he took her hand and escorted her back toward the table.

They made it halfway before the tango music began.

Mary Beth couldn't help it. She paused, making it obvious she wanted to stay on the dance floor.

Knowing what she wanted—he would always know what she wanted—he turned toward her and held her in dance position, still keeping his distance.

He was a marvelous tango dancer, taking command immediately, confidently leading her in long, sweeping steps across the floor, then in turns and rondes. She followed flawlessly, wishing only that he would hold her close, that they might dance together as she knew they could. She glanced to the side and saw a Spanish-looking woman cling tightly to her partner and do a leg crawl, standing on one foot and wrapping her raised stockinged leg about his hip and thigh. Sexy, she thought. The tango was not only about love, but about sex. About life. And she knew that like others before her she was consumed by the tango.

". . . the music," Enrico was saying. "It's stopped."

Mary Beth looked around and saw that other couples were leaving the dance floor.

The band began playing something faster, a simple four-beat rhythm that drew the younger dancers out onto the floor where they would contort their bodies and gyrate free form without touching each other. People not touching each other, Mary Beth thought. Isolation withering living things as if it were a disease.

At the table she sat down, hoping he'd ask to join her.

He read her mind again and smiled. "I'm afraid I have to retire. I have an early appointment tomorrow. Business."

"I thought you were a student."

"I am that. But I'm also still a businessman. A small wine importing business. I have two children to support."

Mary Beth's heart dived into cold water. *Why did he have to tell me?* "You're married?" She'd spoken without thinking. Words, thoughts, were jumping out of her unbidden tonight.

Enrico's smile widened but his dark eyes were sad. "My wife died three years ago in a plane crash. A small private plane. My uncle's. He survived only for another week."

"I'm sorry . . . I shouldn't have been so nosy."

He shook his head. "You freely express your thoughts. I like that about you. I hope we see each other again." He bowed slightly and kissed her hand. He actually kissed her hand.

Speechless, she watched him walk away, his tall figure weaving gracefully among the dancers. She watched him ascend the wooden steps toward the hotel, then stroll into the darkness beyond the floodlit shrubbery, every move like a dance step.

"Quite a fellow," Aggie said.

"He dances the tango marvelously."

"Oh, him. I meant Lonnie."

Mary Beth turned from the direction of Enrico and saw the pudgy man who'd earlier asked Aggie to dance. He had a wide, pale face that Mary Beth thought was distinctly porcine. But he had a nice smile as he extended his hand across the table.

"Lonnie Evans," he said. "From Indiana."

"Mary Beth Adams," she said, shaking his sweating palm. Recently from heaven.

"From Evansville," Aggie said. "Evans from Evansville, believe it or not."

Mary Beth believed.

. . . . .

The next morning some of the tourists from the ship took a tour bus to the town of Diablo Madre, high in the mountains behind the hotel. This bus was spacious and air conditioned, with comfortable, plushly upholstered seats that reclined. Mary Beth, sitting next to Aggie, had the window seat and watched the lush, beautiful jungle glide past, then on the higher roads with their tighter turns the occasional hard-scrabble farm with its shack of a house and meager, canted fields. The beautiful but dangerous jungle had disappeared at this altitude, revealing the rocky earth and poverty that must defeat people early in life if they couldn't adapt. Mary Beth had seen them in her teaching years in the inner city schools, the nine and ten-year-olds who would never adapt but would perish in body or soul like prey animals, and the children who would adapt all too well and become the predators. Destitution and destiny.

"Diablo Madre, or 'Mother of the Devil,' was once a rich and wild silver mining town, like your Tombstone in America," the bus driver who'd told them his name was Carlos was saying into the bus's speaker system. "Then, when the silver ran out, the town almost died. Now the inhabitants make crude furniture and ceramic souvenirs, and some of them farm, though the soil is far from fertile."

The bus squealed and hissed to a stop, and the doors opened.

"Look around for the next half-hour," Carlos said. "Perhaps buy some souvenirs. Your business will be appreciated. But I must warn you about the children. They will try to sell you rocks, saying there is silver in them. Whatever silver is in the rocks is not enough to be of value, and if you buy one of the rocks the children will swarm like bees around you trying to sell you more. You must ignore the children."

"How cold," Mary Beth said.

Aggie sniffed. "Unless you're a millionaire and don't mind buying a hundred rocks. Look."

Mary Beth turned her head in the direction Aggie was pointing and saw dozens, then scores of children running and sliding down a rocky hill toward the tour bus. They were small, skinny, raggedly dressed. They were shouting but few of them were smiling.

By the time Mary Beth and Aggie had gotten off the bus, almost all the children wore mirthless grins and were holding out stones of various sizes, a few of which did glint in the bright sunlight. Mary Beth couldn't help herself. She started to reach into her purse.

But a man about twenty feet away from her was faster. He withdrew a fat wallet and handed a small girl of about eight a dollar bill in exchange for a stone. Immediately the other children swarmed toward him. The man and a woman who was probably his wife stepped back in alarm. The wave of desperate children continued to surge. Their eyes were shining, their teeth bared like those of starving animals. Quickly, defensively, the man tossed another dollar bill onto the ground, buying time to retreat farther.

It worked. As the man and woman hurried toward a corner, the children pursued the breeze tossed bill and fell on it, striking each other and shoving to reach it. A boy about ten finally gripped it, only to have a girl claw at his eyes and snatch it from his hand. Another boy yanked the girl's hair back and bit her until he drew blood and she released the bill.

"Vamoose! Pronto!" Carlos shouted. He removed his thick leather belt, doubled it, and cracked its two sections together, making a sound like gun shots. The children scattered and regarded the bus passengers silently, keeping their distance. The boy who was last to claim the bill jammed it deep into a pocket of his tattered jeans.

"They will bother you no more," Carlos said. "But *cuidado*. Caution. They are poor and want much."

"So sad," Mary Beth said, looking around at the weathered and leaning buildings. Set in a hillside was the timbered entrance to an abandoned mine shaft. Farther up the hill, made accessible by a narrow path, were rows of shanties and open booths that displayed merchandise. Even farther up the mountain, skinny cattle and goats grazed where there appeared to be no vegetation.

"This is the place where you might get bargains in ceramic statuary and hand crafted leather purses and sandals," Carlos said.

Aggie and most of the others took the path up the mountain. Mary Beth, distressed by what she saw, said the heat was getting to her and returned to the bus.

The vehicle's diesel engine was idling like a heartbeat and the air conditioning remained running. Seated in the cool, plush interior, Mary Beth looked out the window at a man diligently hoeing a small garden of what looked like stunted cabbages. Then she noticed a woman seated on a crude wooden stool outside a nearby shanty, nursing a baby. She and the woman locked unsmiling gazes. Mary Beth looked away first.

. . . . .

The next day at the hotel Mary Beth said good-bye to Aggie. Then, on impulse, she rode a battered Volkswagen taxi down to the dock and waved as the *Fiesta Grande* left port. She watched its diminishing form waver and disappear in the distance. Then, closer to shore, she saw another pristine white cruise ship waiting to dock. It would soon disgorge new passengers, new hotel guests, none of whom would be familiar to Mary Beth. She felt an unexpected stab of loneliness as she trudged back to the tiny green taxi waiting for her in the shade of the palms that lined the parking area.

The rest of that day Mary Beth did little more than swim and eat. In the evening she sat alone in a lounge chair on the balcony off her room and watched the sunset. Then she had her second Margarita and sat in the moonlight until she was sleepy, listening to the music from the thatched-roof bar near the lake.

The next day she was able to shake her depression and relax as she'd planned. She swam in the morning in the hotel pool, then had lunch at an outside buffet and watched large and graceful white birds cavort above the lake and occasionally dive for fish.

After an afternoon of reading a boring book, then walking about the nearby small town and its mercado, she returned to the hotel for supper.

By the time she finished eating it was dark. Leaving the restaurant, she heard music not from the bar near the lake but from the pavilion. Another dance. But by now her feet hurt from walking dirt streets and uneven sidewalks. *You're here for enjoyment*, she reminded herself.

Though she was tired, she went up to her room, showered, then put on her blue party dress and white high heels. She decided on some jewelry, including a ruby ring she'd bought for her twenty-first birthday. A gift from herself to herself. Her late mother's wedding ring she removed from her finger and placed in the small beaded evening bag she carried and that when dancing she could loop over the belt of her dress. Then she went down to the dance.

It was as before, the music from the white-jacketed band, the dancers gliding among shadows beneath softly colored lanterns, the dark mystery of the lake beyond. In the warm air was the sweet scent of blossoms in vases of freshly cut flowers on each white-clothed table. A slight breeze off the lake rattled nearby palm fronds and ruffled the hair of the dancers.

"I was hoping you'd still be here."

Mary Beth turned to see Enrico standing a few feet away. He was wearing the same tailored, cream-colored suit he'd had on at the last dance, or one like it. At his feet was a medium-sized blue duffle bag with an airline tag on it.

Mary Beth swallowed the lump in her throat. "I'm glad you're here, too," she said nervously.

Enrico smiled. Like her, he was nervous.

The music stopped. Some of the dancers applauded.

The band began playing a tango.

Enrico cocked his head to the side and held his hand out for her.

Wasn't this why she had come here, for romance?

Mary Beth released the breath she was holding, smiled up at Enrico, and placed her hand in his. He led her gently onto the dance floor.

This time he soon was dancing closer, his body against hers. He led her through more complicated steps, delighted that she could follow. They did Argentine rocks, milonga fans, open swings into side lunges with Spanish drags. The language of dance, of the body. "You have had lessons," he said.

"Did you finish your business?" she asked, as he skillfully guided her through a cluster of less adept dancers. She had complete faith in him and didn't have to twist her body or turn her head for fear of a collision.

"Business?"

"The wine."

"Ah, yes, I had to examine a shipment of grapes that had arrived. They need to be crushed in the presses at just the right time. Very important. But right now, you are very important."

He drew her even closer and took her through a series of pivots. She could feel his muscular thigh between her legs, sometimes barely contacting her groin, the soft but commanding pressure of his hand on her back, his lean, muscular body against hers. He was a wonderful dancer, she decided. Not quite as skillful as David, her instructor. But Mary Beth would much rather be dancing with Enrico.

The tango stopped, but the music remained in Mary Beth's mind and body. Her blood coursed and her breath sighed to its rhythm.

"Can we walk down by the lake?" Enrico asked.

"Of course." Mary Beth's heart felt like a fluttering bird about to escape her rib cage.

"You are afraid?"

"No," she lied, "of course not."

He smiled down at her and hugged her, then held her hand and led her away from the music and dancers, pausing only to pick up his duffle bag. Behind them, the band began a slow rumba.

There were a few other couples walking the slope of lawn or the gravel path that ran along the lake's shore.

Mary Beth didn't know what to say, what exactly to do. "Did you see your children while you were gone?"

"No," Enrico said sadly. "When I return home tomorrow I'll see them. I'm away from them too much."

"I understand," said Mary Beth, who had no children other than those she'd taught.

"There's no reason to be nervous," Enrico said softly, in a faintly amused voice. He stopped walking, held her close, and kissed her gently on the lips. "Are you still nervous?"

"Not in the least!" Mary Beth sighed, leaning her forehead against his chest. She could hear, she could feel, his heart beating.

"Are you still a guest at the hotel?"

Did he want to spend the night in her room? "Of course," she said. He took her arm and they began walking again. "Why do you ask?"

"The boats," he said, "they are available to the guests."

She looked in the direction of his nod in the faint moonlight. Half a dozen small, darkly painted rowboats were tied at the dock, bobbing gently in unison as if dancing.

"We can go rowing," he told her. "It is beautiful out on the lake, calm and quiet. The dancers are a distant vision in the night, and the music floats across the water."

"It sounds heavenly," she said.

"Perhaps it really is. Perhaps our heavens are here on earth."

Mary Beth let him take her arm and steady her as they went down steep wooden steps to where the boats were docked. He helped her into the nearest one and made sure she was seated comfortably. Then he placed his duffle bag in the boat, untied the lines from the dock cleats, and climbed in to sit opposite her.

After using an oar to push away from the dock, he began to row effortlessly with the perfect rhythm he displayed in dancing. They seemed to be skimming over the dark water as the shore fell away. It was like a dream, Mary Beth thought. Like a dream she'd long sought.

At first she'd thought he was rowing toward the center of the lake, but after a while he altered course slightly toward shore.

Mary Beth sat back and let the warm breeze caress her face. Hadn't Enrico said he was a wine importer? Then why was he examining a shipment of grapes to be crushed?

"The people who live near here," he said, "call this Lovers' Lake." He smiled whitely in the moonlight. "Not very original, I'm afraid, but sincere."

"I'm sure."

"Of the sincerity?"

"Of course."

Now they were near the dark jungle that embraced the lake's edge, tall trees and tangled thick vines of a kind Mary Beth had never seen before. Beneath the edge of the jungle canopy, it became very dark.

Enrico stopped rowing. Mary Beth could hear water lapping at the hull as the boat slowly drifted. Enrico removed his white suit coat and at first she assumed he was going to wrap it around her to protect her from the sudden coolness. But he carefully folded the coat and laid it in the front of the boat.

Then he moved toward her. He was kneeling now on one knee before her. "I hope you don't think it was a mistake to come here with me." He reached out a hand and his knuckles ever so softly caressed the line of her cheek. "I would do nothing of which you'd disapprove."

Mary Beth felt her heartbeat quicken. "I believe you."

He smiled and touched the tip of her nose. "But do you trust me?"

"Yes, I trust you."

He moved yet nearer and they kissed. She felt his teeth, his tongue.

"Enrico," she moaned as they pulled apart.

The blade on her throat was at first like ice. Then like fire. She tried to gasp but breathed only fire. Enrico was staring sadly down at her, his expression calm and oddly curious. Above her the stars were dimming. He forced her body toward the edge of the boat and tipped her backward so her shoulders and head were over the water, as if they were dancing.

When most of the blood had run from the gaping wound in the American woman's neck and her heart was still, Enrico pulled her all the way back into the boat and laid her on the sheet of plastic he'd removed from his duffle bag. Then he removed his implements from the bag and set to work. The silver bracelet slid easily from her dead wrist. Her simple pearl necklace he broke removing, but he recovered the pearls, swiped his hand through the water to remove any blood, and slipped them into his shirt pocket. He couldn't work the ruby ring off the woman's hand so he cut the flesh from her finger and it slipped off easily. With his thumb and forefinger he forced open her mouth even wider and used dental implements to remove three gold fillings.

He would sell the bracelet, pearls, and ring in the city where he often sold jewelry. The gold he would melt down and use for currency at the mercado. Using long-bladed shears, he snipped off most of the woman's hair as close as possible to the scalp. This he would sell in his village to the women who made the realista dolls they sold to turistas. He made incisions and deftly peeled away her breasts. They could be sold as soft eel skin leather tobacco or jewelry pouches that fastened firmly at the top with a drawstring.

Finally he searched through the small beaded evening purse she carried and found a few American dollars and another ring, a simple gold one she'd no doubt been afraid to leave in her room when she came to the dance. Enrico would file away any markings and give the ring to his wife, Hortensia.

After shoving the woman's body over the side of the boat, he got several large stones from the duffle bag, placed them in the plastic sheet, and let it slide from the boat into the lake. The weighted plastic sheet would sink and be held by the stone to the lake bottom. The woman's body would be consumed by crocodiles or drift down the lake to the falls and the river that reached the sea within half a mile.

Enrico used a dented tin cup from his bag to wash away what little blood had gotten on the boat. Then he put his suit coat back on and rowed toward the docks.

The few people who were nearby and interested in each other paid little attention to him as he tied up the boat where he'd first found it.

He lifted his duffle bag and walked along the path toward the hotel, then through the lobby and out into the warm night. He was quite calm. In the lobby, a woman smiled at him and he smiled back.

The duffle bag resting on his shoulder now, Enrico strolled along the dark road that wound up the mountain to his village and his wife and children. He wasn't proud of what he had done to the woman. Nor was he ashamed.

It was a poor country.

Tango was her life.

End

CONTRIBUTORS'
Biographies

Trevanian is the most versatile of best-selling authors, choosing for each novel a different genre and "voice." In his latest novel, *Incident at Twenty-Mile*, he masters the Western, creating what some have called the definitive example of that genre. Trevanian's short fiction has appeared in the *Yale Literary Magazine*, *Harper's*, *Playboy*, and the *Antioch Review*, among other periodicals, and most recently St. Martin's Press has published a collection of his short stories, *Hot Night in the City*.

In addition to literary work, **Andrew Kennedy** is the creator of the Theory of Eight system of personality analysis (www.theoryofeight.com) and the Taoist-inspired game of shapes, The Game of Rat and Dragon. He has also made original translations of some of the Taoist texts. He lives with his family on a small hill farm in the Pyrenees.

Ex-journalist **Carole Nelson Douglas** is the award-winning author of forty-some novels and two mystery series. *Good Night, Mr. Holmes* introduced the only woman to outwit Sherlock Holmes, American diva and detective Irene Adler, and was a *New York Times* Notable Book of the Year. The series recently resumed with *Chapel Noir*. Douglas also created contemporary hard-boiled P.I. Midnight Louie, whose first-furperson feline narrations appear in short fiction and novels. *Cat in a Leopard Spot* and *Cat in a Midnight Choir* are the latest titles. Along with her publisher, Forge Books, she has promoted cat adoptions nationwide through the Midnight Louie Adopt-a-Cat program, which has made homeless cats available for adoption at her book signings since 1996. She collects vintage clothing as well as stray cats (and the occasional dog), and lives in Fort Worth, Texas, with her husband, Sam.

Henry Slesar was a mainstay of the fiction magazines of the late 1950s and early 1960s, the last big boom of the digests, which were just the pulps in more convenient size. He did it all and he did it well. A collection of his crime work is long overdue. In the course of his career he has won the Mystery Writers of America Edgar Allan Poe award for novel (1960) and for a TV serial (1977), and an Emmy award for a continuing daytime series (1974). He has written for many TV series such as *Alfred Hitchcock Presents* and *The Twilight Zone.* And he survived many years as the head writer of a long-running soap opera, *The Edge of Night.*

Brendan DuBois is the award-winning author of short stories and novels. His short fiction has appeared in *Playboy, Ellery Queen's Mystery Magazine, Alfred Hitchcock's Mystery Magazine, Mary Higgins Clark Mystery Magazine,* and numerous anthologies. He has twice received the Shamus Award from the Private Eye Writers of America for one of his short stories and has been nominated three times for an Edgar Allan Poe Award by the Mystery Writers of America. He lives in New Hampshire with his wife, Mona. Visit his website at www.BrendanDuBois.com.

Alexandra Whitaker has written a book for children, *Dream Sister;* invented an ingenious game for learning English, *Speak for Yourself;* and collaborated on several original screenplays and adaptations for the screen. At present she is working on a novel. She lives in Spain and has a young daughter.

Ina Bouman lives and writes in Amsterdam. She has written four crime novels featuring Jos Welling, an inquisitive journalist with a social conscience and an open mind. Her books explore the dark side of the medical field, including drug and organ trafficking, unethical experiments, and genetic manipulation. She also writes literary novels and poetry. Her latest novel is *Body at Risk.*

Bill and Judy Crider live in Alvin, Texas, with their three cats and lots and lots of books. Bill is the chair of the division of English and fine arts at Alvin Community College. He has written more than fifty novels, including mysteries, westerns, horror, and men's adventures, since the appearance of the Anthony-award-winning *Too Late to Die* in 1986. He's published an equal number of short stories. Judy has played a big editorial role in all these works but has only now begun taking credit for her creative input on stories like "At the Hop," which was nominated for an Anthony on its original publication.

A former New Yorker, **Joan Richter** now lives in Washington, D.C. A journalist, editor, and short story writer, she was director of public affairs for American Express Publishing Ccrporation in New York, publishers of *Travel & Leisure* and *Food & Wine*. She has traveled extensively throughout Europe and Asia. Her two years with the Peace Corps in Kenya in the mid-sixties sparked an interest in foreign cultures, which continues, and plays a part in her fiction. Her short stories have appeared in *Ellery Queen's Mystery Magazine* and in anthologies.

Barbara Burnett Smith is the author of the Purple Sage mystery series, which is neither western nor historical, despite the title. The first, *Writers of the Purple Sage*, was an Agatha nominee for best first. The fifth in the series will be out this fall. She is also the author of *Mauve and Murder*, in which she used her sixteen-year broadcast career to create morning announcer Cassie Ferris. Barbara has served as the national president of Sisters in Crime, and in her left-brain life is CEO of Catalyst Trainings, specializing in presentations and public speaking.

Linda Kerslake, a new writer from the Pacific Northwest, is a medical office manager by day and spends her evenings and weekends plotting someone's untimely demise. On paper, of course. On a recent trip to New York, she found the Cotton Club and the Savoy, famous clubs of the Swing Era and part of America's jazz history, demolished and gone. After riding the A train and visiting the Apollo, she began this story about a murder in Harlem during World War II. She is now working on her first mystery novel, with a few breaks for more short stories.

Carmen larrera is the only female Italian author currently writing spy novels. Although she earned a degree in political science, she writes full-time, producing short fiction, cartoons, and teleplays. She is the author of the mystery novels *Never with Paintings* and *An Indiscreet Glance*, both co-written with the noted Italian art expert Federico Zeri, which has been translated into German and Japanese. Her short stories have been published around the world, including in *Ellery Queen's Mystery Magazine* and publications in Germany, Spain, and Japan.

Ruth Cavin says, "Mystery novels and related works are the backbone of my list, but I do publish nonfiction and other kinds of fiction as well. I've had a serious love affair with the written word that long predates my weekly column for the college paper at what was then Carnegie Tech—a column shamelessly derived from the *New Yorker's* 'Talk of the Town.' I've worked in public relations, produced advertising copy, been the author of published books (although none of them mysteries), and in the distant past wrote some plays that were never produced. I've had to take seriously my own advice to new authors: 'Don't give up your day job.' But editing is a day job I love."

Mat Coward is a British writer of crime, science fiction, horror, children's, and humorous fiction, whose stories have been broadcast on BBC Radio and published in numerous anthologies, magazines, and e-zines in the United Kingdom, United States, Japan, and Europe. He has received short story nominations for the Dagger and Edgar Awards. According to Ian Rankin, "Mat Coward's stories resemble distilled novels." His first non-distilled novel—a murder mystery called *Up and Down*—was published in the United States in 2000. Short stories have recently appeared in *Ellery Queen's Mystery Magazine, The World's Finest Crime and Mystery Stories, Felonious Felines,* and *Murder Through the Ages.*

John Lutz is one of the most skilled mystery writers working today. His most recent novels are *The Ex* and *Final Seconds,* co-authored with David August. His settings and descriptions always have the ring of authenticity, whether he's writing about the blues scene in New Orleans or the relationships between men and women. His series characters are also in a class by themselves, whether it be the hapless Alo Nudger, or the more traditional detective Fred Carver. A favorite contributor to both *Ellery Queen's Mystery Magazine* and *Alfred Hitchcock's Mystery Magazine,* his work has also appeared in numerous anthologies, most recently *Murder Most Confederate.*

COPYRIGHTS AND PERMISSIONS